The Gift
of
Christmas

AN ANTHOLOGY

Edited by Susan Lute

Windtree
Press

The Gift of Christmas
An Anthology

Edited by Susan Lute

Published by
Windtree Press, Portland Oregon

818 SW 3rd Avenue #221-2218
Portland, Oregon 97204-2405
855-649-0821

ISBN: 978-19400649-9-4
First edition

Cover Artist: Christy Caughie of Gilded Heart Design

Ordering Information:
Quantity sales. Special discounts are available on quantity purchases by bookstores, corporations, associations, and others. For details, contact the "Orders Department" at the address above or email windtree@windtreepress.com.

windtreepress.com

Contents

I have always thought of Christmas time, when it has come round, as a good time; a kind, forgiving, charitable time; the only time I know of, in the long calendar of the year, when men and women seem by one consent to open their shut-up hearts freely, and to think of people below them as if they really were fellow passengers to the grave, and not another race of creatures bound on other journeys.

~ Charles Dickens

ACKNOWLEDGMENTS

Undertaking an anthology requires many people to coordinate the submissions, editing, sequencing, compilation, formatting, and eventually marketing. Every author in Windtree Press had some part in this anthology. However, below are those who went the extra step to make sure this all came together.

Susan Lute, Anthology Senior Editor and Coordinator
Elaura Renie, Associate Editor
Judith Ashley, Associate Editor
Maggie Lynch, Associate Editor, Ebook formatter

Christy Caughie, Cover Design

Jane Killick, Print book formatter,
Interviewer and Producer for podcast and video

Forward

CULTURE, RELIGIOUS UPBRINGING, and secular norms make the meaning of the Christmas season different for each person. Whatever your personal beliefs, you will find both meaningful and joyous stories of the holiday season captured in these twelve stories.

We begin the anthology with a sweet children's story about a little dog, named Metro, in Susie Slanina's "Metro's Mountain Cabin" which extends her series of books about Metro the little dog. Here Metro gets to spend the holidays with his best friends, both animals and humans. This story is written for children ages 7-12, and younger children will enjoy having it read to them.

The second story is the only non-fiction offering in the anthology. Melissa Yuan shares her meditation on life, death, and relationships in her essay "The Cancer Christmas" about her father's diagnosis of brain cancer and the lessons she learned about what's important in life.

Mysteries and Miracles are a part of four stories in this anthology. "Isabella's Christmas Box" brings back Paty Jager's popular anthropologist Isabella Mumphrey and her DEA lover, Tino. Isabella's skills are needed this time to open a Mayan puzzle box. In "The Mermaid's Treasure" Anna Brentwood presents a twist on a historical story of a brooch that may have been worn by Catherine the Great and stolen from the Czar's secret treasure room. Keeping with the treasure theme, Pamela Cowan leverages an heirloom of foreign coins in her story "Christmas Miracles". An heirloom also plays an important part in Courtney Pierce's "The Nest" when popular baby-boomer couple, Jean and Spence Collins, from her Legacy trilogy, find a special ornament at an estate sale.

As many of the Windtree Press authors write romance novels, finding love was bound to be a chosen theme for this Christmas holiday. Though several stories feature loving couples, two of our authors have provided stories specifically in that vein. Judith Ashley's "First Love" explores how one young woman tries to open herself to love in spite of a personal history of distrust and fear. Christy Carlyle explores second chance love in her historical romance offering, "Don't Forget the Mistletoe" where messages play an important role in the story.

The remaining four stories have family relationships as a central theme. Jane Killick's "Christmas with You" features a young family celebrating a special Christmas with their baby. In "Career Conundrum Christmas" Jamie Brazil explores the decisions one often faces when trying to balance honoring the past and looking to one's future. Maggie Jaimeson's "The Hogmanay Stranger" takes her Sweetwater Canyon characters and their families to Scotland to celebrate Hogmanay, and in the process discovering what is most important to each of them as they move forward into a new year.

Finally, Susan Lute's novella, "A Marine's Christmas Proposal", presents two people undergoing difficult transitions, a former Marine and a young business owner. This story explores the question of how we choose to form families and, in doing so, find a way home.

Throughout these authors' works, I found stories of hope, inspiration, kindness, forgiveness, charity, compassion, and of course love. Above all, I found a common thread that no matter the challenges one faces we are all called to be our very best selves. Not only at Christmas but also throughout the entire year.

May your holidays be filled with wonderful memories, both past and present, and may you find your best self in the spirit of this season as you step into the new year.

Sincerely,

Maggie Lynch

Metro's Mountain Cabin
Susie Slanina

SHERRY AND MARGUERITE had been best friends since kindergarten. Now they were eighteen and excited to go on a camping trip on their very own. At first, Marguerite had not wanted to go camping in a tent because she was very glamorous and her idea of 'roughing it' was a five-star hotel with room service.

Sherry had three small dogs: Metro, Tawny, and Gizzy. Marguerite had a big dog named Starbuck. For weeks, Sherry had been trying to convince her friend to go camping with the dogs in a tent. Finally, Marguerite compromised and agreed to go on a trip to the mountains, as long as they got a room, not a tent.

So they tried to reserve a room.

"How about Big Bear, Marguerite? Look, it has a big lake, and the book says it is very dog-friendly."

"Gosh that is a nice lake," Marguerite said, getting excited. "Let's look at a picture on the internet."

The internet showed a picture of a shimmering big blue lake. Marguerite read the description out loud:

"Welcome to Big Bear Lake, a four season resort community surrounded by the San Bernardino National Forest, 100 miles northeast of Los Angeles. It is the perfect getaway high above the smog and the hustle and bustle of the lowlands."

"This place sounds wonderful!" Sherry exclaimed. "Let's start calling!"

First they started with the most reasonably priced lodgings with the nicest features. They all had mountainy sounding names and friendly people answered the phone. But, alas, not one would take four dogs. They did take dogs, but apparently two was the limit.

After the fourteenth call, Sherry hung up the phone in frustration. "This isn't fair! All three of my dogs put together don't add up to what one big dog weighs. It's Wednesday. I have only a week and a half left of vacation. I just want to take Metro, Tawny, and Gizzy somewhere pretty for a few days."

Marguerite was concerned. She looked at Sherry whose eyes were quickly welling up with tears.

"What are we going to do?" she asked her friend softly.

Sherry wiped the tears away. She said in a determined voice, not quite believing herself, "I'm going to get a cabin of my own in Big Bear. That's what! Then we can take all the dogs whenever we want!"

"And how do you plan to do that?" Marguerite asked, dumbfounded.

"I don't know yet, but I have a week and a half to figure it out. Want to help?"

The two friends hugged each other and laughed.

"Yes!" Marguerite agreed, joyfully shaking her head. "But you can't possibly get a cabin before your vacation is up."

Sherry said, "Golly, this is true. I think there is a pesky thing called escrow." Then she grinned. "But when I get it, the cabin will be a cabiny-cabin. You know? Like real woodsy with maybe a stream in the back."

Marguerite was thoughtful. She looked at Sherry and, not quite believing herself, said calmly, "Well … you still have a few days left of vacation. What are you going to do? Ummm, would you like to go on a camping trip?"

Now Sherry's eyes got big. "Do you really mean it, Marguerite? Camping in a tent? You?" Sherry laughed at the thought.

Marguerite laughed right back. "Well, if you can get a cabin, I guess I could do a little camping."

The two friends and the dogs did a little jig of happiness. Camping! And they just knew they would find the coziest cabiny-cabin ever!

Deep in December, Marguerite was visiting Sherry in her little cabin in the forest. Last summer Sherry decided she wanted to get a cabin so that she could take Metro, Tawny, and Gizzy with her on vacations.

"Sherry, just think … do you remember how it all happened?"

Sherry shook her head and grinned. "I still can't believe it! Last summer was the most surprising summer of my life!"

LAST JULY:

*I*T WAS THE evening before the big camping trip. Marguerite and Sherry had shopped for supplies and were packing.

"Marguerite, you know I'm going to hold you to your promise of going camping in the mountains ... and tomorrow's the big day. No backing out now."

Metro was sleeping on Sherry's lap. She looked up when she heard the word 'camping,' sighed contentedly, and fell back into a light snooze.

Metro understood some human words. Camping and mountains were two of those words. She understood the word 'camping' because she had already been on a backyard campout in a tent.

She knew the word 'mountain' because she had gone on a picnic in the mountains with Sherry and Marguerite.

Metro put the two words together (camping and mountains). It must mean that you would get to sleep in a tent ... up in the mountains! She could already smell the green pine trees and feel the clean, crisp air.

She hopped on the couch and thought. In her little doggy brain, she was struggling to define the word cabin. She didn't know the meaning yet, but she knew it must mean something very pleasant, because her human mom sounded happy whenever she said the word. She'd been saying it a lot lately.

"Oh, yes, Sherry I know." Marguerite said. "In fact, I'm actually surprised to say I'm looking forward to it. I was determined to get out of the promise I made to you, to camp in an actual tent, but now it's okay. I'd still rather be getting a room with four walls and bathtub though. Nite-nite, Sherry, I'll be over early tomorrow morning."

"You better be!" Sherry warned. (The two friends liked to tease each other.)

The big day finally arrived. Marguerite came over at 6:00 a.m. sharp. They double-checked everything on the camping list while they ate cereal on Sherry's sunny patio. Even though it was early, it was already warm and the weather forecast said it was going to be much hotter.

"And, don't forget I'm going to buy a cabin in the mountains so that we can take the dogs up anytime we want to. We can make plans for that while we're camping." Sherry said.

Marguerite stirred some cream in her coffee and said, "Sherry, I've been wondering, how exactly do you think you can afford to buy a cabin? You're barely eighteen-years-old."

"Marguerite, I don't know how I'm going to do it. I just know I *am* going to do it!"

"Well, it doesn't hurt to have a dream," Marguerite said.

"I hope it's not just a dream. I'm going to figure out how to make a budget. Mom and Dad used this book for a budget. I'm going to try it." She went inside and took a book from the shelf. She tossed it in with the camping supplies.

Metro looked up at the book. She was puzzled. 'Budget' was definitely not in her doggy vocabulary.

Marguerite and Sherry took their cereal bowls into the kitchen.

"I can't wait to get up to the cool mountains, it's already so hot!" Sherry said.

"I know. This heat is brutal." Marguerite looked at the weather forecast. "It's going to be 104 today in Covina, but in Big Bear the high will be 77. Doesn't that sound lovely?"

She looked at all the supplies spread out in the kitchen. "There certainly is a lot of stuff you need to go camping for a few days. Let's hurry up and finish packing."

She looked carefully at a pan on the counter before packing it.

"Sherry, is this pan dishwasher-cleaned or just dog-licked clean?"

"Uh, I'm not sure — better give it a wash, just in case." Sherry said. Marguerite quickly washed the pan they would use for cooking.

"It looks like that's everything . . . oh wait!" Sherry put the budget book in the duffel bag.

Marguerite added make-up and face masques to her duffel bag.

"Don't forget, Sherry, you promised me that you would try this new make-up I have."

Sherry rolled her eyes. Glamorous Marguerite still had no concept of camping out. Sherry didn't like wearing make up. But a promise was a promise. And Marguerite was a good sport for agreeing to camp in a tent.

"Can I bring my curling iron?" Marguerite asked.

"No, you silly . . . there won't be any electricity."

"Ha-ha, I knew that already, besides I never use a curling iron. That's why I brought these empty juice cans. Look at this magazine. It shows this great hairstyle on how to set your hair with juice cans." Marguerite showed Sherry the magazine.

Sherry looked at the diagram of a head with juice cans set in complicated lines. She thought it looked ridiculous. "I'm not doing that to my hair."

"Don't worry, I'll be glad to set your hair for you! We'll sleep with juice cans in our hair and when we wake up we can style it just like the picture," Marguerite said brightly.

Sherry had a funny image of the two girls on a dusty hiking trail with perfect make-up and bouncy hair-dos.

"Marguerite, I'm surprised you didn't pack gowns, jewels, and high heels for us to go hiking in!"

"No, but how about this?" Marguerite looked innocent as she held up a bottle of fancy bubble bath.

Sherry started to reply that there were no bathtubs in camp-grounds. But then she saw the twinkle in Marguerite's eyes, and knew she was just fooling around.

"Marguerite, you make me laugh! We're all packed up now. Come on, doggies, let's get out of this hot town!"

Just then the phone rang. Sherry picked it up.

"Hello?"

"Hello! Is this Sherry who has a little dog named Metro?"

"Yes, that's me. May I ask who's calling?"

"Well, Miss, my name is Mr. Shady and I am in the advertising business. I'm currently representing a company called Corporate Fat Cats. We heard about Metro's great singing at the opera in Hollywood, and we were wondering if you would consider having Metro sing on a commercial for a new product."

Sherry put the phone on speaker so Marguerite could hear. They looked at each other in astonishment. Speechless.

Mr. Shady continued: "The only requirement is that this has to happen today! If you agree, we will be sending a limousine to your house immediately, and then we leave for filming in Hawaii."

"But, oh my gosh, my friend and I were just leaving to go camping in Big Bear. We are on summer vacation," Sherry stammered.

"The deal is that Kool Kitty Shampoo needs Metro right now! The opera star who was going to be singing the commercial came down with the flu, and she remembered how Metro stole the show. She said Metro has a wonderful howl that would be perfect for the product and Metro is the only one she could think of with a range of voice as strong as hers. She said your dog could really belt out a tune."

Sherry remembered the lady opera star in the heavy purple dress who had beckoned Metro to come up on the stage and sing when they were visiting Hollywood. She smiled at the happy memory. But then she thought about today's camping trip and how much she had been looking forward to it.

"But, but, my friend, Marguerite, finally agreed to go camping … in a tent!" Sherry explained.

Of course Mr. Shady had no idea how long she had tried to get Marguerite to go camping in a tent!

Marguerite put her hand up to Sherry's mouth. "Wait, wait, Sherry! Let's hear what else Mr. Shady has to say."

"Sherry, pardon me, but you need to make up your mind," Mr. Shady said. "Will you be going camping in the mountains or will you bring Metro to Hawaii? She will be paid a tidy sum of money for her work."

Marguerite grabbed a pencil and wrote quickly on a tablet. She showed the note to Sherry.

$$$ 4 CABIN!!!

Sherry got it. If Metro could earn money, then she would be able to help pay for the cabin.

"How long will the filming take?"

"It will take one week."

"And what is the product?"

"It's a dry shampoo for cats. The product is called Kool Kitty Shampoo. We will be showing cats taking baths with funny expressions on their faces because cats don't like water. In the background, Metro will be howling and it will seem as though the cats are howling, except with Metro's beautiful voice."

"Is the product safe for kitties?"

"Oh, yes. It's completely organic, biodegradable, and wasn't tested on animals."

"Hmmm. May I call you back in an hour?"

"No, sorry. The company has a strict filming schedule and owns a beautiful suite in Wakiki Beach right on the ocean. The limousine is currently in Hollywood to pick up the opera singer. You need to decide right now! We will be at your house in one hour. You can look over the contract on the way to LAX, Los Angeles Airport. If you don't agree with the terms we will take you home before boarding the plane and you can go camping in the mountains. It would only set back your timetable by a couple of hours."

Sherry looked over at Marguerite. She was nodding as though to say, "Yes, yes, do it!"

Sherry wondered absently if Marguerite was looking for an excuse to get out of camping in a tent.

She said, "Mr. Shady, this is all very sudden. But since I can change my mind, I need to know if I could bring my friend, and my two other dogs, Tawny and Gizzy. And, also my friend's dog, Starbuck," she said in a rush.

Mr. Shady sounded very pleased. "Certainly, Corporate Fat Cats has deluxe accommodations and will welcome them all."

After the phone call, there was a mad rush. Duffel bags with camping supplies were kicked into the closet. Marguerite ran home and grabbed sun dresses, sun hats, and bathing suits.

When she came back, Sherry was telling her two cats, Butterscotch and Playmate, farewell.

"We will be back before you know it. You be good kitties. I know Lori will take excellent care of you both."

Marguerite glanced out the kitchen window. "Sherry, look at that limousine!" The car was gleaming white and it stretched the whole length of Sherry's house.

Mr. Shady stepped out of the car and beads of perspiration broke out on his shiny, bald head. It was blazing hot. He chewed an unlit cigar and took a handkerchief from his pocket to wipe his head.

Marguerite wrinkled her nose when she saw the cigar. "Eww. I hope he doesn't light that thing," she whispered.

"Eww. I know!" Sherry whispered back, then went up to Mr. Shady.

"Mr. Shady?"

"Yes, are you Sherry?"

"Yes, please come in. I'll just be a minute to leash up the dogs."

Mr. Shady gave Sherry his card. Marguerite immediately took it and did some quick research on the computer. Everything checked out.

He entered the house and looked around, noticing everything. Butterscotch glared at him from her perch on the recliner.

"Holy Toledo! Is that cat wearing a necklace?! She's gorgeous!"

"No, Mr. Shady, it's not a real necklace. See, her markings make it look as though she's wearing a pearl necklace with a white heart pendant." Sherry tilted Butterscotch's head so that Mr. Shady could see the unique *necklace* that the beautiful cat wore everyday.

"Why she would be perfect to show off a line of jewelry for a company that Corporate Fat Cat owns. She has a queenly personality, and the fact that she's hoity-toity is perfect! That's the kind of client we're trying to reach: rich, uppity women with an air of superiority. Can she come to Hawaii with us? She would be working as a model for Pearly Girl Jewelry."

"Oh, Mr. Shady, I would love for Butterscotch to join us! And, look! I have another kitty too. This is Playmate! Can he come with us?"

Mr. Shady looked over the grayish cat and the friendly kitty affectionately rubbed against his legs.

"Meow, meow," Playmate pleaded, purring in a most delightful fashion. He flipped over and showed Mr. Shady his furry tummy. "Meow, meow," Playmate purred louder, and stretched out on his back. His paws reached toward Mr. Shady, inviting him to give a belly rub.

"Nah, that's just a scrawny cat. We can't use him to advertise anything."

Sherry thought fast. She didn't want Playmate to be left home alone if all the other pets were going.

Marguerite was helping Butterscotch into the cat carrier and Sherry was slowly leashing up each dog, thinking frantically.

They started out the front door and were in the driveway, just steps away from the limousine parked on the curb.

"Wait! Wait!" Sherry cried. "Playmate knows how to play marbles!" She remembered one night when Playmate played with a marble on the hardwood floor under Sherry's bed. Every time she reached for the marble, Playmate batted it away.

Mr. Shady stopped on the driveway. More beads appeared on his bald head and he chewed his cigar furiously.

"That cat can play marbles?" He looked skeptical.

"Yes! He's like a pro with marbles. You can't get a marble away from him."

"Hmm. Corporate Fat Cats does own a major toy company, but I don't know if they sell marbles. Maybe if this scrawny cat can play a good game …" He chomped on his cigar, thinking.

Sherry held her breath.

"No. He can't come with us. Every kid today wants those confounded video games. They don't care anymore about low-tech, quiet games like jigsaw puzzles or jacks or marbles. We have to go now. Leave the cat at home."

Sherry's heart sank. She could hear Playmate meowing sadly from inside the house. She knew Lori would take good care of him, but still. She couldn't bear the thought of friendly Playmate feeling lonesome for his doggy pals and even crabby Butterscotch. She took a deep breath.

"Sorry, Mr. Shady, it's such a hot day, and I hear that Hawaii is very hot as well. I think we'll stick to the original plan and go camping in the cool mountains. Thank you for the opportunity, though." She started walking back to the house.

Even though Marguerite was wearing dark sunglasses, Sherry knew she had one eyebrow raised in surprise.

Mr. Shady glanced at his watch and sputtered, "Oh, just bring the silly cat. I'll check with the toy company about the marble business. Now, can we please get out of here?"

Sherry was so relieved. Now all her pets were going to Hawaii!

"Thank you so much, Mr. Shady," Sherry called over her shoulder as she ran back to get Playmate.

The limousine had a circular couch and was wonderfully cold on this hot day. Mr. Shady gave Sherry a black binder with the contract.

Sherry and Marguerite bent their heads over the paperwork.

Sherry had secretly been wondering for days how she could ever afford to get a vacation cabin in the woods. She looked deeply into Metro's eyes. Ever so softly, Metro hummed a little tune to Sherry, it sounded like a Hawaiian song.

Sherry had her answer. She quickly signed the papers, and Metro dabbed her paw print on an inkpad and signed too.

In the cool, climate-controlled comfort of the limousine, Sherry leaned back on the leather seats and sighed. The coolness of the car reminded her of the coolness of Big Bear. Through the tinted windows she could see the mountains. She wistfully waved to them and gave one last thought to the long-planned camping trip. She knew the mountains would wait for her family of pets to come back. It was difficult, but she switched her imagination to Hawaii, and smiled at the thought of Metro in a grass skirt and flowered lei.

Suddenly, there was a loud pop. Mr. Shady had cracked open a bottle of champagne and was holding an elegant crystal flute with golden, bubbly liquid. He drank deeply and poured himself another glass.

"Say, you girls can have anything you want to drink. Help yourself!"

Marguerite and Sherry chose sparkling apple cider in the champagne flutes. It was bubbly like the champagne. They toasted and the crystal glasses made a delicate clink-clink sound. "Here's to a great time in Hawaii!"

When they arrived at LAX, a Lear Jet was waiting on the tarmac. They buckled up their seat belts and flew off to Hawaii. As soon as they stepped off the plane in Honolulu, Sherry felt enveloped by the Aloha spirit, the beauty of the islands, and the warm friendliness of everyone they met. Metro and Butterscotch did fantastic jobs with their commercials. Everywhere they went they were treated like royalty. The dogs swam in pristine beaches. They sailed on the luxurious Corporate Fat Cats yacht that had a helipad and a real helicopter! They flew on the helicopter and saw waterfalls close up. And Metro did look very cute in her little grass skirt and flowered lei.

The week in Hawaii flew by fast and so did the rest of the summer.

Now it was fall. There was a slight chill in the air and the leaves were starting to change colors. Marguerite went back to school at USC. Sherry buckled down with her job and college classes. Every evening when she got home, she was greeted like a movie star by the three dogs. It was wonderful to feel so loved! She greeted them right back like they were movie stars and they happily spent every moment they could together.

T WASN'T UNTIL a weekend in October that Marguerite and Sherry finally had a chance to go camping in a tent. By then the sun was setting earlier. They arrived at the campsite after dark on a Friday evening. After pitching the tent, they sat inside and, under the light of a lantern, they poured over real estate magazines that showed which mountain cabins were available to purchase.

"I definitely want a cabin with two bedrooms so you can visit, Marguerite. Also a deck, I would like to have a deck. And a fireplace too!"

The girls looked and looked through the brochures. They drew circles around the ones with possibilities. They put stars on the ones that looked really good. And they drew lips (kisses) on the ones that were their favorites.

The next morning after a hearty campfire breakfast, it was time to go look at cabins with a realtor. The fourth cabin they saw was perfect! It was bright and cheery, had an upstairs deck and the backyard even had a stream!

"I'll take it!" Sherry exclaimed.

The realtor looked puzzled. He said, "But we have all these other cabins to look at and it's not even noon. Don't you want to see any more?"

They were standing on the deck looking down at the babbling brook, enjoying the happy sound it made. Wind chimes tinkled pleasantly.

"No, this is the one! And now we can take the dogs and play at the lake all weekend instead of looking at cabins."

Sherry disliked any kind of shopping, even cabin shopping! The realtor was happy that he made a quick sale and took the girls out to lunch and then to the real estate office. Sherry quickly signed her initials on lots and lots of papers.

"One question, how long will it take to get the key?"

The realtor said that escrow would take about two months. Marguerite looked at her calendar and figured since it was mid-October now, they would be able to enjoy the cabin during Christmas vacation!

"Wonderful! Thank goodness that's over with! Come on doggies, let's go explore Big Bear!"

They took the dogs on a sightseeing boat ride around sparkling Big Bear Lake, explored Big Bear Village which was like an alpine town one might find in Germany, and visited the solar observatory that was on the lake.

By the campfire that night, they decided to play a game called Doggy Appreciation. It's a very simple game to play. One at a time each dog gets to sit on a lap and be petted. This dog gets all the loving attention. Marguerite and Sherry whispered to the dog how much they loved them, and how proud they were of them, how pretty they were, and how grateful they were to have them in their lives. This could go on and on. The dogs adored hearing all the kind words, and the girls loved to watch as the dogs blossomed like roses under showers of appreciation.

"Starbuck, when I have a cold I love how you stay quiet and never leave my side even though I know you'd rather be outside playing," Marguerite said.

"Gizzy, I love how you tilt your head when I tell you a story, as though you understand each word," Sherry said.

"Tawny, I love how you gaze at me every morning while I have coffee. Then, when I have to get ready for work, you sigh so deeply that I sigh too," Sherry said.

When it was Metro's turn, she sat up straight on Sherry's lap and listened carefully. Her eyes shined with pride as she looked from Marguerite to Sherry. By the light of the campfire, her glossy brown fur shimmered in waves with each pet stroke and her golden highlights sparkled.

"Metro, I love how you always feel what I feel. One time, when I was sad, you limped around the house with your tail straight down. I was concerned, but when I smiled you wagged your tail and stopped limping. Because of you, I try not to be sad. You are just off the charts in your doggy goodness." Sherry's heart felt tender as she hugged the good little dog.

When the fire was safely out, it started to get chilly. The girls scrambled inside the tent, quickly got in their sleeping bags and cuddled with the dogs.   Sherry gazed at the moon through the screen at the top of the tent. "I wonder if sleeping in a cabin will be as nice as sleeping in a tent?" She asked drowsily. There was no answer, Marguerite was already fast asleep.

"What do you think, Metro? Tent or cabin?" Inside the sleeping bag, Metro snuggled in her favorite place, close to Sherry's heart.

I don't care, Mom, just so long as I can be with you.

AT DAWN, THE girls awoke to strange noises. In the dim light, through the screen in the tent, the girls watched in astonishment as squirrels flew high above them from tree to tree. It was like watching a high-flying trapeze act. And the squirrels were making such a racket! In fact, the sound they made sounded like a racket: *rackety-racketa-rackety-racketa!* It was very entertaining to watch and they were wide-awake in just a few minutes!

As the sun rose, they built a campfire and made a big breakfast. While it cooked, they sipped coffee and felt good and alert. It was a good time to concentrate on a budget. Metro's commercial had paid for the down payment to the cabin, but having two house payments would require some careful financial planning. They got out the budget book and looked over some of the categories. There were lots of categories and sub-categories, but instead of getting discouraged, they picked three items that looked easiest to begin with: clothing, travel, and gifts.

"I'll go on a budget with you. Let's tackle clothing first," Marguerite said."

Sherry was surprised because Marguerite loved pretty clothes.

"Maybe we could make our own clothes. That would be fun. My mother has a sewing machine," Marguerite said.

Sherry made a face. "Aww, I don't like sewing. Remember when we took that class in Home Economics and we basted the stitches so carefully? And, then we had to take *out* the stitches? All that hard work for nothing! Bleh."

"But that's what basting is, a temporary stitch. Sewing is wonderfully fun, you just don't know what you're missing. I think I'll look at my mother's dress patterns when we get home and make us dresses. And I'll knit! I'll knit us some pretty sweaters! That won't cost too much." Marguerite estimated a price target for clothing and entered a figure in the budget book.

"Okay. Have fun with that." Sherry wanted no part of sewing or knitting, but she knew Marguerite was a girly-girl and liked that stuff.

"What about travel?" Marguerite asked. "We like going on trips."

"But we'll have the cabin, and we can come up anytime we want!"

"But what about seeing the world? You always said you wanted to see the world."

Sherry thought hard. "You know, Marguerite, someone could offer to show me the seven wonders of the world and I wouldn't go. I just want to look in my dogs' brown eyes, that's wonder enough for me." Then she thought again and grinned. "Well, I *might* go, if the dogs could come with me like they came to Hawaii."

"Okay, good. So travel won't be much of a budget cost," Marguerite crossed travel off the budget book.

The smell of eggs and potatoes was enticing and the dogs were getting restless. "No more budget talk for today, Marguerite. Let's eat and then we'll take the dogs for a hike on the Woodland Trail, okay?"

Marguerite closed the budget book. "That sounds like a good plan."

"Oh, yum," Sherry said, when she took the first bite of scrambled eggs. "Is there anything better than breakfast when you're camping out?"

"Well, maybe dinner!" Marguerite smiled.

Sherry looked closely at her glamorous friend. Maybe, just maybe, Marguerite enjoyed camping in a tent after all!

THE REST OF October and November went by so slowly. The hot, dry Santa Ana winds came and went. The beginning of December was almost unbearable to Sherry. Every morning, while she waited for the train to take her to the university in Los Angeles, she gazed at the purple mountains in the distance. Soon they would be covered with snow. How she longed to be up there with the pups! She couldn't wait to hear if everything was approved for the cabin.

While she was at work on winter solstice, December 21st, she got a phone call from the realtor. "Everything is final. The cabin is yours! You can come and pick up the key now!"

It was perfect timing, a Friday and the universities were closed for a week. No school for Marguerite, no school or work for Sherry!

Sherry was able to get off work early. She picked up Marguerite and Starbuck. After the long, winding drive up the mountain, they stopped at the realty office. The realtor handed them the key. "Have fun," he said and gave the dogs a pat.

"Thank-you so much for all your help," Sherry said.

She rushed to the car and they drive just a few more blocks. "Pups, there it is!"

The cabin looked wonderful in the last rays of the setting sun. The sky was blue with streaks of pink clouds. The dogs remembered Big Bear and they jumped out of the car like synchronized swimmers, wagging their pom-pom tails and sniffing the good forest smells.

Sherry unlocked the door and the insides smelled good too — knotty pine. At once they felt right at home. The previous owners had left a nice note that said, "Enjoy your hideaway!" Next to the note there was a book on how to recognize the birds of the San Bernardino Mountains.

"How nice of them!" Marguerite exclaimed, looking at the pictures of beautiful birds.

It was deep in December, and the day was cold, so different than two hours away in Covina, where the temperatures did not vary much, no matter the season.

They went out on the deck to enjoy the sunset on the first evening in the cabin. By now the pink clouds had turned to silvery streaks across the sky. The tops of the pine trees glistened in a golden light.

"You know, Marguerite, even though it's cold, I'm glad I have a place to come and experience all four seasons. There's something deep in me that needs that. In Covina, it feels like we're in a rut because it's sunny and warm all year long. Up here the seasons are distinct."

"Well, I'm getting distinctly cold, can we go inside now?" Marguerite rubbed her nose with her mitten.

Sherry lit a fire and tuned the radio to a station that was playing continuous Christmas music. Marguerite called for a pizza to be delivered. The dogs cuddled in their beds near the fire.

Looking at them, Sherry said, "Just think, we're really up in the woods now! This is so homey and cozy, Marguerite, just what I dreamed about. Some people name their cabins. Let's think of a name!"

Sherry poked the fire and then took a tablet to the couch. They suggested names and made a list of words they especially liked which would define the character of the cabin.

"Serenity means calm and peaceful. That's a good name," Sherry said. "I want to be calm and peaceful when we come to the cabin. What word can go before Serenity?"

Marguerite said, "how about sweet?"

"Yes! Sweet Serenity is the perfect name." Sherry was already making plans to get a pretty wooden sign made with the name, a painting of pine trees, a snow covered mountain, and a sunrise. She would hang it over the front door.

It was getting late and the fire was dying out. They decided to play a word game to relax after such an exciting day.

Sherry laid out her tiles horizontally and played the word D-O-Z-E. Marguerite added an 'N' to the end of DOZE and played another word vertically that included the letter 'N.' Sherry looked at the first word, which now spelled out DOZEN, then looked at Marguerite with raised eyebrows.

"Marguerite, that is not a real word. I challenge you! Did you think you could get away with a fake word like dozen? Does it mean you were 'dozin' on the couch?"

Bubbles of laughter rose from Marguerite's tummy and emerged. "Oh, Sherry, you are so funny! Did you forget about the eggs? Like a dozen eggs?!"

Sherry felt bubbles of laughter in her tummy too! "Oh, gosh, I must be getting sleepy! I said dozen with a long O, making the word sound like 'dozing'. The two friends laughed and laughed.

Metro liked to hear laughter. She wagged her tail which was her way of giggling.

"Ahh, this has been a such a fun day, but you know, fun can be extremely exhausting. I'm sleepy too." Sherry said. "In fact, I feel like a long doze! Let's take the dogs for a little walk before nitey-nite."

They started to leash up the dogs, but just then the Christmas carols stopped. The radio crackled. A serious voice announced, "We're sorry to interrupt our holiday programming with a special bulletin for the Big Bear area. A surprise snowstorm has just been detected on our radar. It will start snowing some time tomorrow afternoon. This storm will bring over a foot of snow. Blizzard conditions apply. Do not attempt to travel. Please make sure you have emergency supplies and food for the next two days. Stay tuned for further information. Thank you, and now back to our program."

Marguerite and Sherry looked at each other and said together, "Snow! And a lot of it!"

"We better get up early tomorrow and go shopping!" Marguerite said.

"What fun! We're going to be snowed in. Yay!" Sherry exclaimed.

SATURDAY, DECEMBER 22

TRUE TO THEIR word, the girls arose early the next morning, and since it was an emergency, they didn't pay attention to their budgets. Sherry said budgeting could start on New Year's Day. It would be a good resolution. They shopped and shopped. A lot of people had heard the news and it seemed everyone in town was stocking up on supplies.

All the groceries were put away by mid morning. There was no sign of a storm yet. In fact, it was warm enough to eat breakfast on the deck.

The stream was babbling happily below them. Marguerite noticed giant pinecones all over the ground. She had an idea.

"Let's make bird feeders," she said. "The birds might get hungry with all the snow coming."

They took two of the hugest pinecones, lathered them up with peanut butter, rolled them in birdseed and sunflower seeds, and hung them on trees with a ribbon. They looked as pretty as any decoration. Marguerite took the book on how to identify the mountain birds and sat on the deck. They waited. Soon some birds came to enjoy the treat. They recognized black woodpeckers with bright red heads, blue stellar jays with black crowns, and sweet little chickadees.

They took some peanuts and had fun feeding squirrels. Sometimes the squirrels grabbed the nut and ran away to hide it in the ground, but most of the time they stayed on the deck railing and munched it right there so the girls could admire them close up. They quivered as they ate, and then chased each other around.

After an hour, the squirrels seemed to be getting used to the girls being there. Sherry said, "I'm going to try to feed them by hand." She took a wooden bowl full of peanuts. She had to be very patient. It took a lot of practice and most of the squirrels ran away, but finally a squirrel took, one, two, three, four peanuts from Sherry's hand. She felt honored that the squirrel trusted her.

All of a sudden five trusting squirrels appeared on the rail. They looked like a choir with their mouths open, waiting. Sherry was enchanted and gave them each a peanut. But when she got to the last squirrel, he just couldn't wait. He jumped up on Sherry's jacket and all of a sudden she was face-to-face with the little critter.

She was too startled to cry out. She dropped the bowl and peanuts scattered all over the deck. Out of nowhere, a lot more squirrels showed up for the feast. But this squirrel was still attached to Sherry's jacket! He wasn't going anywhere until he got his peanut served to him. Sherry tried to steady herself and admire the beady eyes and quivering nose, but she just … couldn't. His sharp claws dug further into the cloth.

She was afraid. She didn't know how to get the squirrel off without touching him, because then he might take a nip from her. She stood with her arms out, helpless.

"Mr. Squirrel, I dropped all my peanuts, so I can't serve you," Sherry said in a shaking voice. The squirrel's face was getting closer and closer to Sherry's nose.

"Sherry, take your jacket off right now! He thinks your nose is a peanut!"

Sherry shrugged off the jacket and stood on the deck shivering in a T-shirt and blue jeans. The squirrel was still attached to the jacket on the deck, looking everywhere for the nose he wanted for breakfast.

Sherry shuddered. "I'm *never* going to feed squirrels by hand again!"

Marguerite said, "Aw, poor squirrel. He thought he was going to get the biggest nut of them all: you, Sherry!"

"Ha-ha! Very funny, Marguerite," Sherry said dryly. She put on her jacket and picked up the peanuts that had been scattered on the deck. She flung them as far away as she could. "Here, squirrely-squirrels, come and get your peanuts but don't come too close."

One certain squirrel grabbed a peanut and sat down on his haunches to eat it, but before he did, he peered up longingly towards Sherry's nose.

*I*T WAS LUNCHTIME when the winds started to howl. Marguerite and Sherry decided to walk the dogs before the storm. Tremendous dark clouds appeared as if from nowhere. The tall pine trees above them swayed in circles, faster and faster and faster.

As they walked, Sherry happened to look down. Somehow Gizzy had disappeared with his leash still attached. She had been holding the leash with mittens that weren't very grippy.

"Well, he can't be that far away," Sherry said, trying not to panic.

"Gizzy! Gizzy!" they called. No answer. The winds blew harder. The sky was getting dark like twilight even though it was only noon.

Marguerite ran back to the house and got a box of doggy treats. She shook the box of treats. That made a sound that the dogs usually couldn't resist. They always came running when they heard the sound.

"Gizzy!!! Gizzy!!! Treaty-treat!!! Gizzy!!! Gizzy!!! Treaty-treat!!!" They called and called. Marguerite shook the box as hard as she could, but they couldn't hear their voices because of the powerful winds.

They ran further up the street. And, just above a little hill, there was Gizzy in the middle of the road chewing madly on something. As they got closer, they saw that Gizzy had stolen the leftovers of a holiday meal. He looked up and his face was full of mashed potatoes and gravy.

Marguerite shook the box of Doggy Delights in vain. Because, even if Gizzy had heard the box, he was already plenty delighted and he was not about to leave his gourmet feast for a dog biscuit.

When Gizzy was safely back on his leash, they continued their walk around the neighborhood, making sure not to get too far away from the cabin.

They didn't know that a hopeful little squirrel had been following them.

"Is that your squirrel?" A little boy asked.

Sherry said, "No, but I think I know him. His name is Nosey." Marguerite chuckled.

The first few snowflakes started to fall. Marguerite looked down at her black mitten, and the girls marveled at the shapes of perfect snow crystals. Then the snow started falling in earnest and quickly covered the dogs and the girls.

"We better run back to the cabin!" Sherry said, her feet already in motion. Once inside, they shut the door against the howling winds. The dogs shook off most of the snow.

Marguerite turned on the radio. "Please stay inside during the blizzard, there may be power outages," the serious voice announced. And, just as he said it, the lights and radio went off.

They looked out the window. The snow was swirling in all directions and the little cabin shook as though there were tiny earthquakes. The windows rattled loudly. The wind chimes, which had sounded so pleasant, were driving Sherry mad. She braved the storm and removed them.

Marguerite built a fire and Sherry lit candles. While the storm raged outside, the sturdy cabin was filled with a soft, warm glow.

While the dogs cuddled in their beds by the fire, the girls put together a jigsaw puzzle of a snow-capped Big Bear mountain with colorful wild flowers below. It was fun finding the pieces by candlelight. They sang as many Christmas carols as they could remember. And, when they got hungry, they made popcorn in an old-fashioned popcorn grate over the fire. They were having so much fun, that they were surprised when the radio and the lights came back on.

The announcer didn't sound so serious now. "The worst of the storm is over, and the dangerous winds have died down. Please feel free to go outside and play in the snow."

Marguerite and Sherry wasted no time in getting bundled up. Everybody in the neighborhood had the same idea. Parents, kids, and friendly dogs poured out from cabins. Sherry and Marguerite liked the way their boots sounded as they crunched in the snow.

The dogs loved the snow! They skidded, romped, rolled, and dug. Tawny was like a little snowplow — running ahead, quickly pushing snow away with her nose and paws. Snow flew out of each side of Tawny. She made a series of pathways for everyone.

In the back of Sweet Serenity there was a hill and already some kids had formed a line and were taking turns sledding down. Sherry and Metro sledded together.

"Wheeee!" Sherry cried.

"Wheeee!" Metro cried, imitating Sherry.

The dogs ran down the hill with each sled.

The mountain neighborhood echoed with happy shrieks from the kids and barking from excited dogs.

Marguerite and Sherry made fast friends with all the kids. They made snow angels and had great snowball fights. They built snow forts for cover and behind the forts they were able to make many snowball reinforcements.

An inventive young man named Alan showed everyone how to make igloos from packing snow in ice chests and carefully tipping them over to make bricks.

Nosey the squirrel hopped around too. He dug in snow looking for tasty acorns. Hopefully, he had forgotten about Sherry's nose by now.

They played until dusk. The stream was no longer a babbling brook. It had cut through the snow and the roar of rushing water was incredible.

It turned out Alan lived next door to Sweet Serenity. On his outdoor barbecue, he made apple pie treats for everyone. It was fun to barbecue in the snow! They tasted so good and it was such a simple recipe:

Cut apples in wedges
Sprinkle with mixture of sugar and cinnamon
Wrap in foil, barbecue for half an hour

By the porch light they could see snowflakes falling straight down. It was light and fluffy. This snow had a completely different personality than blizzard snow. It had a magical quality, soft and gentle. Then it stopped.

The storm was over. The mountain was eerily quiet and still.

SUNDAY, DECEMBER 23

*T*HE NEXT MORNING, there wasn't a cloud in the sky. It was bluer than blue. Sherry and Marguerite were awestruck by the icicles that hung from the eaves of the cabin. Some were crystal clear and longer than swords! The snow sparkled in the bright sunlight, the pine trees were covered and their branches drooped from the weight. They played in the snow again all day with their new friends.

That night there was going to be meteor showers. The peak would be between three and four in the morning. Marguerite set the alarm, which seemed to go off as soon as they had fallen asleep. She came to Sherry's room.

"Oh, no! It can't be that time already!" Sherry was exhausted from playing in the snow. She looked at the clock in dismay: Three a.m. "Aw, are you sure you want to do this?" Sherry snuggled deeper under the covers reaching for the three cuddly bundles near by.

"Yes, I do, there's going to be hundreds of meteors per hour. We can't miss the show!"

"Oh, all right," Sherry said reluctantly and, trying her best not to disturb the sleeping dogs, she got out of the warm bed.

Opening the back door, a cold wind rushed inside the cabin and banged the door open. It was a clear night, but it was freezing!

"Marguerite, let's just go back to bed," Sherry pleaded. "I'm still half asleep and it's way too cold on the deck. No one in their right mind would be up and outside at this hour."

But Marguerite was already pulling out the reclining chairs. She was a brave girl and unafraid of a little cold weather. As she arranged the chairs on the deck she looked up. WHIZ! WHIZ! WHIZ! Colorful meteors were streaking across the sky!

Sherry rubbed her arms and watched from the warm kitchen.

"You're right, Sherry. It's too cold out here. Let's go back to sleep.

Will you come out and fold up your chair so it doesn't blow away?"

"Can't you just do it, Marguerite? I'm still in my pajamas and you're all bundled up with mittens and a hat." Sherry shivered and dreaded the thought of going out on that cold deck.

"It will just take a second. Come on, give me a hand with this," Marguerite said in a calm manner, as though there was nothing exciting going on in the dark sky above her.

Sherry wondered why capable Marguerite needed help, but she put on her heavy robe and fuzzy slippers and stepped onto the deck, feeling a little grumpy. She started to fold up her chair and out of the corner of her eye, she saw flashes of light. She looked up ... ZING! ZING! ZING! The meteors were falling almost as fast as the snow yesterday.

She was wide awake now. "You brat, Marguerite! This was why you wanted me to come outside! You knew I'd change my mind!" She laughed. "Good one! Well, you're right, give me just a second and we'll watch the show!"

Marguerite smiled. She went inside and made cocoa while Sherry changed clothes.

They brought out sleeping bags and reclined in deck chairs, enjoying the steaming hot chocolate. Even though the wind was howling, they soon felt warm and snug. "Oooh, look to the right!" Marguerite pointed, charmed by meteor with a yellow tail.

"Ahhh, look to the left!" Sherry gasped, seeing another.

"Oooh! Ahhh! Oooh! Ahhh!" The girls were dazzled by the light show.

"The sky is so clear tonight, but just think how it would look at the spot where we took Metro stargazing in the desert. The trees are pretty, but in the desert no trees blocked our view."

Sherry looked through binoculars at the Milky Way. It looked like a pathway of diamonds across the night sky.

She remembered her dad's favorite riddle. "Marguerite, do you think there's milk in the Milky Way?"

"Yes, there is, because there's milk on planet earth, and planet earth is in the Milky Way galaxy!"

Sherry never got tired of hearing the riddle. She snuggled deeper in the reclining chair, gazing at the sky and remembering how her dad's eyes twinkled when he asked her the riddle. She felt glad knowing that all humans, plants, animals, and even milk had a home in a beautiful galaxy called the Milky Way.

ON CHRISTMAS EVE, Marguerite and Sherry made up red stockings for the dogs to hang over the fireplace. The names METRO, TAWNY, GIZZY, STARBUCK were in silvery glitter. They filled them with dog treats and toys.

"But, what are we going to do about presents?" Marguerite asked. "We've always exchanged presents since we were in kindergarten. It's a tradition."

"Gifts, that's one of the items in the budget book, right? I know, this budget thing is getting tricky. Sometimes the best gifts are unusual. I remember one time my mother gave me a box and inside that box were other boxes that got tinier and tinier. The tiniest box of all was a jewelry box and inside was my library card nestled in cotton. She had gone to the library, paid my overdue fines, and I got my library card back." Sherry smiled, remembering. "Come to think of it, a library card is better than jewelry anyway.

"Let's not exchange presents this year. Having your friendship, the dogs, and now the cabin is all I could ever want. Besides, some gifts need dusting. Remember what Thoreau said about dusting? I think I remember it by heart."

Sherry recited the quote in a deep, manly voice. "I had three pieces of limestone on my desk, but was terrified to find that they required to be dusted daily, when the furniture of my mind was all undusted still, and threw them out the window in disgust."

They laughed. Marguerite knew Sherry was referring to a quote by Henry David Thoreau in *Walden*. The girls had studied the book together in high school.

"I'm like Thoreau — terrified of dusting! We'll think of something and make a new tradition, a tradition better than gifts." Sherry said.

"Okay, Sherry, no gifts this year." Marguerite sadly crossed gifts off on the budget book.

CHRISTMAS MORNING

MARGUERITE KNOCKED ON Sherry's bedroom door.
"I brought you something for Christmas, Sherry."

Sherry turned over, looked at the box in Marguerite's hands, and groaned. "Oh, no. I thought we agreed, no gifts."

"I think you'll like this one. Hurry, open it up!"

Sherry lifted the top of the box and inside ... there was Metro!

Sherry gasped. "Oh, my gosh, Marguerite! This is the best present ever! Hey, wait just a minute! Did you steal Metro from me while I was asleep?"

"Ha ha, yes I did, just a minute ago! I was up early thinking about something I could give you that you would really like and I knew just the thing. So ... tell me again, how do you like your gift?"

Marguerite had tied a pretty ribbon with a bell on Metro's collar. The little dog jingled as Sherry lifted her from the box.

Sherry looked at Metro with new eyes. It felt like she was meeting Metro for the very first time. She remembered that day so well.

There, sitting in a cage at the animal shelter, with one paw lifted, had been a tiny puppy looking up at Sherry hopefully. It was love at first sight. Sherry was speechless as she gazed at the perfect puppy. The nice shelter worker put the puppy into Sherry's waiting hands. Sherry held her close and could feel the puppy's little heartbeat next to hers. The puppy whimpered and nestled closer. Sherry's heart flipped over and, in that moment, both their lives were changed forever.

Sherry's eyes misted up at the memory.

"Marguerite, believe me, this is the best gift I've ever received!"

"I believe you, Sherry." Marguerite hugged Sherry and sat on the bed.

All the well-loved dogs tumbled around them. Metro's bell jingled merrily in the mix-up. Marguerite and Sherry laughed as they looked fondly at the best presents in the whole world.

~

ABOUT THE AUTHOR

Susie Slanina lives in Vancouver, Washington. After graduating from California State University, Los Angeles, she went to school in Ireland to study the Montessori approach to educating children. She worked 24 years at CSLA and retired at age 50 to spend more time with her dogs in a cabin in Big Bear. She had been retired for eight years when a poem she wrote about a spider became the catalyst for the Metro book series. She used to enjoy traveling, but discovered that hanging out with her dogs is better than seeing the wonders of the world.

Follow the adventures of Metro the Little Dog *through several chapter books. You can learn more about Susie Slanina and Metro at:*

metrothelittledog.com

The Cancer Christmas

Melissa Yuan

THE FIRST CHRISTMAS after my father was diagnosed with brain cancer, I realized everything had changed.

Up until his diagnosis, my father's life revolved around working. When I was growing up, I found that if he wasn't at the office, he was teaching me how to change the oil on our car, finishing my grandparents' basement, shushing us because he was listening to the stock reports, or forcing me to do fractions well before I understood them.

But he knew how to have fun, too. He was the one who picked us up and hurled us on the bed over and over again, while my brother and I bounced to our feet and begged for more. He showed us how to limbo under a broomstick. And, years later, when my first pregnancy ended in a stillborn baby girl, although he said little, he made her a blanket embroidered with her name and date of birth and death.

The summer of the following year, around his fifty-sixth birthday, my parents came to visit me and our new son, Max. Dad mentioned having trouble remembering people's names and having to work more slowly. Since I was an emergency room doctor, albeit on maternity leave, I asked if he wanted to come to the hospital to scan his head. He said no, his family doctor had referred him to a memory clinic.

On November second, the scan showed a tumor too deep to remove. When he first heard the news, his first reaction was, 'I guess this means I can't work.' His second was to point at my six-month-old son, Max, and say, "I just wish I could watch this one grow up." His third was to tell me and my brother, "I've done what I needed to do. Take care of your mother."

By Christmas, the first treatments had already taken their toll. The anti-epileptic drugs gave him a rash. The high-dose steroids made him dizzy and hungry and moon-faced. And who knew what side effects came from the radiation. But he still kept nearly all of his hair and he looked much the same. He was just very, very tired.

I didn't realize how tired until my family came to visit for

Christmas. Dad posed for pictures in the kitchen. He put presents under the tree. He accepted his stocking. He even offered to take care of baby Max, since his number one goal in life was to be useful. But when I searched for them fifteen minutes later, I found Dad sitting on the toilet lid while Max ripped handfuls of paper off the toilet paper roll and threw them on the floor, cackling with delight.

The environmentalist inside my breast cried out, "No! Toilet paper comes from trees!" The clean freak in me yelled, "What a mess!" But I bit my tongue. I realized that my father was too exhausted to carry Max or push toy cars on the floor with him. The most he could offer his beloved grandson was one treat his mother never allowed: destroying toilet paper.

I wish I could say that I laughed with them, but I wasn't that enlightened. I cleaned up the paper and carted Max away so my father could rest.

The following Christmas, my father was hospitalized. He'd fallen several times at home. He needed two people's help to stand up, so he couldn't even go home on a day pass. And I have to say, despite the candy cane decorations and the tinsel on the ceiling, it saddened my heart that my father was spending Christmas on the cancer ward. But when I brought Max to see him, Dad opened his eyes and started to play.

I was amazed. How could this man, who couldn't even sit up on his own, play with his 19-month-old grandson?

Each patient had received a small Christmas stocking filled with candy. The oncology nurse pulled a small candy cane out of Dad's. Max had never tasted a candy cane before, but he sucked on a small piece and smiled.

My father took a piece of candy cane into his own mouth. Then, using his lips, he pushed it back out toward Max.

Max giggled and reached for it.

Dad pulled the candy cane back into his mouth. Then, after Max gave up, Dad pushed it out again: peekaboo!

Max laughed and laughed.

I stood silently by the hospital bed. My father had lost nearly everything: his ability to work, his sharp intelligence and memory, and even his ability to walk to the bathroom by himself. But this holiday season, he had not forgotten how to love or how to make his grandson laugh.

And maybe I had learned something, too, because when Dad said he didn't want any presents this year, I understood. I asked my family to write letters to him instead. We gathered around his bedside and took turns reading stories about our time together and how much we appreciated him. Dad snuggled in bed and closed his eyes in order to concentrate on our words. And so, before he died in May, we were able to tell him exactly how much we loved him.

I can't say this was my best Christmas because it was mired in sadness. But it did teach me the spirit of Christmas: love.

~

ABOUT THE AUTHOR

Melissa wanted to be a writer since she was five-years-old, but went to medical school first. Now she's an emergency doctor with two kids and a new medical mystery, Terminally Ill, *which Publishers Weekly calls "entertaining and insightful."*

She's been published in Nature, The Dragon and the Stars, Indian Country Noir, Weird Tales, *and lots of other fine venues. She's a winner of the* Aurora Award, Innermoonlit Award, and Writers of the Future. Publishers Weekly *hailed her short story,* Indian Time, *as "impressive" and "moving." But the most exciting thing about the indie publishing revolution is connecting with readers around the world.*

To learn more visit Melissa's website at:

melissayuaninnes.com

Christmas Miracles
Pamela Cowan

*T*HE GIRL ON the corner looked cold. She kept moving, stomping her feet on the hard, frozen dirt at the side of the road. The clothes she wore seemed too thin for the weather, and the hand-lettered cardboard sign in her hands shook. Karen didn't bother to read it. There was only one thing on her mind: getting to Portland. She wasn't going to let anything slow her down. It had been hard enough making the decision.

Less than an hour ago she'd briskly climbed the steps to the attic and opened the door. For a moment the attic was spooky, full of strange shapes and looming shadows. Then she flipped on the light and it became the familiar storage space at the top of the old farmhouse where she'd lived for the past twenty years.

In the center of the room were the bunk beds the kids had once used when friends slept over, or for their pretend trips. She wondered if they still remembered the nights when they'd lay listening to the rain pounding on the tin roof, on safari, tired from exploring a strange and dangerous continent. The striped comforters were partly covered by their abandoned collections of old dolls, worn trucks and tattered stuffed animals.

Around the beds, stacks of boxes held more discarded toys, old school papers, and moth-eaten clothes. In between the stacks were old lamps that Henry pretended he'd eventually fix, fans that didn't move, and chairs that were too dangerous to sit on but could still hold stacks of magazines whose articles she'd never find time to clip.

Karen pulled a pile of half-finished quilts from the top of an old trunk and opened the lid. Inside she found the flaking remnants of a bouquet of roses, a spray of lavender, and an orchid corsage. Beneath the flowers was a small wooden box filled with old love letters, under it, dog-eared diaries with tiny keys attached, old photographs, and canceled plane tickets. All the detritus of a woman's life — too personal to exhibit — too valued to discard.

Also inside the trunk was a small sack sewn from burlap. Karen removed it, pleased by its heft, and carried it to a window seat where the light was better. She unwound the rubber band around the neck of the sack and poured its contents onto the seat beside her. The coins spilled out with a pleasant clinking sound and seemed to gather the light. Unconsciously Karen began to stack them into precarious towers.

How many times in her forty-five years had she done just this, idly play with the coins and dream of all the strange times and places they represented. When she was a child they had belonged to her grandmother and she had only been allowed to look at them. When they'd become her mother's she was allowed, occasionally, to touch them.

She remembered holding coins from France and imagining the Eiffel Tower. Paris. Romance. She could recall fantasizing that the coins from Arabia had once been used to buy exotic spices, silks, maybe even a woman for a Sultan's harem. After the coins became hers, she too had added to them. Here were quarters bearing the birth years of her parents and her children. Here were a few pesos from a honeymoon trip to Mexico, and here, the strangely shaped one from Egypt that she'd had to have.

She felt guilty. The coins would have been her daughter Amy's eventually and they'd have been appreciated. Of the two children, Amy was the one most given to nostalgia and a love of the past. But Amy would understand. She would feel that cheating her of the coins would be less a sin than cheating her brother out of his future.

It was sort of ironic that while Amy loved the past, Tom loved the future and in fact planned to help design and build it. He'd always wanted to be an architect and being accepted to one of the best architectural schools in the country, was the beginning. Anything that forced him to give up on college and come home might end that dream.

Of course Tom's dream wasn't the only one Karen worried about. How many nights had she awakened in an empty bed and heard

Henry, her husband, wandering restlessly downstairs. How often had she found him in his office staring at a spreadsheet, or hammering on his computer keyboard as if he were furious with it for not giving him the answers he needed?

They both knew the only answer was money. The tax bill had appeared with its usual precision and must be paid by January 15th. It didn't care about the bills for Henry's broken leg, or the cost of tuition, or three years of late frosts. It didn't care that Christmas was only a month away and they were afraid to hang lights because the slightly higher power bill might be the difference between making it to the next season or giving up altogether.

Well, this wouldn't be the year, not if she could help it, and she could. She had the coins. She didn't know how much they were worth but it had to be enough. Amy would know. She worked in an antique store in the city. She'd sold those old things of grand-mother's and helped pay off her tuition. Too bad there weren't more old sequined purses or hand-knit shawls around the place. Who'd have guessed they'd be so valuable one day?

The sharp backfire of one of the tractors starting up put a sudden end to Karen's daydreams. Surely Henry wasn't trying to climb onto the tractor with his broken leg. Gathering the coins, she slipped them back into their bag, and then noticed one of the seams was coming loose. Looking around for something to hold them, she remembered the box of love letters. She carefully slid the ribbon-tied bundle out and was ashamed of the bitter thought that came unasked, that at least her letters were safe, since they had no monetary value. Silly to be so attached to things she told herself. The coins were of no importance. Only people mattered.

After slipping into her jacket, Karen tucked her purse under one arm, the box under the other and climbed into her car. She drove down the sloping driveway to the barn then got out and walked up to the attached lean-to, where the tractor stood running loudly, exhaust rising to join the early morning mist. Henry was peering into the engine compartment, leaning on one crutch. He looked up and smiled when he saw her.

"Thought you'd lost your mind and was trying to drive," she shouted above the rumble of the tractor. "Glad to see you're still only half crazy. Where's your other crutch? Didn't Dr. G say you should use both of them?"

"When did I ever listen to doctors?" Henry shouted back." The engine sputtered and died. "You know there's only one person I listen to," Henry said, his volume dropping in the sudden silence.

"Me?" Karen asked.

"Of course."

"Well, you're obviously delirious. You must have a fever."

"Just a fever for you."

"Oh for …" Karen pretended annoyance but the wide smile that reached and crinkled the corners of her eyes gave her away. Putting her hands on her hips she told him sternly. "You're on your own for breakfast and probably lunch too. I have to run into Portland."

"Going to see the kiddo?"

"Yeah, and run some errands. Do you need anything?"

"From Portland? Hell no."

Karen was again reminded of how hard it would be for Henry to give up the farm and live where he could find employment, most likely a large town or city. He'd do it, of course. He'd always known keeping his parent's farm operating at a profit would be tough. That he might eventually have to accept selling it. Still, he'd worked hard to keep it, and last year they'd made a fantastic deal with a winery to plant and grow grapes. The income should be steady and allow them to keep the farm, and even allow Henry to take some time off now and then. But that income was three years off.

"Okay, well I'd better run," Ellen said, snapping out of her gloomy thoughts. "I called Amy and she's expecting me for lunch. Maybe I'll bring something back for you." Karen gave Henry a quick goodbye kiss and got back in the car.

$\mathcal{K}$AREN KNOCKED ON the door and heard her daughter yell, "Come in!"

She opened the door and Amy, standing in the doorway to the kitchen at the back of the house said, "Hang up your coat. I'm burning lunch," then ducked back into the room. Amy was eight months pregnant and only worked on the antique store's busiest days. Today was a slow day, she'd explained when her mother called.

"I hope tomato soup and grilled cheese is okay. It's the only thing I want to eat lately."

Karen laughed. "It was red licorice with me. I must have eaten a tub a week."

"That's awful."

"Really? Because it was slices of dill pickle and whipped cream with your brother."

"Oh my gosh, I'm going to be sick. Promise not to talk about pickles."

"I promise. I promise. Not to change the subject," said Karen, to change the subject, "but, how's Jerry. Is he working today?"

"Yep. No slow days for accountants. He's out earning diaper money, poor thing."

Karen placed the box on the table in the breakfast nook and took a seat. "Your brother called. He said his first final is today and his last is on the seventh. He thinks he'll be here on the eighth."

"Awesome. It's been a long time. Guess Dad will be happy to see him. He must have a list of jobs that he hasn't been able to get to. I don't know why he doesn't just accept that he's not going to be able to do any work this winter. Can't he just sit back and—"

"And what, watch television?"

"Yeah, okay, I guess not," said Amy, with a crooked smile. She stood in front of the stove, stirring a pot of soup that gave off the scent of tomatoes and fresh basil. "I wish we could help," she continued. "We thought about refinancing the house but we just don't have enough equity yet."

"Oh, Amy, that's so sweet of you and Jerry. You have to thank him for me. But really, you both need to stop worrying about us. You'll have a family of your own to worry about soon. And besides, you never know what might happen. It's almost Christmas, a good time for a miracle."

"Well, if that miracle doesn't show up you can always look on the bright side. Living in town can be nice. There are stores on every corner, concerts, no hour-long drive to get anywhere. Besides, if you lived here you'd be closer to your grandchild."

"That's very practical of you. And I'm sure Jerry would love to see his in-laws more often," Karen teased.

"Oh Mom, you know Jerry's crazy about you guys."

"That's because we live an hour away, if the traffic is good, an appropriate distance for in laws. Anyway, I didn't come here for your advice on city living. I came for your advice on antiques. Can you look at these and tell me what they're worth?" Karen removed the lid of the box, revealing the coins inside.

"Oh no, Mom. Not your coin collection."

"Yes. And I know you were meant to have them but I'm thinking of selling them. Do you think they're worth anything?"

"Coins aren't really my thing, but I'm sure I have a price catalog somewhere. It would at least give us an idea." After turning off the heat under the soup, Amy went upstairs and in a few moments returned carrying a large book.

Karen flipped through the book but put it aside in order to eat. It wasn't until they'd finished lunch and cleared off the table that the two women started to work. Karen arranged the coins by country, denomination and year, while Amy looked them up and kept notes.

After an hour Amy sat up, put down her pen and said, "I'm sorry Mom. You've got some nice old coins but none are rare and only the silver dollars are worth much more than face value. The entire box is only worth about three hundred dollars. I might be able to get a bit more on resale but I don't know. I could buy them from you if you like. Give you three hundred now and when they sell give you any difference."

"Minus a commission," Karen said.

"Charge my mom a commission. I don't think so."

"Well then, Ms. Businesswoman, no way am I selling them to you."

"But, Mom—"

Karen waved her hand, dismissing her daughter's argument. "It doesn't matter, three hundred, four hundred. That's just not enough." She put the coins back in the box and slid the lid in place. "Amy McKenzie-Schnable, don't you dare cry. Everything is going to be just fine."

"I'm not crying," Amy said, as tears ran down her face. "Anyway, if I am, it's not my fault, it … it … it's baby hormones."

"You poor thing," Karen said, handing Amy a napkin. Despite her daughter's tears, Karen's mood lifted. The thought of a grandchild had cheered her considerably. Maybe Amy was right and selling the farm wouldn't be such a tragedy. Henry might find a job he didn't completely hate, and being closer to Amy would be nice.

She tried to keep these positive thoughts as she drove back home. It was a relief to exit the highway, leaving the city traffic behind. It was still early afternoon when she reached the 'Welcome to Dundee' sign. As she entered town she saw that the young woman who'd been panhandling that morning was still at it. The sun had come up, burning off the mist and the young woman looked less cold but no less miserable.

Karen pulled up to the stop sign and this time took a moment to read the woman's sign. It said, 'Car needs repair. No money. Please help.' Karen didn't know what impulse caused her to roll down her window. The town held its normal share of hard cases: rough looking men with gaunt cheeks and eyes that seemed to look beyond you. Normally she didn't make eye contact with them. This time she couldn't help herself. Maybe it was because the young woman reminded her of Amy. She had the same dark wavy hair and big brown eyes.

"Your car broke down?" Karen asked, nodding at the sign.

The woman took a step closer to the car. "Yes ma'am, it did. A nice man towed it to his shop and looked at it for me for free, but he says I need a new water pump so I'm trying to get enough to buy one."

"What man?" Karen asked. She knew when she told Henry about this later he'd give her points for not taking the girl's word at face value.

"His name was Bill. He works at a place called Charlie's Chop Shop."

Karen nodded. "Yes, I know Bill, and actually he owns the place. He called it Charlie's because he liked the alliteration. Charlie's Chop Shop sounds better than Bill's Chop Shop."

"And lots easier to say," agreed the girl. She smiled, or at least pulled back the corners of her mouth. At the same time she hugged herself. Karen realized she was shivering. "You need something warm. Hop in and we'll go get you some coffee and maybe something to eat. Did you eat today?"

The girl shook her head but made no move to get into the car.

"Do I look like a maniac?" Karen asked, and then: "The café has pie."

At this, the woman ran around and opened the passenger side door. Karen took the box of coins off the seat and put them on the back floor, making room for her.

*T*HEY HAD FINISHED their burgers and moved on to the promised pie before Karen managed to coax the woman — whose name was Elizabeth — into sharing her story.

"What I don't understand is why the military didn't pay your way," Karen said.

"I didn't ask. We're not married after all."

"But you were planning to be, as soon as he got back. Seems to me they'd take that into account. My dad and grandfather were in the military: Japan, Korea and Vietnam. We should be taking better care of our military."

"I guess so, but Denny said he didn't want us to be a military family. He'd seen too many families torn apart, too many married people living alone. He had one more tour in Afghanistan and then he planned to get out of the service and go into business with his dad. When he got back we'd have the big wedding and start out together."

"But then he got hurt."

"Yes. There was a bomb. It went off when they drove over it. The driver was killed and Denny was pinned underneath the truck. His spine was hurt and he couldn't walk. They were flying him to a special hospital in Maryland to do emergency surgery. His father called a few days ago, told me about the accident and where they were sending him. I had to get to him. I threw some things in my car and took off. I guess I was sort of a mess."

"I can only imagine," said Karen, patting Elizabeth's hand. And you don't have anyone who can help you — wire you the money?"

"If I could reach them. I mean, I don't have family but I do have friends. Only, I don't know how to contact them. When I left I grabbed my phone but not my regular charger. I had the car charger though and one night I rented a room so I could catch up on some sleep. I was getting sort of 'drifty'. I left my phone on the car charger and that night someone broke my window. They took the phone and a gym bag full of dirty gym clothes that were on the back seat."

"Well, the dirty clothes served them right."

Elizabeth nodded and smiled at the idea of the thief discovering what he'd risked jail to steal. "I looked up Denny's dad's phone but he was driving to Maryland, and no one's answering at their house.

Almost everyone else I know has a cell phone that isn't listed, and since they're programmed in my phone I never bothered to memorize them. I know I must sound really dumb. I guess I am. I took off without thinking. I didn't have much money to start with and then I had a flat the first day and had to pay for a new tire. Then I paid for the hotel room, and I bought a bag of groceries so I didn't have to waste money buying food, and that took my last nickel. I figured I'd be okay but now—"

"Now you're stuck."

"Yes ma'am. But I think if I can borrow enough money from people I can get the car fixed and maybe that will be the end of the bad luck. I need two hundred dollars."

"And how is that going? Are you close?"

Elizabeth reached into the pocket of her coat, not much more than a windbreaker, and drug out a handful of crumpled bills and coins. She dropped them on the table and began to count. "Nineteen dollars and twenty-seven cents," she said when she was done. "I guess it's going to take longer than I thought."

"Are you done with your pie?" Karen asked.

"Yeah. It was great. Thank you."

"You're welcome. Shall we go?"

"Sure. I appreciate the ride."

Karen realized that Elizabeth was expecting a ride back to where she'd picked her up. That was not her plan. Instead she drove the young woman across town to Charlie's Chop Shop. She pulled into one of the spaces in front and parked, and then she reached back and lifted out the box of coins. "Tell Bill that there is three-hundred dollars' worth of coins in here," she said, placing the box on Elizabeth's lap. "He can take them to any antique store and sell them for at least that. Tell him Amy will give him that for sure. In fact, tell him Amy's mom says to get a move on and order the part and fix the car."

"But I—"

"But nothing. It will make Bill laugh. We're friends. And it will hurry him up. He sort of runs on island time or something.

"But I can't—"

"Don't you want to be with your fiancé?"

"Of course."

"Well then, say thanks and get out of the car."

Elizabeth, having accepted Karen's help, beamed at her. "Thank you. Thank you very much." She got out of the car and shut the door.

Karen rolled down the window and smiled back. "Good luck, to both of you." Then she drove home, empty handed but happier. At least someone would be getting a Christmas miracle.

CHRISTMAS AT THE farm had been especially lovely, thought Karen as she washed the last of the serving trays. Who was it who said you have to have the bad to have the good? Whoever it was had been wise. With the prospect of this being the last Christmas they'd spend in this old, drafty house, everything had become magical. From arguing eggs away from the crabby hens in the early morning, to canning dozens of jars of food they'd probably not bother to pack, to scrubbing the heavy porcelain sink so it sparkled white as new, every gesture seemed special, a moment to save and remember later.

Henry and the kids had gone off on a moonlight sleigh ride. Henry, his leg propped up on a stack of pillows was up front with Tom who was driving the team. Amy and her husband, Jerry were in back: Amy trying to pretend it was a romantic interlude, while Tom fussed and worried about her pregnancy and the wisdom of letting two large animals drag them around the countryside.

Karen had smiled and waved as they moved away, the bells tied to the sleigh jingling pleasantly long after they were out of sight. Poor Jerry, when the baby arrived he'd not only be outmaneuvered by the women in his life, he'd be outnumbered.

They'd wanted to take her with them but Karen had wanted some time alone with her thoughts. Henry had given her a brief but knowing glance. He'd understood. This was her chance to say goodbye, a moment to give in to her sadness before she pulled on the mantle of adulthood and became her usual cheerful and cheering self. They'd all be struggling with the loss soon enough, and they'd need her to be strong for them.

And so she'd allowed herself this time of weakness. She'd moved through the rooms of her house saying goodbye and then, because she wasn't prone to wallowing in self-pity for long, she took a firm grip on herself. *A house is not a home. A home is the people around you and those people aren't going anywhere.*

She was setting dessert on the table, an apple crisp and a bowl of fresh whipped cream when the stomp of boots, and the wash of icy wind blowing through the front door, announced her family's return

"We're back, Mom. No one was mangled. Not even a bruise. The stockings were hung by the chimney with care," shouted Amy.

"Isn't that supposed to be through the river and around the woods?" asked Tom.

"You mean around the river, dork. Who rides through a river?"

"Oh for the love of … What are you two on about now? Hey, get those boots off, you're tracking snow all over the place. Henry, where the heck are your crutches?"

Tom walked in behind his father carrying his crutches and looking guilty. Karen shook her head at both of them. "Got the mail," Henry said, holding up a double handful of letters. Can't carry all this stuff and negotiate with those things, can I?"

Karen rolled her eyes and swept forward to take the mail. "Now you can," she said. "Not that you will. Dessert's on the table. New pot of coffee. Decaf. Don't complain."

In the calm following the minor storm of their entrance, the family ate and drank coffee, their time outdoors fueling their appetites. As they talked and laughed Karen absently went through the mail, bills in one pile, requests to buy stuff to create more bills in a second pile. Unlike the rest of the mail the final letter was hand-addressed. She thought maybe a Christmas letter from a friend or relative but then saw the name, Elizabeth Parker and a Maryland postmark. She opened the letter and read.

Dear Ms. McKenzie,

I got your name and address from Bill at Charlie's Chop Shop. I told him I was going to send you a thank you letter. Thank you so much for helping me when my car broke down. You are one of the kindest people I've ever met. I want you to know that my fiancé is doing much better than expected. The doctors think he will make a full recovery and there will be no lasting damage. He has been walking more every day. We plan to get married in the spring.

I gave your friend Bill the coins, but I kept the box they were in as a sort of reminder that there are good people in the world. I showed it to my fiancé. The minute he saw it he got all excited and called his dad, who's been staying at a nearby hotel. When Denny's dad saw the box he got excited too.

I think I told you Denny was planning to go into business with his dad but I never said what that business was. He owns an Asian art consulting and appraisal firm in New York. As soon as they saw the box they knew what it was. I'm not an art consultant, and I know nothing at all about Asian art. Denny's dad is also writing you a letter and I'll attach it to this one.

I guess I just want to say, thank you very much, and merry, merry Christmas!

Dear Ms. McKenzie,

My name is William Ross, of Ross & Ross. I deal in Asian art and antiquities. The box my future daughter-in-law has shown me is of the Qing dynasty, the last imperial dynasty of China, proceeded by the perhaps better known, Ming dynasty. We realize you would not *have given Elizabeth the box had you known its value. I admit I'm rather proud that she and my son have chosen to contact you and make you aware of the box's place of origin and its value, which we believe is between $60,000-80,000, and to return ownership to you. I would be happy to speak with you and learn what you know of it and how it came into your possession. Please contact me at the number below and let me know what you'd like to do next. We can insure and ship the box to you or, if you wish to sell, would be happy to contact the appropriate collectors and organize an auction at your behest.*

Sincerely yours,

William Ross

Karen took a deep breath. She hadn't realized she'd been holding her breath until then. She felt a little lightheaded.

"What is it, Mom?" asked Tom.

"I well ... I don't know where to start." Then she told them the story of the day she tried to sell her coins and ended by reading them the letters. When she was done, the family sat staring at her in astonishment for a full minute. Then, they exploded, jumping up and hugging each other, laughing and squealing, even breaking into an odd sort of dance around the table.

"Sit down. Sit down," Karen urged. "Your father has a broken leg. Get back in your chair, old man." Henry ignored her, took her hand and twirled her in dizzy circles.

"Wait a minute. Wait just one minute," said Tom, turning to face his sister. "Didn't you take the box to Amy? How come Miss Knows-All-About-Antiques didn't tell you about the box?"

Red-faced from dancing more than embarrassment Amy said, "I deal in American antiques, not Chinese ones. Besides, Mom didn't show me the box, just the coins, right Mom?"

Knowing the box had sat on Amy's table in full sight the entire time she'd been there, Karen remained loyal and took her daughter's side. "That's right, she was looking at the coins."

"Oh sure," said Tom, humor thick in his voice. "Take her side. How come she always takes your side?" Tom demanded of his sister.

"Because I'm special." A sudden clenching pain spread from her back, around to her naval. She put her hand on her swollen belly, the skin felt firm and tight, just as the midwife had said it would. "Oh boy — Jerry!"

Jerry sprang to her side and helped Amy ease into a chair. "Are you okay?" he asked.

"Well I … Yeah, I think so. But also, well I think I might be going to have that baby sort of real soon."

And that night Karen received not one, but two Christmas miracles.

~

ABOUT THE AUTHOR

Pamela Cowan is best known for writing psychological thrillers. Her mystery novel, Something in the Dark, *won the NSQ award and was a #1 best seller on Amazon Kindle. She recently published* Storm Justice, *a suspense thriller, and is currently working on the second book in that series. Her short stories have been published in* Alien Skin, Argus, Space and Time, Visions, *various anthologies and have been read on OPB-supported* Golden Hours Radio.

An army brat, she was born in Germany and moved with her family seventeen times before her father retired to Oregon, where she has steadfastly remained. She has two grown children and lives with her husband and various four-legged houseguests.

To learn more visit the Pamela's website at:

pamelacowan.com

The Nest
Courtney Pierce

THE CHRISTMAS SEASON officially started on the day after Thanksgiving. In the Collins household, though, the real kick-off was the hunt for a live thirteen-foot noble fir. The prettiest trees, the freshest trees, were in Portland, Oregon, and they could be cut at a farm not too far from their house in Milwaukie, a quiet suburb on the southeast side of the Willamette River. Jean Collins had a discerning eye for one that would fit into the fifteen-foot stairwell — with exact dimensions. The open downstairs rooms in her and Spence's 1960s garden home offered a perfect viewing experience from every angle. It had to be right. Her husband, Spence, tended to be more sympathetic to the trees that had 'issues.'

This year's tree would showcase Jean's latest estate sale score of vintage ornaments. She'd hidden them in the garage for the past three months. Springing the purchase on Spence required meticulous timing. With their mutual commitment to downsize, the deal was that anything new brought in had to be accompanied by something going out.

But by Jean's rules, heirloom ornaments didn't count. She had a nose for finding the unusual, the one-of-a-kind, or those with a colorful history of their own. So when Jean bumped through the mudroom with an armful of age-spotted and torn-cornered boxes, her bright blue eyes danced with anticipation. Spence rolled his big brown ones.

"Check these out! Christmas ornaments," she announced, catching a box before it slid off the teetering stack.

"Honey, we have a ton," Spence griped. "We could decorate three trees with what we've already got."

"But these are antiques — over a hundred years probably."

"And just when did you get them?" Spence furrowed his brow and narrowed his dark eyes, suspicious. "Nobody holds an estate sale in winter."

She grinned. "Back in September — in Irvington. The woman died. Incredible old bungalow, though. Everything she had was amazing. The china was—"

"Jean . . ."

She dipped her head to the boxes. "I've been hiding them in the garage. Timing is the key on these things."

Spence scrunched his forehead. No admonishment needed; the look said it all, but one dark eyebrow rose in the opposite direction. A chink in the armor.

"Save your grumping until after you see them," she continued. "I promise we'll cull out some of our old ones for these."

"Okay, but I'm not committing."

Spence remained quiet. He waved his hand for her to proceed. Jean figured she had exactly fifteen seconds to make her case. But she didn't need to say a word; the ornaments would speak for themselves. She set the stack on the granite island in the kitchen and pulled a white box from the middle labeled *butterflies* in penciled script. The socks-knockers first. The suction from lifting the lid crinkled the brittle tissue inside. Aromas of age and attic rafters wafted around her.

"These had better be good." Spence ran his fingers through his salt-and-peppered hair.

"Just wait." Jean lifted out one of the clip-on butterflies; its silken wingspan measured about four inches across. Shimmery fabric, a dark shade of taupe, had been hand-stretched and sewn over a wire frame. Small cut-crystals in vivid colors — ruby, amethyst, and topaz — dotted the wings, rimmed with a thin cord of soft brown velvet that matched the body. As if springing to life, antennae of fine curly-cues shivered as she held up the butterfly. The crystals sparkled like flawless gems in the overhead kitchen lights.

"Wow! I take back everything I said."

"What'd I tell you? Woe to the man who doubts my abilities to pull off a surprise." She eyed Spence. He nodded, never taking his eyes off the ornament. "I have finally rendered the great Spence Collins speechless." Jean beamed as she, too, admired the butterfly. "We have ten of them in different colors."

Spence rubbed his chin and pointed. "And what's in those other boxes? I'm with you so far."

"All clip-on birds with *real* feathers. The estate sale lady said they're from the late 1800s. It'll be like the backyard crew flew in and landed on the Christmas tree. We'll decorate with our regular ornaments and set these on the ends of the branches as the final touch." Jean opened another box and selected a delicate iridescent hummingbird, bright green with a reflection of subtle pink when she wiggled the ornament under the light. "Hold out your hand." She clipped the tiny bird on the end of his finger.

"I love these. They look so life-like." Spence made a lazy *S* with his forefinger.

If the butterfly wasn't enough, then the hummingbird had won him over. Animals were Spence's passion. He spoiled the critters — all year round — but the hummingbirds received extra treats to withstand the cold, ice, and lack of fresh nectar. And their favorite squirrel, named Jazz Hands, would swish his paws on the floor-to-ceiling glass in the living room for his umpteenth round of peanuts.

A twinkle lit up Spence's eyes. "Let's go get the tree."

"*I* BET SNOW is in the cards this year. Already cold enough," Spence said as he pulled the rope from the trunk. In front of them was a sea of evergreen under a blanket of gray mist. The tree farm was only a few miles from their house. It didn't take long to go from urban to rural anywhere in the area. The fresh pine scent filled the moist air, thick and sweet.

"Smells like snow too." Jean inhaled, energized by the chill and the aroma of Christmas. "I hope you're right. And if we get a tree with a nest, we'll have good luck." She tucked her blond pageboy behind her ears, slipped on heavy work gloves, and then patted the pocket of her fleece jacket for the tape measure. "Let the games begin."

Of the rows and rows of near-perfect trees, by anyone's standards, only one stood tall and skinny above the rest. The one. Jean circled the noble fir with the eyes of a surgeon. After thirty-four Christmases with Spence, she could zero in on one within five minutes — but the measurements made the final decision.

"Thirteen feet on the money," she declared, reeling in the tape with a *whoosh*. "Forty-eight inches around the base. Perfect."

"Looks full too," Spence added. "The branches are separated just right for the lights."

Jean brushed the needles to free them of sticks and debris. In order to check the circumference of the trunk for fitting into the stand, she stuck her hand inside the branches. Her breath caught in her throat. She turned and beamed at Spence.

Catching her elated expression, his eyes widened. "What?"

"A nest. This is the one, Spence."

"Well, that settles it. We'll have this baby up by noon."

Jean pulled out the nest, being careful to not break it apart. A gallon-size plastic bag in the car would keep it intact until they got home. "All white lights will be perfect with the birds and butterflies."

"Maybe use that see-through ribbon. The stuff with the sparkles." Spence summoned a staff member with a hand saw.

With the tree cut and tied to the top of the Volvo, Spence drove as if the tires were made of glass. Over the speed of thirty-five, Jean had that lift-off feeling in her stomach. She breathed a sigh of relief when they turned into the driveway.

Jean helped Spence wrestle the noble fir to stand upright in a bucket of water, and then leaned it against the garage door. She took aim with the hose.

"Spider check!" she warned. "Don't need an eight-legged army crawling all over the ceiling." Jean set the nozzle on the highest force. "I'll rinse and pat it down if you bring in the lights and the rest of the ornaments."

"Righto. Don't forget the nest is still in the car."

*B*Y FOUR O'CLOCK (nowhere close to noon), the tree was finally up and strung with white twinkle lights.

"Ready?" Spence asked, his hand poised over the switch on the crowded power strip.

"Hit it!"

In an instant, the open kitchen, dining room, and step-down living area were cast in a ghostly glow. Jean poured two glasses of cabernet and fired up Dean Martin's Christmas album. The bouncing melody of 'A Marshmallow World' accompanied the light. Her gaze turned to the nest in the plastic bag on the kitchen counter. With a careful hand, she slipped out the marvel of natural engineering: a cup formed of woven sticks and hardened mud, interspersed with leaves and bits of downy fur picked from a small animal.

"Now I feel kind of bad," Jean bemoaned. "A bird worked for days to build this."

"Probably abandoned," Spence added, his expression conflicting with his words.

"Spence, you get to pick the spot."

After careful assessment, Spence pointed to an opening between the branches at about chest level. "Right there. That's where the nest was when you found it."

Jean tucked it on a branch next to the trunk.

Bang!

She gasped. "What was that?"

Spence immediately checked the line-up of plugs on the electrical strip. "Not a short. Maybe something hit a window — down here, not upstairs. You check the sliding door in the dining room; I'll check the ones in the living room and den."

Jean bolted to the dining room. A blast of cold air hit her face when she pulled back the heavy glass door. She flipped on the patio light. No movement, except for her steamy breath dissipating to the melody of 'I'll Be Home for Christmas'. She stepped inside to catch up with Spence. Through the floor-to-ceiling window in the living room, she spotted him outside on his hands and knees in the foggy light of the back patio. He was talking to a tiny owl.

"Is he okay?" she asked in an urgent whisper.

"I think so, but he's stunned. Probably blinded," Spence said. "The optic nerve swells when they hit something hard."

"Shouldn't we leave him alone?"

"We can't, honey. He'll starve. Without sight, he won't be able to eat or drink. And we're in for a freeze tonight."

"I don't know …" Jean hedged. Spence's lack of fear when it came to injured animals never ceased to amaze her. He dove in as a first responder with no regard for personal risk. He should have become a vet instead of the owner of a vintage record store.

Spence raised his eyes. "This is what Christmas is all about, Jean. He needs our help."

When he put it that way, Jean couldn't object. "How long do you think? He's awfully little."

"Couple of weeks at least, provided nothing's seriously wrong. He has to be able to hunt on his own."

"Is he a baby?"

"Not this time of year. He's a Northern Saw-whet. Only the Pygmy is smaller. They're native to Oregon up through western Canada." Spence cupped the owl in his hands. "Go get a shoebox," he whispered. "I'll bring him inside."

Jean dashed up the stairs to the guest room closet where she kept her fabric and sewing notions. She emptied a cloth-covered bin from the hanging shoe holder she used for ribbon storage. At the last minute, she grabbed a piece of remnant fleece and bounded down the steps to the kitchen. Peeking over Spence's fingers were two dilated yellow eyes. A sunburst of white radiated around the owl's petite face; the rest of his feathers were chestnut brown and flecked. Spence set the bird on the soft cream-colored fleece.

"He's adorable," Jean whispered.

Tssssst ... tssst ... eewck. A high-pitched, mechanical squeak was followed by a rapid click of the owl's beak.

"Uh ... I'd better hightail it to the pet store," Spence suggested, widening his already big brown eyes at the reality of the next task.

Jean glanced at her watch. "Five-thirty."

"They close at six."

"Oh ... right. Mice." Jean wasn't thrilled with the parade of rodents that were about to share their holiday.

"Will you be okay with him until I get back?"

"I guess so. I'll keep an eye out while I hang the ornaments on the tree. But hurry. We'll need to take turns with him."

"Don't put on the birds without me." Spence grabbed his keys and headed down the hall to the mudroom.

"Wait! What about a name?" she called out.

Spence's face erupted with a wide grin. He appeared much younger than his sixty-one years when he did that. "Hooters!"

"Hooters?" She waved her hand. "Go on. Git, Saint Francis!"

The door to the garage clicked shut. Jean turned. She couldn't tell if the owl had sight or not, but he blinked twice and puffed his feathers.

Eeeeewck.

"Merry Christmas to you too." Jean dragged the tip of her finger down the back of the owl's head. Soft. His eyes closed slower than before, a sign Hooters was either hungry or getting tired. She glanced at him as she hung the ornaments.

*F*ORTY MINUTES LATER, Spence came through the door with a Plexiglas terrarium teeming with tiny deer mice. He set the clear-sided box on the dining room table.

"A little creepy to put that where we eat, Spence."

"Oh, I don't know. They're dinner." He lifted off the lid. "Should I have a go?"

"I can't look. You do it." Jean turned away, but couldn't resist a peek. Spence plucked one of the mice from the container by the tail. As he stepped closer to Hooters with the writhing rodent, the owl became animated.

"He can see."

Whoo...oo...oo. Tssst. Tssst.

"Just get it over with."

With one fast snap and two gulps, the mouse disappeared. Jean's eyes locked on Spence's. They both turned to Hooters.

"Nothing wrong with his appetite. A good sign," Spence said.

"Ugh. Barbaric." Jean scrunched her face, as though she, herself, had been forced to swallow a rodent. She filled a ramekin with water and set it in the corner of Hooters's fabric-covered box. "I saved the best for last. Let's finish decorating while he rests."

Turning to check Hooters every few minutes, Jean and Spence clipped all thirty bird ornaments on the ends of the branches. The ten butterflies were strategically dispersed around the tree, with one attached to the top. The sparkly ribbon gave the illusion it was carried in the mouths of the birds.

Jean stood back and admired their handiwork. "Beautiful..."

"The bar is set pretty high now," Spence agreed. "This is a winner."

Eeeeeeeewck.

Jean flinched as Hooters launched from his container. Spence ducked as the owl flew past his head, dove into the tree, and settled in the nest. Even in the glow of the lights, the camouflage of the owl's feathers blended in with the other ornaments.

"Spence ... do you—'

"Don't say it. But, yeah, I think that's his nest."

"He followed us home."

*A*FTER NEARLY THREE weeks, Hooters had become quite comfortable in the house, albeit the washing machine worked overtime to bleach the piles of cleaning rags. The twenty-four gobbled up deer mice became somewhat of an Advent calendar in the countdown to Hooters's release. Only three were left. But something started to happen on Christmas Eve morning.

Jean pulled on her sweats. A lot to do. After a cup of coffee and a cleaning of the nest, she needed to start chopping and prepping for the early evening meal of prime rib, Yorkshire pudding, roasted cauliflower, and fresh fruit. A decades-old tradition. This year, she'd add a mouse and a handful of sunflower seeds for Hooters. By four o'clock, she'd be enjoying a glass of wine by the fire with Spence.

Mornings officially began with a touch of the butterfly on the top of the Christmas tree. This one was no different. Jean stepped along the upstairs catwalk and extended her hand to flick the wing. She stopped. The butterfly sat three branches down. Upon descending the stairs, she noticed the ornament shift was more elaborate. The birds had been messed with too. She laughed; convinced Spence had done some rearranging. Six robins had been moved up; four cardinals had been moved down, and eight finches were in different spots too. Every one of the ten butterflies' wings had been repositioned — just enough. Spence was playing with her. A good joke. She pressed the switch to light the tree.

Wuck-uck. Eeeeewck.

"Morning, Hooters." She stuck her finger into the branches toward the nest. The owl shimmied down its length, anticipating a rodent 'over easy' for breakfast. "Daddy's playing a trick on Mommy."

Hooters stared into her eyes and blinked three times. Jean stepped back and studied the ornaments. All of the antique birds and butterflies were in different places. "Maybe you did that," she whispered to Hooters. Something nagged, though. This kind of joke seemed out of character for Spence.

Spence came through the front door with the newspaper, his face animated like a kid's. "It's snowing. Only flurries, but they count."

"Good one, honey."

"What?"

"The ornaments. You must have gotten up pretty early to move these all around." Jean held out the owl. "Time to feed Hooters."

"I already fed him. And, no, I didn't do anything to the ornaments. Why?"

"Look. The cardinal is down two branches." She pointed to different parts of the tree. "That finch down here was up there. The top butterfly isn't on the top." Jean swept her other hand in an arc. "They're all moved around."

Spence followed her gaze. "Huh…" He shrugged. "I swear it wasn't me. I didn't even notice until you said something just now."

"Don't you think it's a bit weird for this to happen on Christmas Eve?"

"Jean … you're talking to a pint-size owl on your finger. Let's talk weird."

"You got me." Jean smiled at Hooters. "Right, little guy?" Her face drooped as she turned back to Spence. "We have to let him go. He's not hurt and clearly not traumatized. We're now officially into selfish territory."

"I know…" Spence stroked the owl's head. "I'll put his nest in the maple tree tomorrow. He's so damned cute, though."

"But what's going on with these ornaments?"

*A*s it did every year, Christmas morning came too soon. At five o'clock, Jean opened her eyes. Spence, already awake, was inspecting her face. Actually, he'd been studying her hair; it had a life of its own. She sensed her blond pageboy resembled an exploded hay bale.

"Nice 'do', dear," Spence quipped. "Merry Christmas."

She gazed into his puppy-dog brown eyes, admiring his long, dark lashes, longer than hers. "Merry Christmas," she whispered, and gave him a deep kiss. "Time to check Hooters."

Jean's 'do' was already up as she pulled back the comforter, reluctant to rob herself of its warmth. She jumped out of bed and opened the drapes in front of the sliding glass door. Snow. Fuzzy flakes blew in opposite directions. Maybe only two inches had fallen overnight, but the branches of eighty-foot cedar trees in the back yard drooped under the weight of white.

"You were right. A snow year."

"Told ya," Spence crowed. "These old bones still got it all goin' on." He snapped his fingers in rhythm. "I'll start the fire; you turn on the coffee."

In their sweats, Spence raced over the catwalk and started down the stairs. Jean followed, but froze in mid-step.

"Spence?"

He stopped on the landing and gazed up at her, concerned by the alarm in her voice. "What's the matter?"

"Look."

In unison, their heads turned. No butterflies. No birds. The stairs creaked as her slow steps descended around the Christmas tree. Only their old ornaments remained: sparkly mercury balls, glass figurines, petite silver bells, and a pickle. All of the ones from the estate sale were gone.

"Where did they go?" Spence flipped the switch at the base of the tree.

"*Hooooters?*" Jean called from the kitchen. She scanned the downstairs.

"Oh my God!" Spence stood on the step that led to the sunken living room.

Hooters sat on the couch — surrounded by birds: cardinals, finches, robins, and hummingbirds. They lined the top of the leather club chairs, loveseats, and hassock. The oversize butterflies fluttered in loops above the furniture, their jeweled wings glinting in the reflection of the white tree lights.

Eeeeeewck. Hooters jumped from the loveseat and sat in front of the sliding door that opened to the back yard. He turned and blinked at Spence.

"It's time, Jean."

Through a blur of tears, Jean smiled at Hooters, memorizing every detail of his tiny face. That face melted her insides. "I know."

Spence crouched and stroked the owl's head. He flipped up the lock and slid open the glass door. A rush of frigid air entered the room, and on its current the birds launched in a line behind Hooters. The butterflies made a quick turn back inside when they hit the cold air. All ten of them returned to the Christmas tree, settling into their original spots on the branches. Upon landing, their wings stilled; nothing more than silk, wire, and sparkling crystals set on a metal clip.

Standing at the window, Jean wrapped her arms around Spence. Hooters. Gone. One after the other, the bird ornaments launched from the bare maple tree and dispersed high into the old-growth cedars. The combination of loss and gain filled Jean with an emotion she couldn't quite articulate. Small moments of magic continually changed their view of life. Her gaze floated toward Spence. His face registered that the morning had, indeed, been a Christmas for the books. They'd never forget the tiny owl, or the magical ornaments.

Spence smoothed down her wild hair. "Can you find another estate sale?"

Jean wiped her eyes and leaned into his chest. "Can you deal with the three left-over mice?"

~

ABOUT THE AUTHOR

Courtney Pierce is a fiction writer who lives in Milwaukie, Oregon, with her husband and bossy cat. After a twenty-year career as an executive in the Broadway entertainment industry, she returned home to finally write the stories that burned inside her. Courtney is Vice President and board member of the Northwest Independent Writers Association *and has completed the* Hawthorne Fellows *program at the* Attic Institute. *Courtney writes for baby boomers. Her boomer trilogy of magical realism,* Stitches, Brushes, *and* Riffs, *is available at Windtree Press, Amazon, Barnes and Noble, and Kobo.*

Follow Courtney on her website:

courtney-pierce.com

Isabella's Christmas Box
Paty Jager

ISABELLA MUMPHREY, ANTHROPOLOGIST and World Intelligence Agency operative, stood in her kitchen making sugar cookies and singing Christmas carols. She hadn't been this excited about the holiday since her sixth birthday.

This was the first time in over twenty years she would have a real Christmas. She'd purchased a fresh — well, fresh for Arizona — evergreen tree. The five-foot noble fir stood in the small living room waiting for Tino, her Venezuelan lover, to return from his latest DEA mission.

During the Thanksgiving shopping crush, she and Tino braved the throngs of bargain shoppers to find ornaments for the tree she talked about buying. Three days from Christmas and Tino was on his way home. She couldn't wait for tonight. They'd decorate the tree, sip wine, and enjoy the first family Christmas either of them had had in years.

Once she'd discovered there wasn't a real Santa Claus, her parents had stopped making Christmas a magical time. Her seventh Christmas she came home from the boarding school and found only the housekeeper at the apartment. They watched Christmas specials on TV and the next morning there were two packages under the tree; a bright colored scarf from the housekeeper and a new coat from her parents. Once she became a teenager, her Christmas present from her parents were their voices in a phone call.

Christmas wasn't about material things. It never had been, but the more her parents drifted away, the more she mourned the way they'd been those first six Christmases. The three of them putting out cookies for Santa and, on Christmas morning, gathering around a designer Christmas tree her mother had had delivered from a department store, to see what Santa had brought. And the Christmas day brunch; one of the few occasions throughout the year when they all sat down together as a family and had a meal. Isabella shook off her melancholy thoughts.

This year was different. She had Tino. This was the first Christmas since he'd lost his family that he'd felt like celebrating. He'd told her how he always took the assignments that would last through the holidays because he'd rather forget there was a family holiday he was missing out on.

Isabella pulled the last pan of cookies from the oven and walked into the living room. There may not be snow and blustery weather outside, but she'd set up a winter wonderland inside with a small village scene, pine scented warming oil, and mistletoe dangling in front of every doorway. She didn't want to miss any chances to capture a kiss from Tino.

They were only three months off the last assignment they'd more or less worked together. As a WIA operative, she'd discovered how and where Aztec treasures were being sold on the black market, and Tino had cracked a notorious Columbian drug ring as a DEA agent. They'd fulfilled their missions, but Tino was still lamenting the fact he didn't shoot the drug lord responsible for his family's deaths and that a crooked DEA agent got away.

They both deserved a wonderful Christmas.

"Querida, this apartment looks like a Christmas postcard." Tino stood in the apartment doorway. His dark gaze drifted around the room and stopped on her. His handsome face lit up with a heated smile. He dropped his duffel bag to the side and closed the door.

A shiver of delight danced up her spine as it always did hearing Tino's accent and knowing he loved her. She'd never dreamed as an awkward, genius-level kid growing up among jeers and fears from the older males in her academic life that she could capture the attention of such a handsome, charismatic man.

She rushed across the room before he stepped out from under the mistletoe and wrapped her arms around his neck. "This is going to be the best Christmas ever," she said, pressing her lips to his and falling into a kiss that made her knees weak and her body hum.

His hands cradled her head as he took the kiss even deeper,

turning his face, melding their mouths, and gliding his tongue over hers in an intimate dance.

Her body sagged. He caught her before she melted into a puddle of desire on the ceramic floor.

"Querida, the way you melt from my kisses gives me a big head."

The sultry words registered in her euphoric mind. "Which head?"

Tino's deep hearty laugh echoed through the apartment and reverberated in her heart.

"Your quick mind is one of the many things I love about you." He kissed her nose. "We have much to do. Christmas is only three days away." He released her and picked up his duffel bag.

"You need help with that?" Isabella asked, following him to the bedroom door.

He hustled through the door and out from under the mistletoe before she caught up to him. "I can manage fine. It smells as if you are baking, no?"

"You wouldn't happen to have presents?" She hadn't received a present from anyone for years. She always gave to charities and helped at the soup kitchen on Christmas Eve.

"If I do, they are a surprise. Go bake." He shot her a mischievous grin and closed the door.

The click of the lock made her giggle. If she really wanted in, that lock was easy to pick. Isabella wandered into the kitchen. Tino had told her of a Venezuelan tradition he missed. She'd scoured the internet and found a recipe for *hallaca*, a plantain leaf-wrapped food that required days to prepare.

"Might as well get started." She placed the recipe on the counter and started placing the ingredients alongside the paper in the order in which she would chop and cook them.

Faint Native American drumming and Alabaster, her cockatoo, shouting "Who's there! Who's there!" sent her scrambling to find her cell phone.

Daddy!

She hit the respond button. "Hi Daddy! Merry Christmas!"

"You sound happy. I'm glad you have someone in your life. But this isn't a personal call. I wouldn't ask you to take on a job right now, but it's in Phoenix and it needs a person who has knowledge of Maya artifacts."

Her happiness was squashed by his immediate business-like tone and that he was putting her to work on her first Christmas she could spend with someone she cared about.

"There are other agents in the area you could contact." She didn't want to sound like a whining, spoiled child; however, she wasn't about to miss this important first holiday with Tino.

"That's true. But none have your expertise. I promise, this won't interfere with any Christmas plans." He cleared his throat. "It's not classified. If you want to drag Tino along, I give my permission."

While she wasn't excited to even do the mission, having Tino along might make it go faster.

"Okay, what's the mission?" She strolled over to Alabaster's cage and handed him a Brazil nut to chomp on.

"A package will arrive by messenger in an hour. There shouldn't be any problems but keep in touch."

The connection clicked.

She wandered back into the kitchen. *Should I keep making this or am I going to have to go right out and get started on this mission?* Staring at the ingredients, tears burned behind her eyes. *I finally have a chance at a normal life and Daddy has to call.*

Strong arms wrapped around her middle and Tino placed his chin on her head. "You're making *hallaca* for me?"

The warmth and excitement in his voice swept her misery away. She spun in his arms.

"Yes. You mentioned how you missed this dish. I only hope I can make it as well as your mother and grandmother." She placed her head on his chest listening to the rhythm of his beating heart. She didn't have a doubt in her mind, she loved this man.

"You already have the main ingredient: love." He kissed the top of her head.

Isabella tipped her face upwards and was rewarded with another knee-buckling kiss. If he kept this up, she'd be nothing but a puddle of needy woman by Christmas.

He drew out of the kiss, dropping soft kisses over her face. When he no longer kissed her, she peered into his eyes.

"Did I hear Alabaster yelling 'Who is there?'" Tino asked, picking up a cooled cookie.

"Yes. Daddy called. I have an assignment."

Tino swallowed the bite of cookie. "But it's only three days until Christmas. Our first Christmas together." His brow furrowed.

"He said it was local, only I could get it accomplished, and it wouldn't interfere with Christmas." She rubbed a hand up and down his arm. "And he said you could help me."

Tino's hand raising the cookie to his mouth stopped halfway there. "I can help? Your father doesn't like anyone but WIA to work your cases."

"He said it wasn't classified." She bit the cookie waving around in front of her nose.

"What is the assignment?" Tino popped the rest of the sweet into his mouth and picked up another one.

"I'll find out when the package is delivered." She stepped out of his one-armed embrace. "While we wait, how about helping me make this?"

An HOUR LATER, the doorbell rang.

"Door! Door!" shouted Ally moving back and forth from foot to foot, bobbing his white plumed head.

"I have it Ally, pipe down." Isabella opened the door.

A man in his mid-twenties wore a baseball cap with the insignia of a local delivery service. "Isabella Mumphrey?" he asked.

"Yes."

"Sign for a package." He held out an electronic clipboard.

She signed her name. He handed her a carved wooden four-inch by four-inch box.

"This is it? No envelope?" she asked, running her fingertips over the intricate carvings on every side of the cube.

"That's it." The man pivoted and left.

Isabella slowly closed the door, staring at the box. Why would Daddy only send her a small box? What was the assignment? To open the box? To discover where it came from?

"Did you get the assignment?" Tino walked out of the bedroom, a towel draped around his lower body. He'd headed for a shower when the first batch of ingredients were in the pot simmering.

Seeing Tino in only a towel, Isabella's thoughts dove straight to the bedroom and how they could celebrate his return home.

He snapped his fingers in front of her. "Where did you get that box?"

She shook off the steamy ideas swirling in her head and turned the box over and around. "It was delivered without a note or anything." Her fingers continued to trace the carvings on the box. Her mind hummed, going through the photographic files in her brain, trying to remember where she'd seen this type of symbol before.

"It's Maya. Pre-classic period." Her finger dipped into each crevice and over the swells. "Some of the symbols were still used today, others ... I need to go to the university library."

"It is closed for the holiday," Tino said.

"I have keys."

"To the library?"

"No, but I'm good at picking locks." Isabella slid the box into her backpack, covered the cookies and turned the burner off under the simmering mixture of meat, spices, and vegetables. She strode into the bedroom and grabbed her survival vest. What had started out as a security blanket of sorts at the age of ten, now was an essential piece of clothing when exploring and on missions.

"Why do you wear your vest?" Tino grabbed a pocket and pulled her against his now clothed body.

"This is a mission. I wear it on all missions." She pulled a lightweight jacket over the vest and picked up her backpack. "Are you coming?"

"I came home to be with you, so yes, I am coming." Tino slipped his feet into loafers and shoved his arms into a windbreaker. "Do you wish me to drive?" he asked, grabbing the keys to her Jeep Compass out of the tray by the front door.

"Please. I want to keep studying the symbols on the box." Isabella followed Tino down to the parking garage and slid into the passenger seat. "Park in my usual place at the university. We can go in through the anthropology department door."

On the drive, Isabella pulled out the box and continued to trace and decipher the symbols. Exhilaration raced through her as the story on the box became clearer.

"I don't know what I'm supposed to do with this box, but I just about have the saying on the side figured out. I'm missing several important symbol meanings."

Tino pulled into her parking slot and turned to her. "What do you think this is about? You weren't given any instructions what to do with the box."

"The instructions are on the box." She kissed him quickly and dug in her backpack for the department door keys.

Once inside, Tino touched her arm. "Does the library have security?"

"Only in the archive section. We shouldn't need to go in there." She walked down the hall to the library and knelt in front of the doors. Plucking her pick tools from a vest pocket, she inserted the small metal picks and went to work on the lock tumbler.

She'd worked less than a minute when the clicks verified she was in. Smiling up at Tino, she turned the latch, pushing the door open. Due to the hours she spent in this part of the building, Isabella knew exactly where the book was she needed. Using a small flashlight from a vest pocket, she made her way through the rows of books straight to the section that housed all the university's books on the Maya.

One by one she read the titles until she found the large tome that would help her decipher the box.

She set the book on a table and stared at Tino. "I don't understand what this box has to do with WIA or how Daddy knew I could handle the job here when the box is clearly a Maya artifact."

Tino shrugged and sat down in the chair next to hers. "That looks like a one person job."

Isabella nodded. "I know which section to look at. You must be bored."

He leaned over, kissed her briefly. "I missed you and would rather be bored with you than miss our first Christmas together."

Her heart ached with happiness. "I feel the same way."

He kissed her again, then tapped the book. "Figure this out so we can go back to the apartment and celebrate."

Isabella opened the book to the section she needed. Within minutes she found the symbols she didn't recognize. "Hold the light, please." She dug in the inside vest pocket for her journal and a pencil. She placed them on the table, and picked up the box. Turning the box in the light of the flashlight, she determined the beginning of the message.

Matching each symbol with a word or phrase, she spun the box counterclockwise. Writing the words and phrases down, her heart raced. This was a box made for a lover. The symbols told of binding their hearts with what lay hidden inside the box.

"What did you find? Your eyes are shining and you glow as if we have just made love."

Tino's voice reminded her she wasn't alone.

"This is a box given from one lover to another." She gazed into his eyes. "I have to figure out how it opens."

Isabella turned the box over and over in her hands, feeling the corners, edges, and top. It appeared a solid carved block.

"Have you figured it out?" Tino asked softly, rubbing her shoulder closest to him.

"No, not yet." She shifted her attention from the box to Tino. "Let's take it back home. I have some books on ancient puzzles. I might be able to come up with an idea skimming through those."

"I am getting hungry." Tino stood and extended his hand toward her.

"Oh, I planned a wonderful dinner for us!" Guilt ate at her conscience. "I'll work on this after dinner."

"Are you sure you will not burn dinner with your mind on the box?"

Isabella understood Tino's valid question. Once she latched onto a project her mind wouldn't let it go. Grimacing, she kissed Tino's cheek. "Probably not."

He laughed and pulled her into a one arm hug as they walked out of the library. "Then I will make dinner while you study the box."

"Thank you!" She still couldn't believe how lucky she was to have found such an understanding lover.

"You know that fascinating mind of yours is what adds to your appeal." He kissed her temple, motioning for her to leave the building ahead of him.

Isabella slipped into her car, waiting for Tino to start the vehicle and pull out of the parking lot before she once again tumbled and rotated the box, all the while pressing the symbols.

When they pulled into the apartment parking lot, she wasn't any closer to knowing how to it opened.

"Maybe it isn't a box. Can you hear anything when you shake it?" Tino suggested as they walked to their second floor apartment.

Isabella shook the box. There wasn't a sound or vibration of anything moving inside.

She shook her head. "It has to open. It would be a cruel trick for a lover to play — giving his love a solid block with a message saying to open it."

Tino unlocked their door.

Isabella crossed the room straight to her extensive collection of research books on nearly every Native American Culture.

The first time Tino saw her apartment, he'd strolled along her wall-to-ceiling bookcase reading the titles out loud. "You were not kidding when you said you take your career seriously," he'd said, then surprised her by asking if she let others read her collection.

She lent her books to other anthropologists and anyone who was interested in a topic or culture she had a book about.

"I will start dinner," Tino called from the kitchen.

"Mm-hum," she uttered, reading the titles of books on the fourth shelf. There it was. Her section on puzzles in history. She'd found more than one culture who enjoyed making up puzzles and asking their family and friends to find the answers.

She leafed through the section on stone works of art that could continue standing, even when most of the base was removed, and others that crumbled to ruin by the snatching of one specific stone. These were used against enemies.

Here it was. A section on ancient puzzles. She scanned the pages, locking them in her photographic memory. An account of a box similar to the one sitting on the table above her book caught her attention. The one in the book was made of stone, a much harder substance to carve and manipulate into a puzzle.

Reading the analysis of the construction, Isabella picked up the wooden box, once again running her hands over all the sides and corners. The pad of her thumb found the slight notch on a corner. Still wearing her vest, she pulled out her survival tin, opened the lid on the Altoid-sized metal box, and plucked the x-acto blade from the bottom. With care, she slipped the tip of the blade into the notch, gently prying until a crack wide enough to slip her fingernail in appeared. Using her nails and fingers, millimeter by excruciating millimeter, the gap widened until one puzzle piece came off the corner of the box.

"Dinner is—"

Tino's voice penetrated her concentration.

"Have you found a way to open the box?" He knelt on the floor beside her desk chair.

"Yes, the construction is tight, and I don't want to ruin anything on the box." She glanced at Tino. His gaze was fixed on the object in her hand.

"Do you know if the contents are safe?" he asked, placing a hand on her arm.

"The inscriptions on the outside cite this to be a box between lovers. I doubt there is anything harmful." But his question did spark a thought. What if the box had a Romeo and Juliet misfortune?

She peered into Tino's dark brown eyes. "I don't know if I'm supposed to open this or just decipher the message on the outside. Daddy didn't send any instructions." She tapped her finger against the top of the box.

"Call him and ask for more details." Tino grasped her hands. "But first come enjoy a meal with me."

Isabella's gaze lingered one last time on the slightly askew box. When her mind was preoccupied with a project such as this, she had a hard time concentrating on anything else. However, her longing to have a normal Christmas with someone she loved, drew her gaze back to the man who loved her unconditionally.

"How about I call him tomorrow morning? Tonight is our night. You've been gone three weeks and I want to show you how much I've missed you."

$\mathcal{I}$SABELLA WOKE THINKING of the box sitting on her desk. She peeked at Tino still deep in sleep. A smile formed on her lips. They'd enjoyed the dinner Tino made, then spent the remainder of the night naked, making love and watching an Indiana Jones movie.

She slipped out of bed, pulled on her robe, and padded on bare feet to her desk in the other room. The box remained as she'd left it.

Daddy was in Washington D.C., two hours ahead of Phoenix. Retrieving her phone from the table by the sofa, she dialed his number.

"Did you finish the mission?" Daddy said with a lighthearted tone she hadn't heard in years.

"No. I'm calling to find out exactly what I'm supposed to do with the box." She pushed her hair out of her face and stared down at the puzzle.

"Have you cracked the symbols on the side?" His tone was once again professional, not cold, but distant.

"Yes. The box appears to be a gift from one lover to another. I started to open the box and a comment Tino made had me wondering if I was supposed to open it."

"Yes, the client wants to know what is inside."

"And what do I do with whatever I find?" She spun the box, once again making sure she'd deciphered the symbols correctly.

"The client has faith you'll know what to do with the contents."

The line went dead.

This whole mission was odd from the start. What did he mean the client had faith in her?

She placed the phone on the desk and picked up the box. Tracing the symbols, spinning the box, she once again fell under the spell of needing to know what was hidden inside. Small victories were being made on the box, when Tino's cologne filtered through her concentration.

"I see you are still obsessed with the box."

His husky early morning voice swirled heat through her body, drawing her attention. He stood an arm's length away in low riding camo-colored pajama pants.

Drool started to slip out the corner of her mouth at the sight of his tanned torso, flat stomach, sprinkling of dark curls, wide shoulders, and muscular arms that were crossed as he stared down at her. She noticed his gaze on her leg, bare from her foot up to where the robe hung open at her hip.

"Querida, no matter how many times we make love, I will never stop wanting you. You are a drug I cannot live without." Tino leaned down, capturing her lips in an incendiary kiss.

Never had she dreamed of having a lover, let alone one who craved her as much as she craved him. Growing up with a genius IQ and always being years younger than her fellow students she'd been ridiculed, the butt of many jokes. It hadn't helped she had a metabolism that allowed her to eat like a lumber jack, yet have no curves or womanly attributes. And to think, her Venezuelan lover, loved her for her mind as much as her stick-figure.

The kiss stole her breath and heart all over again.

She wrapped her arms around his neck and Tino picked her up, carrying her back to the bedroom. The box could wait. It hadn't been opened in centuries. What did a few more hours matter?

*A*FTER THEIR LOVEMAKING, Isabella made breakfast and she and Tino made the next phase of the *hallaca*. While that simmered, Tino settled onto the couch to watch the news and she sat back down at the desk.

After peeling away one layer, she discovered a box inside of the box. The inner cube was slick and unadorned with symbols. This time she found the notched corner right away and began the slow process of discovering the lines and pieces to open the object.

"Ezzabella," Tino's voice penetrated her concentration.

"Yes?"

"I read there will be a version of the Charles Dickens' *A Christmas Carol* being performed tonight. Would you like to go?"

Isabella glanced up. Tino had never suggested they go to a play together. "Do you like *A Christmas Carol*?"

"Sí, it has always been one of my favorite Christmas stories." Tino folded the paper he was reading. "If you get changed we can have a nice dinner before the play."

She studied him. He wore his dress khakis and nice button-up, long-sleeved shirt. He had already dressed to go out.

"Did you ask me about this earlier?" She searched the recesses of her brain to see if she'd missed a conversation earlier today.

"No. I want to go with or without you." He stepped close to the chair. "But I would prefer with you." He placed a kiss on her lips and stepped back.

Isabella opened her eyes, shoved the box to the center of the desk and stood. "Then I guess I better get dressed."

(A)LL THROUGH DINNER and the play, little bits and pieces of the past couple of days played in her head. Lots of things about the box weren't adding up. Tino was sticking to her closer than he had since moving in. Granted it was going to be their first Christmas together and the first Christmas with loved ones they'd both had in years, but there was something else. Something she couldn't quite grasp.

Back at the apartment, Tino danced her into the bedroom. Under his wonderfully heated ministrations, she lost herself in the ecstasy of being thoroughly loved. She dozed off and woke after midnight. The box was on her mind. She had to discover what was inside before any more distractions drew her away.

A quick peek revealed Tino was sound asleep. She slid out from under the covers, donned her robe, and headed to her desk. The desk lamp cast a soft, warming glow on the inner box she'd left in the middle of the desk.

Holding the small box, she once again began the process of discovering the cracks that revealed the way to open the box. An hour had passed when the box popped open. A small satin bag fell onto the desk.

Satin wasn't a cloth the ancient Maya would have had access to. She frowned and studied the bag shining in the light. The client wasn't going to be happy to find their ancient box had been tampered with. Would they think she stole the contents? Daddy would defend her, but why would someone play such a prank?

Plucking the bag from the desk top, the weight told her there was something inside. She pried the top open with her fingers and tipped the bag upside down. A silver ring inlaid with turquoise and diamonds dropped onto the desk, shimmering and blinking in the lamp light.

This wasn't ancient craftsmanship. She picked up the band, turned it and peeed at the inside, where she found a printed inscription: *You are my heart.*

Her fingers shook as she slipped the band onto her ring finger. Tino had said that several times since meeting him. Tears trickled down her cheeks and her heart felt too large for her chest.

Tino and Daddy had set up this 'mission.' Everything that had happened since receiving the call from Daddy now made sense.

Tino had found the perfect way to get her attention and deliver her present.

She slipped back into bed, pressing her body against Tino's, waiting for his arms to circle her and draw her closer.

She felt his arousal at the same time he kissed her.

"What are you doing awake so early?" he asked, moving his hands to cup her bottom as he pressed his arousal against her mound of curls.

"I couldn't sleep thinking about the box."

His body stilled. "And?"

"Thank you for the beautiful ring!" She kissed him long and lingering, transmitting her emotions to him through the kiss. Drawing out of the kiss she focused on another matter. "How did you find an ancient box to put the ring in?"

"It is not ancient." He kissed the tip of her nose. "I noticed the books you had on puzzles and took one to a master wood crafter. I asked him to build the puzzle box with the ring inside."

"But the Maya symbols on the outside box ... They were carved so realistically."

"Remember the old man in the village in Guatemala who allowed you to read his tablet?"

Her mind buzzed with the memory and the honor the man had bestowed allowing her to read and photograph the tablet. "Yes."

"I visited him and asked him to carve the saying."

The pride in Tino's voice and love twinkling in his eyes overwhelmed her senses. No one had ever taken the time to learn what made her happy. "That's a lot of trouble for a Christmas gift," she said as tears of happiness welled in her eyes.

Tino held her head in his hands.

"Ezzabella, the ring is more than a gift. It is my commitment to you. It is an engagement ring. I wish to marry you as soon as you pick the date."

Her mind stopped and her heart raced. *Engagement ring!* She knew his feeling for her surpassed any he'd ever had with anyone else. She'd hoped he would want to marry her someday.

He touched their noses. "Marriage is what you want, no?"

"Yes! I've wanted it since Guatemala, but I didn't want to pressure you into making a decision you weren't ready for."

"Querida, the ring tells you the truth. You are my heart. I would be empty without you in my life." He sighed heavily. "My only regret is that I was not by your side when you discovered the ring. I wanted to wait for the delivery of the box, but your father thought you would need the time to figure it out."

Isabella laughed. "Do you really like *A Christmas Carol*?"

"No. I only said that to get you to leave the box alone. I had hoped you would open it on Christmas Day."

She laughed until her sides hurt. "I'm sorry. You know how I get obsessed."

"Sí, that is one of the many things I love about you." He slid a hand down her side.

Her body shivered with anticipation.

"I would like to give you one more early Christmas present," Tino's hands glided over her body as his lips caressed her neck and shoulder, moving lower toward her nipples.

"This is my best Christmas ever!" Twirling the engagement ring on her finger, she knew her life with Tino would be as challenging as the puzzle box she opened, and over-flowing with love.

~

ABOUT THE AUTHOR

Award-winning author Paty Jager has seventeen published novels, five novellas, and three anthologies. They include an action adventure series with Isabella Mumphrey, historical and contemporary western romance books, and a historical paranormal romance trilogy.

Paty and her husband raise alfalfa hay in rural eastern Oregon. On her road to publication she wrote freelance articles for two local newspapers and enjoyed her job with the County Extension service as a 4-H Program Assistant. Raising hay and cattle, riding horses, and battling rattlesnakes, she not only writes the western lifestyle, she lives it.

Visit Paty at her website:

patyjager.net

To those who venture for to
realize a dream & those who like to
read about them....
Enjoy!
Anna Brentwood

The Mermaid's Treasure
Anna Brentwood

All that is gold does not glitter, not all those who wander are lost; the old that is strong does not wither, deep roots are not reached by the frost. From the ashes a fire shall be woken, a light from the shadows shall spring; renewed shall be the blade that was broken, the crownless again shall be king.

~ J.R.R. Tolkien

SEPTEMBER 7, 1893
REVAL HARBOR, TALLINN, BALTIC SEA

RUSALKA-MERMAID, NAMED for the mystical sirens of lore, was, in her first incarnation, a glorious warship in Czar Alexander's Imperial Russian Navy. Twenty-five years later, she was living out her retirement as a training vessel assigned to the gunnery squad.

Armed forward to aft with all manner of nineteenth century weaponry, from nine to fifteen-inch smoothbore Rodmans to Obukhov rifled guns, the top and side-heavy matron had willingly sacrificed speed and range for armor and armament, though in truth, the dear old lady had never fired a single shot in battle.

That day, the skies were blue and clear. The sun was shining and the beach winds blew as light as a mother's touch. The skilled and hardy crew of the *Rusalka*, twelve seasoned officers and one hundred and sixty-five rugged crew members, were tending to last minute preparations and awaiting orders to depart. And only one man, Captain-Lieutenant Petya Yaroslav, the captain's right hand, would remember that something about that day was unusual; that his superior officer, the sensible and rigidly proper, Viktor Hristianovich Ienish, Captain second rank, was acting quite odd and completely out of character.

First, the methodically punctual captain boarded the ship forty-seven minutes late with the excuse that he'd been to the hospital for a relentlessly painful headache. His usually tidy gray uniform was mussed; his neatly coiffed hair pecked, but most disconcerting was the look of dismay on his normally placid face. He hurried aboard, ignoring the multitude of expectant faces watching him and barked at the captain-lieutenant to accompany him.

Used to following orders, Petya Yaroslav complied, and though he was puzzled by Viktor's behavior and curious as to why they were headed below deck instead of to their immediate posts, he didn't ask. Nor could he not help notice the elaborate gilded and carved box the captain clutched, as tightly as a barmaid her coin, under his right arm. Petya hardly gave credence to the incredulous tale the captain spouted once he locked the door of his cabin.

Exactly thirteen minutes later, captain and captain-lieutenant at their posts, the *Rusalka* sailed from the harbor at 08:30 for Helingfors, escorted by the gunboat *Tucha*.

And while a gale was forecast, there was nothing to indicate it. Their departure was smooth, two-foot waves and gentle breezes. Seventeen miles north of Tallin, the fleet ships were within a half-mile of one another. The waves continued to grow in size and force, but it wasn't anything the crew hadn't been through before.

By noon, sixteen to twenty-knot winds had the ship bobbing like a cork. Whale sized waves blocked sight of everything but the agitated waters surrounding them.

Dropping *Rusalka*'s speed considerably, the distance between the ships widened as the fierce Baltic storm strengthened, graduating to forty-knot winds.

The waves became rolling walls of water, twenty feet high and more, punishing as they battered the iron lady like a randy pugilist's fists.

Every hand was on deck, each seaman never more alive or equal than when challenging the seas, fighting to survive, to tell another tale.

Unlike her fleet escorts, the *Rusalka* did not appear in either Helsingfors or Tallinn the next morning. The commanding officer of the gunnery training squadron, Rear Admiral Burachecka, ordered a search by all available ships in the area.

Nine days into the search, the body of a seaman washed ashore. The lookout from the *Rusalka* was the only one of the one hundred and seventy-seven aboard the *Rusalka* ever to be found.

For one month and seven days onward, dozens of ships crossed the Gulf of Finland to search for the missing battleship and its men, only to find broken remnants dazedly moving from the tug of the sea, lifeboats with empty mouths agape — never to be filled.

Later, a court of inquiry dismissed the commander of one of the escort ships from service for leaving the *Rusalka* during the storm. Rear Admiral Burachecka was found negligent in ordering the ships to sea with bad weather on the horizon. It was concluded the *Rusalka* went down with her entire crew.

And, in 1902, on Kadriorg Beach in Tallinn, a granite monument was erected: of an angel, arms outstretched and pointed at twenty-three degrees, the course the *Rusalka* took towards Helsinfors. History records that there were no survivors, and to this day, flowers and wreaths are laid at the feet of the angel in honor of those lost men. However, history can oft times be inaccurate; sometimes angels appear in the most unlikely of places and oft times the lost don't wish to be found.

December 24, 1893
Ellis Island, New York

CAPTAIN-LIEUTENANT YAROSLAV arrived shoreline on the eve of America's Christmas Eve festivities and celebrations, weary and empty, a different officer than the one who had boarded ship at Helsinki.

Despite the excitement of those around him, he was of no mind for celebrations. Well aware of the chill of the winter air, the fog from his breath, he remained unaffected because he'd spent much of his childhood in the frigid tundra of Siberia. At thirty-one years of age, he was older than his years, a serious, scholarly man content being alone and unmarried. He thrived on living a simple military life of precision and order. He never would have envisioned becoming the lone survivor of a terrible shipwreck and failed mission. A ghost, tasked by his captain, commander and comrade at the eleventh hour, with a mission that had not only puzzled him, but had succeeded in sparing his life and for whatever it was worth changing it irrevocably and forever.

Through some quirk of fate, his unwavering obedience had led him here, to this day, this moment. And, though he suffered what some called survivor's guilt, feeling he should have gone down with his ship, he wasn't dead. Not in the conventional sense of the word anyway. After much anguish and planning, Petya Yaroslav, aristocratic son and descendant of a Varangian prince, of men with names like Vladimir the great and Yaroslav the wise, made the only choice he could; he left his country.

He could no longer remain a decorated officer in the Great Russian Navy, or the son of deceased but respected idealistic, aristocratic rebels who had believed in equality, willing to take a stance and defy a monarchy. Instead, he must become someone else: a civilian, a humble fisherman, bourgeoisie, a sometime ship builder with the common name of Pyotr Marchencko. The few family left to mourn his death would believe his soul resided in a watery grave deep below the Baltic Sea. He knew a man could plan forever, but life had other ideas. He accepted that one had to do what one must to adjust to life's changing tide. He would emigrate to a new land and take on a new identity.

He would always remember his country, his comrades and his captain. As boys, both Viktor's and his family had been involved in Decembrist plots and had survived the uprisings. Exiled as rebels, then later revered, forgiven and returned to their homeland, their lands restored.

He'd learned a valuable lesson in politics and philosophy, and Pyotr now stood in Petya's stead.

The ship made its way toward America's New York harbor. Watching through the same green gold eyes of his doppelganger, both tied to the sea, he was a little awestruck at his first glimpse of the famous lady holding her torch. The mother of all exiles, the

Statue of Liberty proclaimed with silent lips; 'give me your tired, your poor, your huddled masses, yearning to breathe free.'

Petya's eyes moistened, his chest filled with unexpected emotions. His strong heartbeat quickened, as he stood steady on the deck. The magnitude of this new experience was humbling. Whether he'd wanted it or not, he was being given a chance for a new start.

The boat anchored mid bay as the crew readied to tender the passengers to Ellis Island. There were other ships and thousands of people. First and second class passengers like him could disembark and pass through Customs at the pier ahead of hundreds of others, spared the long lines and scrutiny of the less fortunate, those passengers traveling coach or steerage.

Despite being raised in privilege, Petya valued simplicity. He shared his parent's ideals that men should be judged by their worth, not their birthright; that no man should rule or own another. This new land, this America purported to hold those same high values yet, like any human endeavor, was fated to be rife with contradictions.

Touted as the land of the free and the brave, America was the country born from philosophies that posited all men were created equal. That all people were entitled to life, liberty and the pursuit of happiness. Yet he already saw the obvious discrepancies between the dark and the white, the rich and the poor, and those who settled here longer to those like him just getting off the boat.

Satchel in hand, gold and valuables sewn securely into his shirt and pants, and blade hidden in his boot, Petya said a final, silent and emotional farewell to what was and what had been.

Now, it was Pyotr who paused, took a deep breath, and clasping his bag tight in hand, walked forward, his gait slow but sure. Carrying hidden promises as the ground pushed back against his heels, he stepped up and off the plank and onto the solid soil of his newly, adopted country — America.

America the beautiful. America the melting pot. America the land of opportunity. The air was contagious with promise. No matter the challenges, he vowed to forget all that came before. For here, with no past to bind him, he only had the future and the possibilities were suddenly endless.

FEBRUARY, 1894
LOWER EAST SIDE, NEW YORK

*H*IS FIRST THOUGHT upon seeing her was that she was the most beautiful woman he'd ever laid eyes on. His second was that he would marry her.

He immediately felt uncomfortable for his foolish and unsettling fascination with the deli owner's pretty niece, yet he'd come to this deli for every meal since.

The owners were Russian, the staff friendly and the place smelled of home, of warmth and comfort, of grilled onions and beets and dill from the brine of the pickle barrels; from fish and meat, from cheeses and breads and all manner of baked goods.

"Pyotr, welcome, how nice to see you again." A woman as beautiful as any sea siren smiled at him, a pot of hot water in her hand. "Good to see you back."

"Considering I am here every day," he said, watching appreciatively as she set the pot down by his teacup. "I should be saying zat to yoo."

"I only help out here when I can, I have another job. Being here is just fun for me."

"Da, I do know you have other job. I hear you are artist with needle but unfortunately, I don't wear dress. Every day you are here though, is how you say ... better day for me. For aunt and uncle too. Nyet-no?"

Color rushed into her face and she tossed her golden hair even though, except for a few rebellious tendrils, most of it was bound into a tight coil of knots and twists. Her wide eyes were exotic, a warm amber that reminded him of Russian forests.

"I think you'd look silly in a dress, and I also think you sir, are a bit of a flatterer. No?"

The sound of her laughter lit something dark inside of him. "What is that word — flatterrrer?"

He'd been studying since he'd arrived and his English was improved, but many words still eluded him. Grateful the restaurant was not crowded, he paused gazing into her eyes. She started back but finally broke the silence by asking him what he would like to order, adding, "And, I suppose first you will want your usual, borsht with sour cream?"

He nodded transfixed, wondering if something was going wrong with his brain. And his manners. By rote he ordered the roast and potatoes too, and the challah bread he'd come to like. He was child-ishly encouraged she remembered the borsht, then chided himself. It was her job to be nice. He was a customer.

Keeping his head down, he couldn't resist stealing glances at the woman, a girl really, as she laughed with the clerks, bantered with her aunt and uncle and greeted patrons by name, escorting some to their tables, checking on others.

He had never been in love, yet he'd never felt as fascinated by a woman before. It was as if he were bespelled. To talk to her even as a good customer should be enough. To wish she might even consider him in a romantic light was foolish, stupid. Yet, he could not stop wishing it. The thought that she might be promised to another bothered him far more than it should.

Four weeks after his arrival, he began to understand much of the English. By eight weeks, he spoke well enough that he rather fortuitously landed a civilian position at the American naval yard tending boats, cleaning up around the docks, and maintaining engine supplies.

He learned the girl's aunt and uncle were Russian Jews and

quite religious. She'd been orphaned and came to live with them in America as an infant. Raised Russian Orthodox, he was more a man of science than supposition. He supposed the girl, Irena, was of the Jewish faith too, their beautiful niece whom he could not stop thinking or dreaming of.

Even if there weren't the differences of religion, what would she want with him? He was a man of thirty-two with old world values, foreign and honed by years of rigid service. Far too jaded for someone full of hope and innocence. But logic wasn't working for him anymore.

He'd settled in an old tenement apartment on the lower East side of New York, an older neighborhood populated by Eastern Europeans; Russians, Poles and Germans. His European counter-parts were working class, or poor, or of the Jewish faith. Having been of the nobility he had little experience with diverse peoples or people with a history of being persecuted for their religious beliefs or affiliations, their lack of means or perceived odd behaviors.

His first real comrade was his neighbor, a cheerful German. Jacob lived in America for five years and made his living as a butcher, the trade of his father and grandfather before him even though in his country he'd been an accountant. Being a foreigner often meant not having the same opportunities as the real Americans, who by definition were those peoples who had been here longer and had assimilated better.

Pyotr understood men and their hierarchies. He knew such was the lot of an underdog, starting from the bottom. On the other hand, anyone here, no matter his or her birth could overcome such obstacles. Many did, succeeding beyond their wildest dreams. It suited him to be ordinary and considered the same as everyone else and he did his best not to stand out.

Bringing him his check, before she turned to go, Irena said, "Pyotr, I know you are new to this country and are just getting set-tled in, but I never see you at synagogue. I understand you live in the neighborhood. Attending services is a great way to meet people."

She said she never missed Saturday morning services, and had the audacity to wink. "I hope to see you there someday soon."

"Yes!" He blurted it out before he could think and, shocked at himself, lowered his head and stammered, "Um … maybe ….maybe you will." He almost meant it.

Smiling awkwardly, his face felt as warm as a just out-of-the-oven biscuit. He hoped it wasn't red. He knew congregants didn't necessarily attend a church because of a deep religious calling, but he didn't want to purposely be deceptive.

Still, the temptation to see Irena and accept her invitation was strong. A belief was intangible. Was it anyone's business if he believed as they did or not, as long as he respected their right to believe as they chose?

He could well imagine his pagan and Christian ancestors spinning like tops in their graves over the very idea of one of their own converting or even considering it, but they were all gone and as far as anyone who'd known him before, he was gone too.

As he stood, he gathered his coat and his hat and braved one more look at the beautiful girl who had captured his heart. Who was he kidding? He wanted Irena for his wife. If sharing her faith or attending religious services would somehow make that possible, he'd do it even if his deceptive soul roasted in Hell for all eternity.

DECEMBER 8, 1904
MANHATTAN, NEW YORK

PAULINA ALEXANDRA MARCHENCKO, bristled with all the exuberance a petite nine-year-old body could contain as she arrived home from school. She raced up the stairs to the family apartment and opening the door, shouted "Mama, I am home."

Usually her mother met her downstairs at the front of their building, but she hadn't been there today to greet her. She called out again, but there was no answer.

Maybe she went to the store? Maybe she was at Bubby and Zayda's or Auntie Ruth's and had forgotten the time?

Paulina loved Fridays! Tonight was the sixth night of Hanukah too, which made it even more special. All around, a sense of holiday was in the air from the beautiful decorations in the stores, to the Christmas carols they learned at school. She wished she could celebrate Christmas too, it seemed such a wonderful holiday, but as Jews, they only celebrated Hanukah.

For seven days and eight nights every December, Paulina never got tired of her mother's potato latkes, of lighting the menorah, singing songs, spinning a dreidal, playing nut games and eating special candies like her favorite chocolate jelly rings. She loved getting money for her bank and a present each night for eight nights. But on Friday nights she most looked forward to hearing one of her papa's wonderful stories.

All day her friend's words blurred at times. Even the teachers called her out for not listening, but she couldn't help it; she was restless for the day to end so she could hurry home, help Mama serve supper, light the Sabbath and the Hanukah candles and wait for Papa to return from *shul*.

Last night, Mama had been feeling tired and had gone to sleep early, so Papa had tucked her into bed and kissed her good night. She'd begged him to tell her another one of his own stories, a new and longer story and one not from a book. They argued and she persisted, until finally, he stopped, grew quiet, and then told her in his deep, raspy voice, tomorrow he would tell her his best story ever. Tonight, he had to take care of her mother. Tomorrow was tonight. She couldn't wait.

She loved hearing about his adventures in Russia on the sea as a boy, about how he took one look at her mother and knew that she was the woman he would marry. How they had fallen in love and married within three months of meeting one another; but the best stories were the ones he told her about the sea, about ships and shipwrecks, mermaids, sirens, sea serpents, about kings and queens and treasures.

She reached high to hang her coat on the hook, taking a deep whiff of the delicious smells permeating the apartment. The aroma of her mother's baking, fresh challah, apple cake, cookies made with honey and almonds, reached through the air in patches that changed as she walked, tendrils of taste that on an inhale tugged her very tummy.

The *cholent*, a stew prepared from fresh vegetables, herbs and meats simmered in a big pot on the stove.

Paulina grabbed her school bag off the floor where she'd dropped it. She ran down the hallway toward her room, but noticed a light on in her parent's bedroom.

"Mama?" She called out then peered inside the room. Mama's bedside lamp was on. She walked in to turn it off, and was startled to find her mother lying on the rug, staring up at her.

"Paulina, darling," she whispered in a voice so faint, Paulina could barely hear her. "I'm sorry I didn't meet you."

Heart racing, she felt scared seeing her mother curled onto her side with her arms holding her belly, her face as pale as the white of her blouse and her honey-colored eyes dazed and dull. In a too quiet voice, she said she had a bad cramp and was waiting for it to pass. "As soon as it goes away, I will get up."

Her mother closed her eyes even as she kept telling Paulina not to worry. That she'd had spells like this before and usually they went away.

Paulina sat down on the floor beside her mother, worrying her lip and waiting for what seemed like forever. As if to assure her daughter she was fine, Irena occasionally reached out to pat her on the arm.

Finally, grasping her hand tightly in hers, her mother took several deep, fortifying breaths. Opening her eyes, she looked as scared as Paulina felt and said, "Paulina-angel-a, mine. Be a big girl … go next door … get Ruth … tell her … I need a doctor and to please get Papa."

Paulina glad to be able to do something, immediately ran to do her mama's bidding — praying with all her heart mama would be alright, not at all aware that even the most earnest of prayers aren't always heard.

SIX YEARS LATER
NEW YORK CITY

𝒫AULINA AWOKE TO birds singing outside her bedroom window though it was still quite dark outside. It was too early to dress for her new job as a feller hand — a seamstress at the Triangle Waist Factory. She'd taken the job and dropped out of high school before graduation because the opportunity had come and she didn't intend to be a burden on anyone, least of all her best friend and neighbor, Mina, or her boyfriend, Elliott. If it wasn't for them — and Elliott's family, who she was coming to like and know — she was alone in the world.

Both had been upset by her decision to quit school, but finishing her diploma had to wait. As her Papa always had said, people plan but life has other ideas. It wasn't as if she had aspirations like Mina who wanted to be a doctor. She didn't have a family business to inherit like Elliott, who worked in his father's jewelry business. No, all she'd ever wanted was a simple life with her mama and papa, and to marry Elliott and have a family of her own someday. She suspected Elliott had been planning to propose after she graduated high school, but then tragedy struck and everything changed.

She glanced around her tiny, almost sparse bedroom, at her mahogany dresser with its ornate princess mirror, at the gilded, framed photos of her great aunt and great uncle, at her beautiful mother and handsome, distinguished father, all of them vital and alive. Just thinking about living in a world without either of her beloved parents made tears come, and she had no time for that. Mama had raised her to be strong, caring and practical. Papa had raised her to work to the best of her abilities, to expect the unexpected and make the best of life's surprises.

And she would.

She blinked her eyes several times, wiping at them until any sign of her weakness left.

So many changes. Could she afford to eat, to keep her home? What would she do? Where should she go? She forced herself to put aside her worry and grief in order to sort through a lifetime of family momentoes and memories. Deciding what to keep, what to give away. Last night she'd all but dropped to sleep out of sheer exhaustion.

She got up out of bed as agitated as the day before. Why was she nervous? Not because of the job, a job she could do with her eyes closed. Sewing was a skill her mother had taught her as soon as she could hold a needle, and she was fast and accurate stitching on a machine too so that wasn't it.

She headed toward the kitchen, a wraith in a white cotton gown padding down the hall, bare feet on hard, well-worn planked wood floors. In spite of herself, she glanced at the new elephant in the room, the pile of belongings dumped on the living room floor in denial last night. They would have to be confronted.

Papa never woke up after his injury, so she hadn't known his wishes. She preferred forgetting but could not avoid the stack of foreign-looking papers. Or the small, ornate chest that she'd discovered hidden under a false bottom in his desk.

That, and a rough drawing of what had turned out to be a diagram of the bedroom floorboards where papa, who never really trusted banks, kept his money.

She hadn't been surprised to discover her inheritance there: stacks of fifty and one hundred dollar bills and silver coins, enough that if she remained frugal, she could keep the apartment and her life on course for another year or two. It was a relief knowing she would not have to move in with Mina or feel hurried to plan a wedding in the midst of her grieving.

Paulina nervously wiped her palms and walked over to the pile of her father's belongings. She was taken aback to discover he had secrets. It was all so confusing.

She had been scared, scared because though unexpected, this hadn't surprised her. And now, unable to deny her curiosity, she knew she must try and understand why her simple father had a hidden drawer with a locked chest that looked like something that belonged in a museum. Inside, she found a gray uniform with golden yellow stars and lines, a slew of official looking military service papers in Russian, and a diploma from a prominent Russian University. All belonging to a Petya Yaroslav.

Paulina understood some Russian, but she could only read and write in English. If she decided to investigate further, she'd have to get help with the papers, but she also had to consider papa kept his secrets for a reason.

The eerie truth was that the chest looked exactly like the one he'd described in the bedtime stories he'd told her since she was a child. She would have bet those stories were all from his imagination and that he never lied to her, but now she wasn't so sure. Were his stories or parts of them actually real?

She strained to lift the ornate box with both hands. It was small but very heavy. And locked. She hadn't found a key so she could not open it. Why had he hidden this? Why did he have it? What did it all mean?

Riffling through the papers, her fingers traced the strange letters as she tried to make some sense out of her find. Papa had been well read and smart, but formally educated? She knew Petya was a pet name for Pyotr and this Petya had attended a large university for there was a graduation certificate and Russian naval military papers with a faded photo of him. He'd been an officer and the photo showed a man, a younger version of her father? Who was this stranger, this Petya Yaroslav?

She would never be able to ask papa anything now. An accident in the shipyard. She was still troubled by it. At least they had seen her mother's end coming, but accidents were too sudden.

Looking at the dates on the papers she knew this man was no stranger. He was Papa. Papa had been him. These things, they were his. She told herself to believe it already.

The box felt warm, or was it vibrating in her hands? Was she that nervous? She bent, her intent to place it on the floor. It dropped to the carpet with a heavy thud, the sound of something inside rattled. Jewels? Gold?

Rattled, she covered it over with a sofa pillow and left it where it sat. She didn't have time to explore this mystery now. She had to go to work. She had to think about what all this meant. What to do? Who to confide in?

Heading to the kitchen, she found the honey, sliced a lemon and brewed herself hot water. Life could be so wonderful, but it also could be very harsh. She forced herself to focus on the now as she readied her breakfast, slicing an apple, buttering a piece of fresh bread she'd baked the day before.

The morning sun pierced through the bathroom curtain as she prepared herself for work; it shined through the small, high-set window and fell on her long, bound auburn-toned hair. She resembled her mother and had her pert, tipped nose and delicate chin, but she had her father's bright green eyes, dark hair and narrow lipped smile, though her lips were much fuller than his had been.

Her mama, the beautiful Irena, had been a wonderful homemaker and a talented seamstress — sewing, knitting, or crocheting whenever she could. And that is exactly what Paulina felt she could do too.

She looked down to the sink as she pulled the plug and let the water out. She had to get to the bank. She had to take out the garbage. The bathroom needed a good scrubbing, but chores would have to wait. She had taken too long thinking. Only if she hurried would she be on time.

So she rushed. She stuck her sewing needles and pins into the lapel of her favorite pink sweater. It had been her mother's; one she'd knitted. Sometimes when she closed her eyes, she felt as if her mother's arms were wrapped around her, comforting her. It was nonsense, but wearing the sweater always made her feel better.

Gathering her things, she put on her coat and hurried to leave and catch the trolley. She ran down the stairs, opening then closing the door to hop down the remaining twelve steps to the sidewalk, dodging the slowest of passers-by.

Who had he been then, her papa whom she'd loved so deeply? The gentle man who had called her mother *solnechniy*? His sunshine, and indeed she had been.

Her mother had the kind of beauty that radiated from within, one that came from possessing the most loving and nurturing of hearts. Ironic that Irena's own heart, as big and loving as it was had failed her, taking her mother away far too soon. After Paulina had found her lying on the floor that sixth night of Hanukah, she died a year later on the first night of Hanukah.

Subsequently, Paulina refused to celebrate Hanukah because the winter holidays made her sad instead of happy. That papa had died early in January made it even worse now. She didn't even want to think about what she'd do or how she'd get through the next holiday season. She dreaded it!

She went to school and kept true to her faith after her mother died, but nothing was ever the same. She'd thankfully had papa and they'd carried on the best they could. He provided well, worked hard, went to *shul* on Friday nights and had been a good, loving father. Even at ten-years-old, while she never doubted he loved her dearly, she knew when he lost his sunshine — her mother — half his heart had died too.

MARCH 15, 1911
NEW YORK CITY

*I*T WAS DARK outside when Paulina returned home, sore and aching and tired. The work was more demanding than she would have thought, but she could get used to that. What she didn't like was being treated like a criminal, locked in a large room with hundreds of others, with only thirty minutes off all day long.

Her hands hurt. She rubbed them together. Her fingers were stiff and sore, her nails too short. She'd frayed her fingertips pulling seams and pins well past reasonable and decent hours. There was no negotiating, only following what everyone else did at those long tables, slick floors leaving residue on her shoes, and matted balls of fabric scrap piled in baskets around the room like the eyes of the dragon commandants observing and monitoring everyone's production.

She even had to ask permission to use the bathroom and, if the manager thought anyone took too long, he'd threaten to cut their wages or hours. It was so embarrassing that most of the seamstresses avoided drinking.

For one dollar and fifty cents a week, Paulina worked on the eighth floor putting together the materials for the popular shirt-waists the company was famed for. The factory inhabited the top three stories of the building and employed over four hundred people.

Even with the windows open and overhead fans, the space was sweltering hot and muggy. It smelled of fabric, dyes, metal, oil, perfume and human perspiration. With spring coming, it wasn't only flowers blooming. Flies broke out of winter stasis and buzzed along with the incessant hum of a hundred or more sewing machines. The noise and the rules discouraged conversation. Any violators caught talking were suspended without pay. A normal day began at seven thirty in the morning and ended at five o'clock or, at peak times, nine.

Because she had so much time to think, she spent much of it wondering about the mysterious papers hidden in papa's desk and what might be in the box. Something about the box had ingrained itself into her mind since she touched it. She also could not stop questioning if many of the stories he'd told her might have actually been true and were not just from his imagination.

When she got home that evening and the telephone rang, she was almost glad for the break. She picked up and said hello. Mina sounded tired too, but was as feisty as usual.

"How was your day at the factory today?"

Paulina sighed, trying to stretch out some of the kinks in her neck. "If I hear the word hurry, hurry, faster, faster, one more time, I will have to kick someone in a soft place with my boots on. They lock us into the room and inspect us before we are allowed to leave; afraid we might sneak off with something. It's porky, but jobs are hard to find and at least it is honest work."

"Well, I wish you would quit! You should go back to school, graduate and than let Elliott marry you like he is dying to do, poor boy. That is what you wanted before ... what your father wanted for you too, and I want to be a bridesmaid."

She and Mina bonded at nine when Paulina's mother passed away, and her father hired Mina's mother, Sonya, to care for her before and after school when he was at work.

"Mina, one must allow the proper time to grieve to pass. I can't think about getting married until the year passes."

"That's old-fashioned thinking. I understand not wanting a wedding yet, but you can still grieve and be engaged!"

"I know, but Elliott understands I need some time. I won't do that in the shadow of papa's death."

"I understand too, but you might feel differently when more time passes. Didn't Elliott offer you a job at his father's jewelry store?"

"Yes, but I wouldn't impose on the Rosenthal's like that and I prefer sewing to filing. I am fine where I am for now. I have a year to study and take the test to earn my diploma."

"Will you do that, stubborn girl?" Mina was relentless. She added. "I know how you feel, Paulie, I do. There isn't a day that goes by when I don't miss my mother too, but I also know death is part of life. We all will die. It isn't a choice of when. When our time comes, it comes. The trick is to cherish and enjoy the people and things in your life that are happy while you are living. None of us are promised tomorrow."

Mina's wisdom went beyond age and religious difference. Her logic about life and death helped.

Paulina sighed, rubbing her eyes. "You're right, but that doesn't make it easier to bear. I will get my diploma before the year is out, but I have too much to do and am too tired to do it all right now."

Sharing this type of hardship with her friend when she herself had just lost her own parent was a horrible thing. Mina's mother had died just eight months ago.

Paulina sat down on a chair and yawned. "How are you doing with school?"

"Studying constantly, worrying about tests, never enough time with my volunteer work at the hospital, the usual." Mina stalled, and then blurted, "I didn't get the two scholarships I was hoping to. Those went to boys too since I have been told more than once that women are more interested in marriage and having a family. Am I a dodo bird wanting a university and a medical school education?"

"No, Mina, and I am so sorry," said Paulina. Mina worked hard for her grades in the parochial school she attended and had sat with a comatose Pyotr whenever Paulina needed a break. She was a natural caregiver and hoped to start school as soon as possible.

The medical profession was a male domicile. Medical institutions encouraged men more than women.

"It's not unexpected," Mina sighed, sounding resigned. "People say I am chasing a rainbow."

"I don't!" Paulina was emphatic. "If anyone should be a doctor, it's you! You said there are women who persevere and become doctors. You will too."

"There is a reason why I love having you for a best friend," said Mina, chuckling. "But the truth is, the women who make it either have a father who is a doctor or money for education. I don't have either. Mother left enough for me to pay for necessities. It will be okay, though. You know me, I will keep trying even if I become the oldest female doctor in the United States."

Paulina laughed, knowing Mina meant it. "What will you do now?"

"Old Dr. Brooks has offered me a job working in his office through summer. Maybe next year too. If I save enough money, I'll apply next year and the next after that if I have to."

They hung up and Paulina leaned into the cushioned chair. She knew whatever it took, Mina was determined to follow her dream. Thinking of dreams ... the box and items loomed in her vision. What if there really was a treasure? What if she could actually help Mina somehow?

She stood, stretched. She needed answers. She couldn't even think of starting a new life if her old one was a lie! What if her father had been a spy or a thief?

Her whole being rebelled at that idea. Her father had been such an honest, compassionate, loyal and loving man. He wouldn't have done anything to hurt anyone. She sat down on the rug, uncovered the box and wondered if mama had known about the papers and the box, or if papa had hidden it from her too. Now she would never know. She needed to find the key.

Perhaps the key was in the folded uniform she had dumped on

the floor? Papa's desk and bedroom were the only things she hadn't explored thoroughly yet. As a child, she hadn't been allowed to even touch his desk. She hoped the key was somewhere in there or in his closet.

Staring at the box for some time, Paulina troubled herself with the next complication. There was still so much to go through. Looking at the clock on the mantel, seeing how late it was already, she knew she'd have to postpone searching for the key.

The next morning, Paulina had to force herself to get up and go to work with what little sleep she'd had. She hurried into her cramped space and resumed what she thought she did very well. Her stitching was straight and even, she kept her space neat and worked quickly like her mother.

Another week disappeared as her work at the factory kept her too exhausted to do much more than go home, bathe, talk to Mina and Elliott on the telephone, change and stare at the messy house and all the things she still had to do but was too tired to.

She thought she was doing well until one morning, thirty minutes early even, the floor boss yelled, "Go up a floor, we don't need ya here."

"Will I be doing the same thing?" She asked, encouraged.

"Suppose so! Get up there. Stop wasting more time."

"May I ask why you're sending me?" Paulina pressed, curious and hopeful she was being sent upstairs because she worked fast enough to be considered one of the better seamstresses, but knew she shouldn't have spoken so freely.

He looked up with a puffed chest. "Replaced ya with someone who'll get the amount done that needs doing!"

She deflated as he turned his heavy head away from her, dismissing her all at once. "And, make sure you use the freight elevator!"

She took her things, straightened up her station and waved goodbye to her co-workers. She wondered if she'd see Yetta and immediately found herself nervous again.

Returning home in the darkness, having stayed later than ever, she was glad that in three days she would be spending time with Elliott. She had one Saturday off a month. They would meet for Saturday morning services, then an afternoon at the park to see a show and supper at his parent's house. She looked forward to it. She missed seeing her friends at Saturday services and needed a break, a laugh, something to do, somewhere to be away from all the work she had left to do, all the things she had to figure out. Upon coming through her door, she did her best to ignore the mess and collapsed into bed. She sat up to rub some rose petal lotion on her blistered fingers.

She lay down again and tried closing her eyes, but felt as if someone was in the room with her. Uncomfortable, she scanned the room, but found nothing.

Until that moment, she realized she hadn't thought about the chest for several hours. The contents all came to her in a flash. What if they were photographs from Papa's childhood? She would love to see that, and getting up, forced herself to fight the exhaustion and go look around her papa's room.

An hour or so later, she found the box as she'd left it. The latch looked sound, but iron can rust. Believing any key could fit the hole and possibly work, she used a skeleton key she found hanging behind Papa's shirts in his closet. She fiddled with it for some time.

To her delight, the locking mechanism crunched at the tenth turn. Bits of black and red shavings mulched out of the hole into a fine grated dust that was the lock. She opened the lid; it protested, but she protested back.

In a final jolt, the hinges gave way. The lid flew open and the box fell to the floor with a clatter, some of its contents tumbling out.

What was she looking at? She couldn't believe her eyes. She was dreaming. She had fallen asleep, surely! This wasn't his. Her father had told her stories about treasures, sunken ships and pirates, mermaids and sirens and kings and queens, about the Czar's palace all her life. They could not be true. What if they were?

One story he'd told often was about a cursed treasure and a Russian battleship that sank in the Baltic Sea near Finland with almost two hundred men aboard. How one man had survived and found the treasure. Wanting to die himself, the man had swam for miles and, as his strength was waning, had come upon a beautiful sea siren who, instead of luring him upon the rocks to his death to finish him off, as was a siren's wont, had reached out her hand and saved him.

As it happened, the treasure hadn't been cursed but instead blessed. Though they were from two different worlds, they fell in love, overcame all the odds and together, lived happily ever after.

The shipwreck story always made Papa's eyes mist. He said it was because it had really happened and many good men lost their lives that day. Sea sirens were mythical creatures, and the one in his story always sounded identical to her mother. Tears stung her own eyes. Odd that she'd just realized all this now.

She felt excited but tense. Restless, she picked up a newspaper off the floor, dusted off the table nearest her with her hand. She looked around the room nervously, feeling some shame that she should be questioning the stories her father had told her, remembering the stories she'd adored all her life and now dissecting them. However, the more she mused, the more it seemed possible the answers she sought were within her own memory if she could sort truth from fiction.

"A secret treasure filled with items stolen from the Czar's treasure room. That people had died for."

Guilt flooded her, but why should she feel guilty? It wasn't hers, but it was hers. Who else would the box and its contents belong to now? She touched the box, stared at its contents in open-mouthed disbelief. She looked away only to feel the pull to look again and again. A trembling ran through her as her shock settled. Fingers, sore from holding a needle all week, began to cramp, as did her stomach.

No! Pyotr Marchencko had been what he seemed, a devoted

husband and father. A man, who went to *shul* every Friday night, had close friends and worked at the naval yard. A man of very modest means with little formal education. Yet, a man who loved to read voraciously and spoke several languages. Quiet, a very private person, he never liked to talk much about his life before he came to America and met her mother.

Faintness tugged at her. Going over what she knew of her father only made him sound stranger, a pirate from some other time and world … but what of her mother? She could not have known of this.

Paulina didn't want to know either. She grabbed the fallen treasure and stuffed it back into the box, pushing the lid down, trying to go back, to remind herself, to reassure herself that she hadn't just seen so much wealth in front of her.

Mama had been a simple, devoutly religious and happy woman. They were all simple! Papa had been much older than her mother, not as devoutly religious, and as Paulina was starting to suspect, maybe never a Jew at all.

"And though they were from two different worlds, they fell in love and overcame all the odds, and together lived happily ever after." Thinking of her father's words and the siren and the sailor story, she wondered if he'd loved her mother enough to accept her beliefs so they could live happily ever after. Oh no, she was only making it worse, finding irregularities to his character.

She thought of him and saw him in her mind's eye. He'd doted on them so. There was little he enjoyed more than relaxing each evening after supper with his vodka, his pipe, the newspaper and a good mariners tale. Nor was there a night when he didn't ask her about her day and listen to her girlish chatter or indulge her with one of his wonderfully imaginative stories.

Shaking her head, she sniffed, tears sliding down her face like a summer storm as she swiped at her face with the back of her hand then forced herself to open the box again. There were five odd looking rocks and a bunch of ancient looking coins that might have been gold, but they were dirty. Some were dull and some shiny, and there was a variety so she didn't know if any of them were rare or worth anything. What interested her most was probably the most valuable thing in the box. It was a beautiful jeweled brooch. She examined it in awe, turning it different ways to see how it's brilliant stones refracted the light. It was ornate and fancy, gold and diamond-encrusted, a perfect songbird with eyes so blue and shiny they had to be sapphires? Oh! She would be robbed, put in danger! Arrested!

She couldn't keep these things lying around if they were valuable, but, but … something tugged at her about the brooch.

Papa had told his stories and how many had involved a beautiful diamond and sapphire pin that had once belonged to Catherine the great. The jewels in some of his stories had magical powers or a curse but she was certain he'd once talked about a brooch reputed to turn into a bird that flew between the worlds connecting the living to the dead. Was it this brooch that had somehow wound its way into papa's elaborate stories? Surely, the brooch in front of her was real and as solid as the stack of old coins it had been nesting on.

She picked it up, and in a flash saw her father staring back at her through the reflection in the shinier coins. She dropped it as if it were a hot coal.

"Papa!"

She violently turned to look behind her, suddenly frightened she would see him standing behind her, but nothing was there. Why should she be afraid of her own papa when she'd give anything to have him back?

She attributed her nerves to exhaustion. She was so tired, not sleeping, not eating or drinking enough and working too hard.

She had to do something else. This place was a disgrace. She had to find the strength to empty the dirty dishwater, gather up the garbage, put away the dishes and tidy up the house. Surely she had other things to do!

She entered the kitchen, heart pounding, her vision blurry. She made herself some hot milk and put a snippet of vodka in it for good measure to calm her jangled nerves. She cleaned for as long as she could stand, sipping her toddy, glad to be doing something.

Resting against the counter edge, her eyelids grew heavy. She yawned, her body telling her it wanted sleep. She wasn't sure if she could sleep, but finally decided to go to bed while there were a few hours left. In the morning, she was meeting the loving and patient man she planned to marry.

She hid the chest in a large cabinet. Should she confide to Elliott or Mina about what she'd discovered, or wait until she knew more? What would they think? She had to think about what to tell or not. She didn't want to cast aspirations on her papa's character. She put the uniform and the papers back into the hidden drawer and closed it. Yawning and beyond tired, she went to bed.

*

He FOLLOWED HIS superior officer back to his bunk, astonished when the captain ordered him to shut the cabin door behind them; the wood hammering against the steel, the sea disappearing from their ears, only the sway of the ocean still in the room.

He watched as the captain, little confidence gained with his darting nervous eyes, gently lowered the box he'd been holding, and set it down on the table with a weighty thud. His expression became fierce. Looking him directly in the eye, the captain's usually ruddy jowls quivered. His eyes were fervent and glazed as he requested that he listen carefully and not speak, they only had minutes.

He said, "Ve hrrave known vun another since boyhood and I am commanding officer. You must trust vat I will tell yoo without question for there is no time left. Both of us grew up amidst seeds of revolution so we know the plots of men. Upon my Ahncle's death, it fell to me to be guardian of certain documents and items remaining from rebellion of 1825. In box are blue diamonds cut from infamous Le Tavernier, and several valuable ancient artifacts and gold coins. But the brooch! The brooch once rode upon the bosom of the Great Catherine herself! It is made from Spanish gold, Ceylon sapphires and diamonds. It is reputed to have power to connect the living...," he swallowed deeply and his voice shook, "to the dead! Those who wear it most like carry its secrets, whether treasure, or curse — I cannot say."

Reaching into his uniform jacket, he pulled out a thin goatskin packet, sealed entirely in wax. He placed it on the table by the box. "You must slip off ship ven we are away from port. No one must see. You must swim like fish. Take papers and box and see them safe until I return from voyage. If I don't return, you will have memorized name and address of person to take them to. Do this immediately if I don't return, and tell no one of this — ever."

"Of course." Petya was uncertain why Viktor would not return or why all would not be well. He was an excellent swimmer and trained almost daily in the cold Baltic seas, but the hard part would be to sneak off the ship without anyone in the fleet spotting him. That would be nothing short of a miracle. He said as much to his captain.

"What if I am spotted?"

"Yoo won't be — can't. I know I ask of yoo a lot, but consider this a mission of the utmost importance. I have not enough time to tell yoo, so understand once. Someone tried kill me. Papers in wrong hands endanger many. Can cause another uprising. Treasure was taken from Czar's winter palace, diamond room many years ago. Some believe these objects inside were given to Paul the first, by the devil himself and have much mystical powers."

Where before he was dutifully planning how he would escape unnoticed, being a man of science, Petya could only grunt and say, "With all due respect, Captain, surely you don't believe that nonsense?"

Viktor sighed, rubbing his temples. "Ven my dreams show me my own death and those images flood my head; ven I feel salt-sea through my nose, filling my lungs and see ship going straight down on sea floor like spike, feel and hear steel buckling, see men fighting till end, *all lost in ship's steel embrace, I wonder. This morning, despite storm comink, Admiral Burachecka ordered us to sea anyhow."*

Petya had shivered seeing how worried the captain was. He would not risk life unnecessarily. If Viktor was the secret guardian of these objects and was feeling endangered, he understood why he would want to safeguard them. And why he'd trust him to see to it.

"It's burden. Sometimes I think better for them to disappear, but not my call to make."

Looking at his timepiece, Viktor quickly outlined his plan. He made Petya memorize the name and address of his contact should anything happen to him. He would leave his cabin door open so Petya could retrieve the items after the ship left port. He vowed to divert the attention of the crew and the following ship at just the right moment. The two men calibrated their stories and their timepieces. They embraced in a quick show of affection and luck before hurrying up deck to their stations.

Petya did as ordered. He left the ship undetected, swam to shore and remained hidden, staying out of sight as agreed until he received Viktor's call. Days later when the ship didn't return and all aboard were feared lost; he was devastated to discover Viktor's dream was a prophecy.

Weeks later, knowing he could not hide forever, he went to the address he'd been given to turn over the objects. To his horror, he discovered the contact shot dead in his country home, a single bullet wound through his skull, his home rifled beyond measure. Stuck with the proverbial hot potato, himself presumed dead, Petya burned the dangerous papers to ash, but could not bring himself to destroy the beautiful objects. He was not a man prone to silly superstitions. Perhaps the pin brought bad luck, but he'd had the pin, not Viktor, so that made no sense. Nor had either of them been wearing it. He decided he'd keep the pin and gold coins hidden, for if they remained obscure and unworn, no one would be the wiser.

*

$\mathcal{P}$AULINA TOSSED AND turned as warmth flooded her face and heated her limbs. She kicked off her blankets, the room uncomfortably warm. Opening her eyes, only when she sat up did she feel the real chill of the room, and realized that it wasn't warm at all. The dream was still with her, a vivid experience real enough to have startled her awake several times. Each time she fell back to sleep the dream continued where she left off. Her father had been without doubt the Petya of the uniform and the hidden papers. She didn't know what to think but she was convinced the dream had meaning. That maybe Papa was trying to help her understand from beyond the grave?

She got out of bed, weary but looking forward to the day ahead. She tried to push the memory of the odd dream to the back of her thoughts. Taking time with her appearance, she pinched her cheeks a little harder. She applied more rouge than normal for she was far too pale and had lost weight. For months she'd been wearing black. She wished for the first time in weeks that she could wear something with a little color, something a little more cheerful, but she was in mourning and would do what was expected and proper.

When she heard the knock at the door, the urge to share some of her burden was strong, but she knew she wouldn't tell Elliott everything — not yet, maybe never.

"Elliott!"

"Paulina!"

He looked handsome and happy. He hugged her too tight, but it felt so comforting to be in his arms after such a long time that she fell into him and molded into his lift.

As he gently set her down, arms tightly grasping her shoulders, his gaze swept over her. He looked concerned when he saw tears beading her eyes.

"Paulina, darling. What's wrong? I know these past months have been difficult and you are working too hard, but you look … beautiful as always, but frightened!" Elliott spoke softly, but his warm and beautiful brown eyes were filled with distress.

She swiped at her eyes, mad at herself for the tears. She would not do anything that could hurt her father's memory or betray his trust. She owed Papa his secrets but she trusted and loved Elliott and knew he loved her. He cared for her father too. He would never do anything to hurt her. She didn't want to lie to him and it hurt her to think she might never be able to tell him all of it, but she had to share some of her concerns with someone.

She said, "I don't know what to make of it. You know I have been sorting through my parent's things. Maybe you can help me?" She pulled him inside; she had never done that before, always behaving so circumspect and ladylike yet her aggressive action made him laugh.

"What's gotten into you, Paulie?" He asked, stepping inside further and remembering his manners, instantly pulling off his hat to hold it with both hands at his waist like a nervous boy.

She knew he'd been ready to propose after she graduated but the unexpected death of her papa changed his plans. She also knew from Mina that he'd asked for her father's approval and had gotten it. Knowing one another like they did, Paulina knew Elliott understood her well enough to respect she didn't want the specter of her father's death hovering over their future. Though he didn't like that she quit school to work, he understood and just hoped she didn't make him wait too long.

She couldn't ever consider another fellow. She'd fallen in love with Elliott when she was only twelve-years-old and him, fourteen. He made her laugh and feel loved and appreciated and her papa had heartily approved of him. He had said, "a strong and promising young man, and he shows respect, and I can tell he loves you the way he should. That's all that matters to me." Papa's blessing meant everything to her.

Looking up at Elliott, holding both his hands, Paulina said, "El,

I need you to promise me whatever I tell you today, you will never do anything or say anything about it to anyone without my agreement. That you will respect my wishes to do what I need to do, as I feel I need to do."

He agreed and listened in astonishment as she told him about the money that she had found, about her father's hiding spot under the floorboards and about the fancy box filled with things she believed might be valuable.

She explained. "I already took the money from inside Papa's hidey hole to the bank. It is enough that if I am frugal and work, I don't have to move out of my home until I am ready. People won't think I am marrying to be supported, but for love, and I can sort through my parent's things without being rushed. I hope you understand—"

"I do, and that's good news," he said, hugging her. "I know how worried you were and knew Pyotr would have provided for you. What does Mina think?"

Looking sheepish, she said, "She thinks I should quit my job and go right back to school. I didn't tell her about this yet. I've just told you."

He smiled, hugging her again. "So, are you going to show me this treasure box you found?"

She pulled him into the living room and got the box out, but was puzzled that it was latched and tightly closed again. "I thought I broke the latch. I guess not."

While Elliott admired the workmanship on the box and remarked on its weight, she got the key. He tried to open it but this time the lock that had seemed rusty and damaged before was solid and tight and unwilling to relinquish its secrets.

"I cannot believe this," said Paulina growing exasperated as she watched him fiddle with the latch. "I swear. It opened before."

"Oh well," said Elliott, shrugging as he put the key down and turned to smooth a wayward curl from her face.

"How about we tackle this later or we will be late for services and I've a special day planned. If you'd like, we can stop by the store and I can put this in the vault. It will be safest there. I can have our locksmith work on opening it if this key won't work. Once I can see what is inside, I can better work on determining value."

She knew Joseph Rosenthal and Sons Jewelers was highly respected and a leader in the sale and design of precious stones and jewels of the highest order but felt panic blossom in her chest at the thought of giving up the box. She shook her head no, adamant.

"Thank you, I will want you to do that, of course, but not ... not yet. I want to keep it here with me until I get more figured out."

His voice was patient. "Paulina, darling, if the contents are as valuable as you think, you should not keep it here for too long. If anyone else finds out about it, you're likely to get knocked off or someone can break in and take it."

Paulina waved away his concerns and patting his cheek, told him not to worry. She scooped up the box and placed it back where she'd hidden it. "I do want your help when I am ready, but not today. Not yet. No one knows about any of this except you and I and we've never been burgled. I would like to keep the items here for now. When I decide what I want to do and feel ready to part with them, I will bring them to you."

Elliott nodded, accepting. "I appreciate your trust. I will help in any way I can, when you are ready."

Locking up the house, they headed out hand in hand to enjoy their special day together.

MARCH 24, 1911
NEW YORK CITY

ℐT WAS ONE o'clock in the morning and, not sure what motivated her except pure stubbornness, she went out of her room to get the box. She turned on her lamp and sat on her bed trying to open it again. There was no logical reason why the key had worked once and would not work again or why it hadn't worked the first night she tried, or the third. But tonight, not being able to sleep well anyway, she decided to try until it worked. Her persistence paid off and it opened. Riffling through the contents, she couldn't quite say why, but the brooch interested her the most.

Taking it from its pillow of leather and gold, she studied it and then pinned it to the collar of her nightie.

Paulina stood to look at herself in the mirror. The brooch sparkled against the white cotton of her gown, far too fancy for her. She was a simple girl and proud of it.

Still, being a woman, she could not help but appreciate the beauty of the piece and the way the diamonds shined, emanating beams that reflected when she turned this way and that. She posed with her chin up, face haughty, using one hand to hold her hair up and then letting it fall. She spun, feeling young and carefree once more and laughed at her own silliness.

It was ironic that she was going to marry a jeweler. She didn't dream of wearing or owning jewels and expensive baubles. All she wanted was a roof over her head, food in her mouth and the people she loved to be well and happy. Still, it was comforting wearing something her father had held special and she saw no harm in enjoying the extravagant brooch in the privacy of her own bedroom.

Yawning and tired beyond measure, she tiptoed to the bathroom. She placed the box at the far end of her bed, but kept the brooch on.

Lying back against her pillow, eyes to the ceiling, she thought about who might have worn the beautiful songbird with the sapphire eyes brooch before, who it might have belonged to. Could it have been a family heirloom or was it possible, as in Papa's stories, it had once belonged to Catherine the Great? Had it resided in the Czar's treasure room and been stolen by disgruntled revolutionaries? Was the story of the ill-fated *Rusalka* a true one? Her mind spun trying to figure out what might have been said about the brooch. Did it really possess mystical powers?

She resolved that despite its beauty, she would not keep it for herself. Forget about magical powers, if she lost it, she'd never forgive herself! No, she didn't need or want such an extravagant item to sit hidden in her drawer. She would much rather have it find its right place with the right person and give Mina the money for school.

It was late. Paulina felt as if she were drifting, a growing feeling of weightlessness came and went. Heat. Cold. The air grew dense and harder to breathe. She must have a fever coming, and trying to remedy herself, gave up and let herself go, falling into a deep sleep.

*

*F*ALLING AWAKE, HER *eyes dashed open to a black smoking void, and she couldn't move, could only watch, feel, and hear the sound of machines clacking, screams and blood-curdling cries. Smoke drifted over her vision, and a sense that her father was near. She called for him.*

"Papa?"

"My Paulina," he answered, love for her in every syllable.

She yearned to see him and felt his smile. "Oh, Papa, I miss you."

"I miss you too, my angel," he replied and stepped forward so that she could see him, but in what a state! She felt such melancholy for his transparent form; where had he been, gone, where was he now?

"What is this?" She whispered, wondering if she were awake or dreaming, not sure.

At that, people she didn't know began to surround and crowd them. People who did not look familiar. They were dressed differently, from different times. They were getting in the way. She backed up, turned and considered pushing past them to flee but didn't want to abandon papa who stood still beside her.

First, there was a ruddy-faced, uniformed man with a beard soaked with what smelled like seawater; she recognized him as the ship captain who had given Petya/Papa the treasure and who'd drowned with his ship though he looked so placid and calm. It was like watching pictures in a nickelodeon, images flashing quickly, next a beautiful dark-haired woman in such a dress, as she had never seen, the brooch hanging as a necklace around her deep cleavage, her long neck on an angled, almost haughty face of serene command. She sensed rather than saw her father. She wondered where her mother was and called out. "Mama!"

There was no answer and suddenly she was alone and scared and so warm ... burning up ... terrible heat!

Next she was at her new workstation on the ninth floor, the whirl of the machines deafening. She tried to work faster but it was like slogging through sludge. Frustrated beyond measure, she felt desperate and knew she had to leave no matter the consequences.

She heard someone yell, 'Go to the light!'

She didn't see anyone, but then she saw the light. Fire! She ran to the door. She tried to open it but it was locked. Frantic to leave, she kicked it, but it would not budge.

Confused and scared, she ran, trying door after door knowing that if she could not get out, the flames of red, yellow and white would claim her and everything with it.

"No, no," she screamed over and over until her voice was gone. "I am too young to die."

She lay paralyzed on the factory floor with people just piled on top of one another, all of them choking and gasping for breath as helpless to stop it, they watched the fire inch closer, taunting them all with the knowledge it would consume them.

The sewing needles in her lapel burned into her skin, glowing hot as frantic faces and blackness swirled her vision.

*

SHE OPENED HER eyes some time later to realize with great relief that it was just a dream. She was safe in her bed. Safe! She burst into tears. Her mother! Her father! All those people. What a terrible dream. What did it mean?

She rocked back and forth, holding herself together and feeling far more emotional than she should. It was a nightmare, not a dream and thankfully, not real!

She felt for the brooch where she'd pinned it to her gown. Hot! Heat scorched the tips of her fingers!

Startled, she chided herself for being foolish. There were no such things as curses or magical powers. Her head was full of Papa's mystery. She was being ridiculous!

Ridiculous but remembering how Papa said the brooch was part of the mermaid's treasure then how the story became more obscure, changing each time he told it, until he wouldn't tell it anymore. She took off the brooch.

She kept seeing Papa in her mind's eye as Petya, then as himself telling his stories of treasure. And, the madness and evil of man, the escape of a single man with a treasure he hadn't wanted, who hadn't wanted escape, and of lost comrades.

That was him! Some of the stories had to be his stories! She thought of the military garb and shuddered to think of her father almost being killed on a sinking ship.

Holding the brooch in her hand, she admired its cool beauty. She told herself she must have been dreaming that it was hot, that an inanimate object could not direct dreams. Or connect the living to the dead. Nonsense!

Placing the pin down beside her, blankets tight around her legs, she reached for the pillow that had fallen eschew and settled it back under her head. She didn't believe in such things but she'd also never had such a terrifying dream before. She would give the pin and the treasure box to Elliott for safekeeping and appraisal. As soon as possible. Tomorrow!

MARCH 25, 1911
NEW YORK CITY

*T*HE SUN WAS a shiny sliver rising over the blue, yellow and red horizon. The streets of New York City bustled with people going about their business and workers beginning their day. Trolleys, buggies and horse drawn carts, a milkman beginning his route, a line already formed at a food cart selling delicious smelling pastries. On almost every corner, young newsboys in knickers and caps hawked papers, shouting, 'hot off the press'.

Paulina got off the trolley near Washington Square Park and hurried towards the Asch Building. Glancing at a clock, she was too early and slowed her pace. After all, she didn't have to clock into work for another thirty minutes and she would still be early. She had time to breathe, to savor. She admired the beauty of having a park in the middle of the city.

Like many New Yorkers she was numb to the crowds, and the garbage. She saw what she wanted to see; colorful stores with interesting signs, the green of the trees, the array of colors on newly blossoming buds and flowers.

Shifting the large bag she was carrying from her left shoulder to her right, she was more than anxious to shed her burden and didn't want to take it inside to work with her and chance the inspectors questioning her.

Elliott had kindly offered to meet her by the Greene Street entrance to pick it up. He'd been pleased she managed to open it again.

"Good, that saves us from involving the locksmith. We do not know why your father kept it hidden, but if it is as valuable as you suspect, I can inquire discreetly and see that you get what it is worth."

"Yes, discretion is most important. Papa left me enough money to survive for some time and I am capable of work. If the treasure inside the box is actually worth something, money is always helpful to have but if I had more than I needed, my greatest wish would be to be able to help Mina become a doctor."

"What a good person you are," Elliott replied, cautioning her not to be hasty. "It is never wise to make serious decisions in the midst of crisis or grief, however if that is what you want to do for Mina, I understand, but be warned researching an item's history and worth and finding the right buyer takes time."

Paulina shrugged. "I am in no hurry. Even if I am able to gift Mina's education, she would have to apply for admission to school for next year. Still, it would make me very happy to be able to do that and surprise her."

"If it is worth something significant and I can sell it, it might be feasible you'd have it in time for Christmas."

Paulina nodded, dreading the thought of the impending holidays, but said, "Being able to help Mina would be wonderful any time."

Paulina arrived twenty minutes early at the spot where she was meeting Elliott. While the air was pleasant, the temperature sixty-eight degrees and brisk, she felt as if it were ninety degrees outside. Despite the cool air, she was beginning to perspire profusely and, concerned, decided to take off her coat.

Holding it and her bag with the box in it tightly to her side, she paced, checking constantly to see if any pickpockets were near or if she could see Elliott.

She walked from one end of the block to the other and back. She had eighteen minutes to go.

As she passed in front of the factory building the second time, her heart pounded hard and loud. She felt as if she'd run a mile. The sound of her own heartbeat resonated from her ears to her toes.

Taking a deep breath, she turned back to walk towards Greene Street. She started to feel even worse, as if she were spinning inside of her own body.

Sixteen minutes.

Did she have a bad heart and failing kidneys like her mother?

Having never fainted before, for a second, Paulina was sure that this was it, though it didn't feel painful, only interesting and jarring. She did her best to hide her fear; walking as if she had a purpose. She didn't want anyone watching to think anything was wrong with her.

A tall brick building dominated the opposite corner and seemed to grow taller as she stared at it. She turned, pacing back and forth from her vantage point at Greene Street and Washington. Still no Elliott.

Thirteen minutes.

Passing the address marker on the front of the factory building at 23-29 Washington Place, a searing dash of heat bloomed in her pocket. Her legs went weak, knees buckling and she staggered, reaching for the nearest wall. She pushed against it so hard she scraped her palm. When she pulled it back, she saw she'd left a streak of blood on the cold brick.

Dizzy and nauseous, she paused feeling as if she were going to collapse from the sheer rush of adrenaline shooting through her veins. Why — what was happening to her?

With a gasp, she jumped back just in time as a woman's body hurdled from the sky, dress and fabric billowing, down, down, smacking hard on the pavement ... and kept going right through the pavement. Disappearing.

Eleven minutes.

Was she losing her mind?

Shaking, she turned to see if anyone else had seen what she had seen but nothing seemed out of the ordinary then.

She screamed, stumbling backwards when another body dropped a few feet from where she had just been standing. It too disappeared.

What did she just see! What was she seeing?

Before she could answer her own questions, there were more people falling from the sky.

This could not be real!

Her hand over her mouth, she watched in mute horror as another person crashed to the ground, then another, this time a young woman she recognized from the ninth floor.

Oh no!

Dora.

Tessa.

Then a man, one she had seen in passing. He was holding onto several screaming girls who began dropping one by one. The look of horror on his face matched hers and then he jumped, following the women to his death.

She didn't think she would ever forget the screams or the terror or the dull thud sound of bodies hitting the hard concrete one by one.

Hunched against the wall as if trying to go through it, a part of her wondered if she should she warn someone, but another part was hesitant. After all, each time she looked back at the sidewalk where people had dropped, nothing was there.

The people walking by were staring at her curiously, maybe thinking she was nuts. Was she?

This wasn't real, wasn't happening.

She was either losing her mind or maybe … the brooch … she wasn't wearing it, just carrying it. Could it be giving her another nightmare even though she was awake? It had to be the brooch.

She glanced up at the building and to her shock, saw bright orange and black flames shooting out of the eighth, ninth and tenth story windows. Before she could visibly react, they disappeared.

Unable to contain her fear, she sprang from the wall and burst into a run. All she knew is that she had to get away.

Nine.

She couldn't go into work today. She could be fired but she could not go!

She felt so sick, so frightened. The thought of going back toward the factory or anywhere near that building terrified her. She could not think!

Her gut told her not to go to work today, not to go near the factory.

Something was wrong with her, very wrong!

Where was Elliott? He had to be on his way.

One block down from where they were to meet, she flew across the street, running and walking and practically hurling herself into Elliott's arms.

Elliott's arms came up around Paulina, who was sobbing inconsolably, as he exclaimed. "What is the matter, what happened, did someone hurt you?"

"Oh, I am seeing terrible things," she cried shaking harder than a leaf trapped in an autumn wind gust. She blurted out what had happened to her, what she'd seen. She knew she sounded like a crazy person, but could not calm down. "No one hurt me, but something is wrong! First I feel hot, then I see a fire and bodies falling from the sky, people I recognized, people from the shirtwaist factory. They were terrified, screaming and then jumping out of windows, it was terrible and..."

Holding her shoulders gently, Elliott stared down at her his dark eyes wide with concern and said, "Paulina, please darling, calm down, it is okay. You are safe. I can see the building from here and none of that seems to be happening."

"I know, but I kept seeing it, feeling it, a fire, all those people trapped."

Using one hand to wipe her forehead, he exclaimed, "My God, Paulie! You are hot, burning up with a fever. No wonder you are imagining things!"

She felt exhausted, confused. "But. My work..."

"Forget it, darling. You aren't well. You have fever."

He took her bags, her coat and put his arms around her. "Come. I will get word to them. We should go to my parents' house and I will call our family doctor. He will be able to help you."

*P*AULINA FELT AS if she were a train emerging from a deep dark, tunnel. She felt the rush of air around her and heard a low hum she realized were voices. She vaguely remembered what happened, the horror of another nightmare taking hold and finding Elliott, feeling safe in his arms. She knew he'd taken her to his parents' house. She heard him call the doctor but beyond that, her memories were hazy.

Someone came in the room and touched her head as gently as a butterfly's wing. "Her fever is finally gone," she heard Mina say, recognizing her by her scent, rose toilet water, before she even spoke. Then. "Are you awake, Paulina?"

She extradited herself from the lethargy pinning her down and finding her voice said, "Yes."

She blinked open her eyes to see a most welcome sight, Mina and Elliott smiling down at her and her coat, bag, and the box on the chair nearby.

Elliott came rushing over and, kneeling by the bed, took her hand and kissed it. His lips were as warm as his whisper. "Darling, we were so worried but, thank God, you look so much better already."

"I feel much better, thank you for taking care of me, both of you. How long have I been sleeping? What time is it?

"Five o'clock," said Mina, hovering close.

"What!" She sat up. She'd never slept a whole day away in her life. Her mouth opened in shock just as Mina, never one to miss an opportunity, stuck a thermometer right into it.

Her fever disappeared with her symptoms. Even the doctor shrugged, unable to explain what it was or why it had come as quickly as it had gone.

Glad to leave the box and the pin in Elliott's care, and not wanting to cause a scandal by remaining at his home without his parents there, Paulina insisted on returning home. Mina agreed to spend the night with her just in case of a relapse.

Once home, bathed and back in her own bed, Paulina listened as Mina told her how Elliott had called her and how alarmed he'd been. "I hope I find someone who loves me someday as much as he loves you. He is a good man."

Paulina agreed and said she felt fortunate. "I wish for you the same someday."

"Not until I become a doctor," said Mina firmly and not unexpectedly, for helping sick people was all Mina ever wanted to do since they were children.

"I know that," said Paulina admitting she didn't have a strong calling like Mina did. "I am not sure I have a job after today, but I don't care. I don't want to go back to that place ever again."

She told Mina that she'd found her papa's nest egg and that he'd left her enough money that she didn't really have to go back to the factory or lose her home. "I would have told you sooner, but there never seemed time."

Mina understood and was relieved for her.

The next day, they were awakened when Elliott knocked on the door. He had been on his way to work until he'd seen the morning paper. As soon as he had, he rushed right over to tell them that yesterday at about 4:30 pm there had been a terrible fire at the Triangle Shirtwaist Factory.

Waving the paper, he looked disbelieving as he said, "One hundred and forty-six people; all but twenty-three of them young women died a horrific death. But, even more chilling, is what Paulina saw in her delirium actually came to pass."

Mina crossed herself. Elliot looked as if he might need a stiff drink. Rushing over to Paulina, he embraced her as tight as he could. Shaking his head he looked at her and said, "Do you realize if it hadn't been for your mysterious fever and delirium yesterday, you might have been inside that building when the fire occurred? You ... you could have been killed too."

Paulina felt sick all over again. Elliot was right. She had no idea why she had been spared when so many others, including the two young women she'd sat between on the eighth floor, Dora and Tessa, had been among those killed.

Mina reached for her hand, squeezing it. The three of them just stood together for minutes, paused in silence and locked in their own thoughts.

Each day that passed, people could talk of nothing else. Paulina learned later that her neighbor, Yetta, had been spared too. There was no logical explanation for any of it; but for Paulina, already burdened with grief, it was overwhelming and she could not stop crying for days.

Mina remained close to her side and Elliott visited every day before and after work, always bringing something that his mother sent for them to eat for supper.

Hugging both of them to him, Elliott said, "Special prayers are being said at synagogue for the lost. Because of this, I find myself reflecting more and more on the randomness of tragedy and death. On God."

"God does work in mysterious ways," agreed Mina, as she pulled away to gather her things to go. With a perplexed expression, she admitted she had no explanation for what Paulina had experienced. Or why what she'd seen in her delirium came to fruition.

But Paulina — her father's image, his words, his hidden cache and all the dreams she had popping into her mind — knew exactly what had happened and why. She said, "God's presence in all things noted, as crazy and unexplainable as it might sound, I have no doubt I am here today because I was warned by Papa and my loved ones and others beyond the grave and saved by one, yes very mysterious but beautiful, songbird with sapphire eyes brooch."

DECEMBER 26, 1921, EARLY EVENING
NEW YORK CITY

SHREDDING POTATOES, SLICING onions and cracking eggs, the turkey roasting in the oven since early that morning, Paulina hummed to the holiday music, playing from the Victrola in the hall, as she lovingly prepared the ingredients for the latkes.

Within hours, Mina and her beau of just a few months would be joining them for supper and celebration. Both worked at City Hospital in New York. Mina was a first year resident working in the burn unit. Dr. Glenn Frank, her beau, one of the senior staff surgeons.

Paulina looked forward to lighting the candles on the first night of Hanukah with her family, and to celebrating a belated Christmas with Mina who for the past nine years had been too busy studying and working over the holidays to have much time to celebrate anything.

Paulina had the table set with her finest cream laced tablecloth and Chanbord patterned china. The gold trim and pink roses on the plates matched the crystal vase filled with imported pink roses. Roses were an extravagance this time of year and one she'd chastised her husband about; but after almost nine years of marriage, Elliott knew how to placate and spoil her. He'd said it was an early anniversary gift so she could not quite quibble.

Their new home was spacious with large windows, hardwood floors and wainscoted walls of black walnut and oak. Candles were lit throughout the house, their sweet beeswax scent mixing with the delicious smell of all the foods she'd prepared. The fresh cut, evergreen spruce and fir boughs on the fireplace mantel and the stairs brought the holidays inside. She hoped the evergreens would provide Mina a sense of her own childhood celebrations, too.

In addition to the roasted turkey for dinner there would be

cornbread stuffing, potato latkes, mashed potatoes, cranberries and string beans she'd canned herself. As for sweets, aside from chocolates, nuts and oranges, there was homemade apple sauce, apple kreplach, honey and butter cookies with poppy seed filling, pizelle waffle cookies made with anise and tzimmes made sweet with apples, pears and plums.

Drying her hands on her apron, Paulina took a quick assessing glance at the white and blue tiled kitchen with its large counters, country sink and all the modern appliances a twenties housewife could dream of. Everything that could be ready was.

She thought about her loved ones who were no longer here. She realized one never stopped missing those they lost, but learned to cherish their memories and life itself. For life was short, mysterious and never to be taken for granted.

Paulina was convinced the brooch saved her. She would not be alive and, if not for Elliott and Mina, she would have never gotten over dreading the holidays!

She smiled, entering the living room to see Elliott finish the last of the holiday decorations by peppering the greenery with pinecones, red ribbons and popcorn strung by the children in honor of Mina's holiday. He was doing his best to keep the three kids out of her hair.

Whether one celebrated Christmas or Hanukah or anything else, she'd learned every day was what you made it. The essence of every holiday was about counting one's blessings, giving and sharing and spending time with loved ones who mattered to you most.

She was shaken out of her reverie when her oldest daughter Irena shouted, "She's here, she's here."

The eight year old was at the window peering out. She let go of the curtain and began twirling spirals as if she were performing the *Nutcracker Suite* for an audience of one hundred. Her younger brother, ever restless, jumped up and down like a grasshopper on hooch.

"Auntie Mina, Auntie Mina!"

"Kids, settle down right this moment," Paulina said trying to sound sterner than she felt. "You sound like a bunch of squealing banshees. Please!"

She scooped up baby Katarina, toddling at a fast pace right behind her two wilder siblings and her father, just as he reached the door.

Holding the squirming child, Paulina stood by her husband and, despite the warmth of the house, felt the immediate rush of chilled air as the door opened wide. Mina and Dr. Frank, arms filled with gift-wrapped packages were swaddled and bundled tight as mummies. They were covered in white, a white dulled by their smiles at the sight of them and their dancing children.

"It's snowing! It's snowing!"

A new chorus of enthusiastic shouts broke out as the children saw the large snowflakes trying hard to create a picturesque winter scene on all and sundry.

Elliott helped Glenn with his bounty, quickly closing the door behind them as they entered to shouts and hugs.

"It looks as beautiful in here as it smells scrumptious," said Mina with a quick hug to Paulina and Elliot as the baby practically jumped into her arms.

Mina laughed, sounding very pleased. She tickled the curly haired baby, said she was getting big. She took in the touch of Christmas that Paulina had blended with their holidays for her. Tears filled her pretty blue eyes as she thanked them.

Putting the baby down gently, Mina proceeded to unwrap herself; coat, hat, gloves and scarf coming off faster than cotton candy spinning at a carnival. Kneeling with arms outstretched, she braced to catch the three little rapscallions impatiently waiting to rush right into their auntie's arms.

DECEMBER 26, 1921
NEW YORK CITY

THE EVENING WAS noisy, pleasurable, and full of food, laughter, conversation, games and gift exchanges, but like all enjoyable evenings, it flew by far too fast.

By the time Elliott poured himself and his guests another glass of wine and they had discussed everything from the state of the union to the problems in Europe, to Prohibition, gangsters and flappers, and had gone through another two bottles of wine, Mina and Paulina had cleaned up the kitchen, put the baby to sleep and had bathed the two oldest children, now playing upstairs in their rooms.

Mina had confided to Paulina that she and Glenn were heading toward matrimony. She said, "We have much in common and the same commitment to our work and very strong feelings for one another. The truth is, I have never felt like this with another human being, besides you, and this is even more than that."

"I should hope so," said Paulina, laughing. Mina looked happier than she'd ever seen her.

Her beau, Dr. Glenn Frank was in his thirties. He was intelligent, committed to his profession and had a kind and sincere manner. He insisted they call him Glenn and he and Elliott seemed to hit it off right away.

For the third time that evening, he thanked them for their hospitality. "I am very impressed with your holiday spirit. I never observed a Hanukah celebration before and I enjoyed how you added a touch of Christmas for Mina. Longer than Mina, I cannot remember when I didn't work over the holidays. People are always sick or needing help. You probably cannot understand, but sometimes the holidays are a miserable time of year for so many so I actually like to work."

Paulina said, "I understand. I lost both my parents during the holiday season and if it weren't for Elliott and Mina, I would have never gotten over my dread of the holidays."

The story of the treasure box came up. Paulina told of how it had taken Elliott almost nine months to discreetly check for provenance and figure out the value of its contents. How, as she'd guessed, all of the items were valuable.

She rubbed her hands together as she spoke. "I thought the brooch was the most valuable thing in that box, but I was wrong. Its monetary value didn't compare to the rocks, which were rare, blue diamonds. Or the coins, which were worth the most. Some of them were very old, rare and highly collectable, easily worth double and triple of everything else."

Dr. Frank was fascinated. He asked what they were. When she explained, he said, "Surely, you wanted to keep such valuable heirlooms in your family rather than sell them?"

"No, not at all," said Paulina. "I nor my papa had any sentimental attachment to the items inside the treasure box. You might even say it was a burden. I wanted Elliott to keep the stones to make his beautiful jewelry since he would not take payment for all his hard work on my behalf. He agreed to keep only two if I'd keep the brooch." At that, she exchanged a loving and knowing gaze with her husband before continuing. "Being a jeweler's wife, Elliott hoped I might feel differently about keeping the brooch so he purchased it for me himself, but I didn't want to wear it. He kept it in the store vault."

Looking lost in memories, she helped herself to a cookie. Took a bite, chewed and swallowed. "More than anything else, I wanted money to help Mina with her schooling. That to me was more satisfying than owning a fancy trinket I never felt right about wearing."

Elliott reached to his wife and affectionately rubbed her arm. She looked at him and smiled inviting him to tell the story of what had happened next.

Nodding, he sat forward and, looking more than a little proud, explained how he'd suggested to Paulina that she throw Mina a little holiday surprise party as an excuse to gift her with the money.

He said, "It was already early December and I knew if Paulina had something to plan, she might not have time to dwell on her grief or think about the coming holidays. Mina and I were both concerned. Mina suggested the only way to make the holidays happy for Paulina again would be to overlay her sad memories with very good, happier ones."

Elliott and Paulina exchanged several loving glances as he told how he kept Paulina busy planning Mina's surprise, and how the surprise party Paulina thought she was planning for Mina turned out to be a surprise party for herself too.

"Again, with Mina's encouragement, I got down on bent knee and proposed to Paulina in front of all our family and friends."

Dr. Frank and Mina exchanged affectionate gazes as he chuckled in amusement. "Why am I not surprised Mina is involved. She excels at helping people whether it is in the hospital or out."

They all agreed and, laughing, Paulina held out her hand to show Glenn the ring Elliott had designed for her using one of the rare, blue diamonds.

"Beautiful ring," said Glenn, admiring the small square cut blue diamond surrounded with delicate rows of tiny regular diamonds. "I am impressed with your craftsmanship, Elliott, and the story."

He asked if anyone minded if he lit a pipe, and no one did.

Elliott lit a cigar and Paulina brought them both an ashtray.

Setting up his pipe, Glenn looked a bit puzzled. "Mina has told me all you've done for her and I admire the close relationship you all share. As a doctor, I am a man of science but one of my personal interests is studying things that often cannot be explained by science. In other words, I am fascinated by how you believe that the brooch may have saved you by keeping you from work on the day of that terrible factory fire at the Triangle Shirtwaist factory."

Paulina, having confided in both her husband and her friend her feelings about that day, explained.

"I was deep in my grief and busy sorting through a lifetime of family memories and stories I'd been told as a child. I wasn't taking care of myself properly and was having trouble sleeping and strange dreams. I wanted to give Elliott the treasure box for safekeeping and evaluation. That morning, the day of the fire, we were to meet before my shift at the factory. I got there early."

Mina confirmed they'd never figured out a reason for Paulina's sudden illness or a suitable explanation for why Paulina had foreseen what would happen that day.

Paulina admitted she hadn't had any unusual dreams or visits from the dead since. She said, "I know it sounds unusual and far-fetched, but I do believe the brooch does have special abilities. Any time I wore it, I felt strange. My papa used to tell me stories about a bird that had the ability to connect the living to the dead. I have reason to believe many of his stories contained truth."

Glenn acknowledged her statement and said, "I truly believe some people are more sensitive to experiences like that as well."

Elliott, showing support for his wife, held her hand and said, "While I believe what Paulina experienced was real, I am not inclined to accept that the cause of her experiences were all brought about by a brooch. However, I do agree there is no plausible explanation for what occurred the day of the fire and, since many of Paulina's papa's stories have turned out to have some base in truth, who am I to say different. Life is full of mysteries that cannot be explained."

"True," agreed Glenn. "And I am ever glad for that. It makes life interesting and even men of science, sensible, logical, will admit the unexplainable does happen. Do you, perhaps, still have this mystical brooch?

Elliott shifted in his chair and shook his head. "No, actually I do not. My wife convinced me to sell it and I did, about two weeks ago. Paulina never warmed to the idea of wearing it and a few years ago, I began displaying it in a special case in the store with a not for sale sign on it.

"It just so happened, we got a customer about a month or so ago who decided he had to have it. The fella was a tough guy, a gangster I'd guess by the looks of him and not someone you'd want to make mad at you. He wanted it for his girlfriend. He wouldn't take no for an answer! Said his girlfriend had eyes the exact same color as the songbird and was in fact, herself a singer, a songbird. He insisted he had to have it for her.

"I told him it was an old family heirloom of my wife's and not for sale, but he insisted everything was for sale at the right price. He was quite convincing and a bit intimidating. I said I would talk to my wife about it. He wouldn't leave so I called Paulina. She told me to sell it, but only on the condition I told the buyer the whole story that came with it."

"Did you?" asked Mina and Frank in unison.

"Yes," said Elliott, rolling his eyes. He relayed how he told the man that even though he had no papers to prove it, Catherine the Great herself reputedly wore the brooch. That it had mystical powers that could connect the living to the dead. That it could make its wearer dream."

Glenn asked. "What happened, what did he do?"

Elliott snorted. "First, he looked at me like I was nuts." He said, "So you're sayin' this pin has a curse?"

"I said not a dangerous one necessarily, but yes. He laughed. He said he didn't believe in crap like that. I agreed to sell it to him, but there would be no refunds if he changed his mind. He told me not to worry. He pulled a roll of bills out of his pocket like I'd never seen one man carry. He counted out ten grand in one hundred dollars bills."

Paulina, as immersed in the story as all of them were, jumped up when she heard a noise from upstairs. She glanced at the time. "It's the kids. Time to get them tucked into bed. Please excuse me."

Mina said she'd finish cleaning up and began to clear the table.

"That really isn't necessary," insisted Elliott knowing Paulina would prefer to do it. "Paulina won't want you doing that. She won't even let me employ a live in or a live out housekeeper to help her."

"Of course not." said Mina laughing, as she chased the two men off. "I know Paulina enjoys tending to her loved ones herself and no amount of money will ever change her course or her as you well know too."

"I do," Elliott agreed, not at all displeased as he led Glenn towards his den to show him his rock collection.

Mina finished cleaning up the table and the kitchen and, when she was done, she tiptoed up the stairs. She didn't want to excite the children or wake them if Paulina had already managed to get them to sleep.

Seeing a dim light coming from Irena's room, she paused and smiled as she heard the two older children begging for a bedtime story. "Mama, please, just one story, just one, please."

Paulina sounded tired but resigned. "Just one and a very short one at that."

A soft girlish voice. "Mama, the one about the princess and the magic bird."

A much louder voice. "No! I want the one about pirates and treasure."

Paulina's voice was patient but firm as she admonished her son. "Petya, we must speak softly as to not wake the baby. Tonight, I am going to tell you a story about real treasures, those of family and friends and the truest meaning of the holidays."

Moving closer, she listened to the rustle of the children settling in, to the creak of the oversized rocker and the cadence of her best friend's lovely voice as rolling with each rocking, she began.

"There are all kinds of beliefs, celebrations and holidays, but the most important thing to remember is one must never stop believing … in magic, in mystery, in the love of family and friends, in the good of people and in the hope and wonder that is our universe and God."

~

ABOUT THE AUTHOR

Anna was a bookworm almost since birth and was recognized as a writing PRO by Romance Writers of America *in 2002. An active member of* Willamette Writers, RWA *and the* Rose City Romance Writers. *Anna grew up in Philadelphia and graduated from Philadelphia's,* University of the Arts *where she majored in Illustration. She pursued a successful and versatile career in children's book illustration, graphic arts, publications and public relations in Southern California before being lured to the Oregon wilderness by her desire to write and her former Navy Seal husband.*

You can learn more about Anna and her books at:

annabrentwood.com

Don't Forget the Mistletoe
Christy Carlyle

"*Y*OU'RE NOT GOING to marry Eliza Hobbs, are you?"

The question took Benedict Poole utterly by surprise, so much so that he nearly tripped over his own feet. One moment he had been indulging in the pleasure of playful banter with the prettiest girl in the room and the in the next she had shocked him to his boots.

Always expect the unexpected from Amelia Westerley. It was a precept he'd held since making her acquaintance at the age of ten. She'd been only seven on that cool autumn day when her mother had called on his mother. Newcomers to the village, his family had been eager to find their place in the close community of Clovebury.

He'd been acutely aware that Amy was younger and hadn't expected much from their forced acquaintance, yet she turned out to be the cleverest and most unexpected girl he had ever met. Still was. And she always managed to surprise him.

He regained his balance quickly but couldn't keep the discomfiture from his voice when he responded to the young woman at his elbow.

"Amy, whatever makes you say such a thing?"

He loathed gossip on principle, but the notion that he was the subject of rumors made him shudder. Not that he was opposed to marriage altogether. The petite interrogator standing next to him knew that all too well.

"You spent a good deal of time with her at the Newland's dinner party and I heard that you accompanied her to the ball tonight."

The facts as stated were true, but collectively they came to nothing. He had known no one else at the Newland's dinner party. Eliza Hobbs had offered familiar if lackluster conversation, and her family owned no carriage. As a neighbor, it would have been beyond rude not to offer to deliver her to the Westerley's Christmas ball in his own carriage.

Was that a flush of pink he saw on Amy's cheek? He noted that she was suddenly very interested in studying the cut of the crystal glass in her hand.

"I offered her the use of my carriage. I delivered her to the ball. Not the same thing at all."

He had as much interest in Eliza Hobbs as he did in any of the other eligible young ladies in his circle. Which was very little, if the truth be told. Oh, he did his duty — danced when necessary and offered the use of his carriage when needed — but none of them endangered his heart. His heart was secure. Uselessly, pointlessly devoted to the one woman who had no interest in it at all.

"You aren't going to marry her then?"

Amelia Westerley was nothing if not tenacious. It was one of her qualities that he most admired. But her newfound interest in his marital status was a shock. More than a shock, it was a great irony. He had only ever asked for one woman's hand in marriage, and Amy had refused.

"Are you so eager to marry me off?"

He wondered, for the first time if their continuing friendship was as difficult for her as it was for him. No, not difficult exactly. He prized her friendship above all others, but it was bittersweet. And painful for him in ways it certainly would not be for her. So why would she find their friendship difficult to bear?

Ah, perhaps she simply wanted him married off so that she might be secure from any more of his unwanted declarations of love.

The Westerley's spacious home suddenly seemed too crowded and the fire in the drawing room grate blazed too high for comfort. Benedict began devising an excuse so that he could make an early departure without causing too much offense.

"No!" Amy must have felt the heat too, as her cheeks were clearly flushed with color. He felt the light pressure of her hand on his upper arm. He savored the heat of her fingertips as they grasped him.

"Don't marry her, Ben."

He looked into the mirror over the mantle and studied her as she turned to him, practically pleading with him. She looked strikingly beautiful, with that pink flush in her cheeks and a sparkle in her eyes. His hopeful heart thought, for just a moment, that it read a glint of desire in those glistening eyes. No, she did not desire him in that way. They had crossed that ground already. That was the way of pain. Those notions were the road to folly.

When he didn't speak, she continued.

"I have heard things about her."

"Amy, you know how I detest gossip. Spare me a recitation of the latest girlish tittle tattle."

He lifted his cup and drank down the final swig of Mrs. Westerley's warm Christmas punch, determined to put an end to this evening. He had looked forward to it for weeks, mostly for the opportunity to see Amy, but no amount of overly spiced punch could blunt the pain of discussing matrimony with the one woman who would not consider it with him.

"I am not a girl anymore. What you call gossip may simply be facts shared among friends. Facts that one should know before yoking yourself to a woman for life. I know you are eager to marry, but—"

"Who says I am eager to marry?"

Amy didn't answer. She opened her mouth as if to speak and he could see that she was nearly bursting with some emotion. But still she said nothing. He wanted to help her, to draw from her all of the emotion that he could read in her lovely face, whatever it might be.

He wanted to recapture the ease they had shared in each other's company earlier in the evening. Conversations that ambled from wide-ranging topic to unrelated topic and good-natured mutual teasing had been the hallmarks of their interaction almost from the moment they had met.

Before he could speak and say something benign to cut through the growing tension between them, she struck him speechless by reaching out to take his hands. As she was at home, she had not worn gloves and he had shed his own with his coat and hat.

It had been so long since he had touched her bare flesh. He recalled the moment the previous September when he'd held her hands, caressed her face. He had been the one pleading then. A surge of pain came with the memory, fresh and sharp, as if her rejection had been just yesterday.

"Amy, I must go—"

"You can't go."

"I'm sorry, but I must."

Nothing she could say could persuade him, not even her supple hands still holding him tightly.

"Have you forgotten about the mistletoe?"

"Mistletoe?" His lips formed the word, but his thoughts scattered as if a stiff wind had just blown through the Westerley's too hot drawing room.

Amy tugged at his hands, pulling him a few steps into a corner of the room, not far from the glow of the fragrant, candlelit Christmas tree. A sprig of mistletoe hung from a red satin ribbon above their heads.

"You do know what you must do under the mistletoe, don't you?"

Benedict sensed no tension in Amy's expression now. Indeed, a smile curved her lips and she stood close, achingly close to him.

He slid his hand along the sleeve of her dress, grasped her arm, and pulled her closer.

"Amy, if your feelings have changed..." Hope flared in his chest like an ember.

"Yes." Her voice was quiet, almost a whisper.

Benedict leaned closer, relishing her nearness — the warmth of her body and the tickle of her breath against his chin. His voice grew husky, the words thick in his mouth. "Shall I kiss you, Amy?"

She didn't answer, not with words, but she lifted up on her tiptoes and pressed her mouth to his.

Benedict slid his arms around her waist and held her as tightly as he dared, gently, fearful of breaking the spell that had placed his heart's desire back in his arms.

All too soon, she pulled away from the kiss, but she did not move out of his embrace.

"Amy…" His heart was so full, his hope so acute, that words were difficult. He took a deep breath. The air was tinged with the scent of pine needles and the sweet lily scent Amy sometimes wore. "My dear, have your feelings changed?"

His chest constricted as he waited for her answer. It was a painful anticipation, and familiar. He'd waited for her answer before.

Amy nodded her head, causing the wavy wisps of chestnut hair framing her face to brush across her cheeks. "Everything has changed."

Her smile was brighter than the candles glowing on the tree nearby, and he was warmed by the sight of it. Another question filled his mind and heart. A question he had asked once before and vowed never to ask anyone again. He could not have imagined her change of heart or surviving the pain of another rejection. Now, with Amy in his arms and a love that mirrored his own shining in her eyes, he thought Christmas might just be the perfect time to risk his heart again.

~

ABOUT THE AUTHOR

Christy Carlyle writes historical romance, usually set in the Victorian era or Regency period. She loves heroes who struggle against all odds and heroines that are ahead of their time. A former teacher with a degree in history, she finds there is nothing better than being able to combine her love of the past with her die-hard belief in happy endings.

Learn more about Christy at her website:

christycarlyle.com

First Love
Judith Ashley

JUNE 10, 1987
DECLAN, ALABAMA

𝒜SHLEY ANN CARLYLE's breath caught in her lungs, her heart skipped a beat and her mouth formed a silent 'O' before a squeal of delight burst forth.

"You're engaged!" she hugged her friend Maybelle tight. Her throat constricted and tears welled. She stepped back, held Maybelle's hands and looked her in the eyes. "Y'all better tell me every little detail."

Ed Denton stuck his head in the office where Ashley and Maybelle worked. "What's all the noise about? All that squealing will scare off customers. Get to work," he barked.

"At break," Maybelle whispered, her smile lighting their work space.

It wasn't easy to stay focused on her work when Maybelle's diamond engagement ring winked at her every time Maybelle moved her hand — which was constantly.

Ashley and Maybelle both worked for Uncle Ed's New and Used Car Dealership, a fixture in that part of Alabama. Ashley's job was to enter the information from the sale of cars on a form that was sent every night to the Department of Motor Vehicles. She also did transfer of title documentation and ordered parts for the service department. Maybelle took care of all the billing, correspondence and other odd jobs. Ed's wife was the cashier and handled the money.

At the stroke of ten, they put their work aside, grabbed their colas and headed out to their bench under the pecan trees along the side of the service department. Their bench was the one on the end, closest to the service department that gave them a perfect view of the mechanics working in the service bays.

Momentarily distracted by the flashing grin and nod from the man working in the first bay, Ashley stumbled. Maybelle's steadying hand kept her from falling.

"Thanks." Ashley took a sip of her cola, thankful it hadn't spilled all over her new skirt and blouse. She took the offered handkerchief from her friend and wiped the sticky liquid off her hand as best she could. Sticky hands could wait. "Tell me everything!"

"I tell you it was so romantic. Walt drove me out to the lake to our favorite spot. He was all dressed up. Wore a new shirt and everything. He'd even cleaned up his truck, well, pretty much anyway."

"So you're at the lake," Ashley prompted, noting Maybelle's unfocused gaze and goofy grin.

"Yeah, we were at the lake. I knew something was up because Walt talked to my dad in private when he came to pick me up and he's never done that. I saw them through the window talking real serious like and then they shook hands." She sighed and reached for Ashley's hand. "Walt asked my dad for permission to propose. Isn't that just the most romantic thing ever?"

Ashley squeezed her friend's hand, hoping to move the story along. They only had fifteen minutes for their break and she wanted to know the whole story before they went back to work.

"He asked me to walk along the lake with him. We've done it before so I didn't think too much about it. Then there's this place with mossy logs under the weeping willow — sort of private and all? Do you know the spot?"

Ashley shook her head. She'd made a point to not know those spots. "Go on."

"Well, he held the willow branches apart so I could duck under. We sat on the logs and he kissed me. After a bit," Maybelle's face flushed pink. "Well, then he stood in front of me and got down on one knee. That's when I knew he was going to propose. He said, 'Maybelle will you do me the honor of becoming my wife?' and I said 'yes' and when I went to kiss him, I knocked him backward. We laughed because we almost rolled into the lake. That would've been something!"

"It's your turn next," Maybelle said, turning to Ashley and hugging her. "Y'all are the only one in our class still in Declan not married or engaged. After all, you're nineteen now. Don't wait too long or you'll be an old maid."

Ed poked his head out the dealership door. Break was obviously over. The friends walked back to the office and went back to work. Every time Ashley glanced over at Maybelle, her friend was gazing at her engagement ring. Ashley wondered what it would be like to be engaged. Gram always said no need to rush into something like marriage at a young age. Live a little life first. There's plenty of time to get married and have kids.

During lunch they talked about wedding dates, wedding dresses, wedding cakes, engagement parties and honeymoons. The conversation continued during their entire afternoon break. Ashley was on a rollercoaster: high on a high peak with Maybelle and then dropping into a deep valley when looking at her own life. Walt showed up at five and Maybelle clocked out. Watching the couple walk off, eyes only for each other, his arm around her waist and vice-versa, Ashley's chest twinged. She looked away.

Ashley picked up her purse, clocked out and started toward the door. The walk to Gram's house took about fifteen minutes. She looked forward to a tall glass of iced sweet tea and a few minutes on the front porch before helping put dinner together. The door leading outside opened just as she put her hand on the handle.

Yep, there was Art Kenner, the mechanic in the first bay, the man who'd been pestering her to go out to the lake with him since they first met. Her mom had gone out to the very same lake with her dad almost twenty years ago and she'd been the result. If it hadn't been for Gram, well, she didn't even want to think about what her life'd be like if Gram hadn't talked Mom into letting her stay with her when she reached school age.

"Hey there, Miss Ashley," Art said, holding the door wide and gesturing her through. "Can I give you a ride home on a hot day like this? I've got air conditioning."

"Thank you for the offer, Mr. Kenner, but I'd rather walk. I get stiff sitting all day."

"Heard Maybelle and Walt are getting hitched."

"Heard the same thing."

They crossed the lot. When they reached the sidewalk, Art moved so he walked on the street side. Just like a perfect gentleman. But she knew his reputation. He'd been out with every unattached woman in town and then some. Gram didn't trust him. She didn't really tell her why but she's a good judge of character.

"Looks like you're staying busy," Ashley commented. "You've got a list of ladies who don't want anyone else working on their cars." She glanced up and confirmed her suspicion that he had his hang-dog look on his face. Clean cut dark blond hair with sun-bleached streaks and brown eyes that reminded her of Gram's chocolate lava cake when the gooey middle oozes out. Those eyes that also had an old hound dog quality were trained on her. Ashley looked away. *Makes no difference if he looks at me like that.*

Art attended all the community events: the monthly dance, the summer concerts, the picnics. While he danced with others, he danced the most with her. He sat close by if not next to her at the concerts and picnics. What he'd paid for the basket she and Gram had donated for the charity auction was more than for any other basket. He'd done his best to charm Gram while they ate cold fried chicken, potato salad and that chocolate lava cake. She still didn't trust him but she'd softened a little since then.

Even on a sultry summer day, Art walked her all the way home. At the gate he turned to go. She fanned her face with her hand and a bead of perspiration trickled down the side of her face. "Want to sit a spell and have a glass of sweet tea?" she asked. Her heart skipped a beat, her mind awhirl. She'd never been the one to start anything. She turned on her heel but in the heat ambled to the porch.

Gram came out with a sweating pitcher of sweet tea and three glasses filled with ice on a tray. She set them on the low table in front of the front porch swing and rocking chairs. Ashley hid a smile as Gram settled herself in the middle of the swing. She must've seen them coming.

Art followed her up the walk to the porch. She'd observed him at work enough to know his face wore his most charming smile. Using his most charming manners and in his most charming voice, he bowed and said, "I heard you make the best sweet tea in town, Ms. Carlyle." He handed Ashley the glass just poured and, after Gram picked up a glass, took the remaining one before settling in the rocking chair. Gram ignored the compliment and sipped her tea.

"Heard the news?" he asked her Gram a few minutes later.

"About Maybelle and Walt?" Gram asked. "Her folks have been telling everyone in town. She's the last of them. Don't know what they'll do now, but with grandkids close by I figure they won't move far from Declan." Gram used the toe of her foot to gently move the swing.

The creak of the chains and a bird's song seemed muted by suffocating heat. Ashley rubbed the cold glass on her forehead and down her left cheek. Sure was hot for this early in the summer.

"Did you know Carolee is having a baby?"

Ashley's languid movements stopped at Gram's question. Shocked by the news, she didn't immediately answer.

"Another one of your friends in a family way?" Art asked.

While Carolee and Ashley had gone to school together, been on the cheerleading team together and sang in the school choir together, they had not been friends. At nineteen, Carolee was married and divorced and, she'd just learned, having a second baby. A lump in her throat, moisture in her eyes mirrored the mantle of sadness that wrapped around her shoulders. Carolee had been married just long enough that her little girl got her daddy's last name. *I must be old fashion or something. I do want to have kids but I want to be married first and I want to know it will last.*

Ashley cleared her throat and blinked the unshed tears away.

"Know her from school and all, but we weren't friends," she said in response to Art's question. "When's the baby due?" she asked Gram.

"Six months or so," Gram replied.

"So it's not Bubba's baby." The lump in her throat choked the rest of her words. She didn't really even like Carolee. But she didn't hate her. Ashley shook her head to erase the errant thoughts about what Carolee's life was going to be like. She sipped her tea. "He'd left town by then. Must be that drifter guy that's sometimes around and most of the time is not. Can't remember his name right now."

That was not the life Ashley wanted for herself. She wanted to travel some, see some places, have a husband who was hers and hers alone.

"Pernault," Art said. "His last name is Pernault. Haven't seen him around for over a month. Carolee being in a family way must be why."

Ashley heard the disgust in Art's voice. Family must be important to him.

Art finished his tea and stood. "Thank you kindly, Ms. Duncan. I appreciate your inviting me to sit a while and cool down." He turned to Ashley. "See you tomorrow."

Ashley sat with Gram sipping a second glass of tea. Words were not spoken which meant Gram had not really changed her mind about Art. There was something about him she still didn't trust. *If she wants me to know, she'll tell me.* He was a good worker, treated her good. Ashley paused and shook her head. Well, he did want her to go out to the lake with him but all the guys want to take the girls out to the lake.

*T*WO DAYS LATER, Ashley and Maybelle sat on their bench in the humid shade. They both had fans that they used in measured movements to stir the air without them breaking a sweat.

"Denton chewed on Art but good this morning for spending so

much time loitering in the office," Maybelle said. She moved her hand this way and that so the sun caught the diamond. It sparkled and rainbows danced on the asphalt.

"Missed that. Art talked his way out of it? He's one smooth talker. Y'all know Gram says smooth talking is like molasses on Sunday morning pancakes — leaves you wanting a little more." Ashley took a sip of her cola.

"He's interested in you. Has been for some time.' Maybelle turned so she faced Ashley. The fan in her hand stopped moving. She tapped Ashley's arm for emphasis. "Do y'all want to be an old maid? You've crossed off the name of every boy we went to school with."

Ashley bristled. "I want someone who's working, who can hold down a job."

Maybelle sniffed and resumed fanning herself. "Art has a job and he's good at it. Mechanics make pretty good money. Walt said Art has plans for himself. Maybe even set up his own shop someday."

Ashley scowled at her friend. "Didn't know Art and Walt were such good buddies."

"Ash, you know everyone knows everyone's business in Declan. Didn't say they were good buddies. And I didn't even say Art told Walt — only that Walt knows."

"It's too hot to argue, and breaks over," Ashley said. She wafted the fan as she ambled across the lot to the office. In the break room she put her empty cola bottle in the flat before getting another cold one from the refrigerator. "Sure wish Ed'd put an air conditioner in the office like he has for himself," she muttered as she sauntered down the hall.

Back at her desk, she thought over what Maybelle had said about being an old maid and Art's interest in her. Gram's words 'molasses is sticky and takes some work to clean up' reminded her to be careful.

At the end of the day, watching Maybelle and Walt leave together, her chest tightened with a longing that swallowed her up. Her eyes burned. She would not cry over this. She sniffed, wiped her nose with her handkerchief, picked up her purse and walked out the door. No Art greeted her, or walked her home, or sat for a bit and shared a glass of sweet tea. Was this going to be her life?

After dinner the phone rang.

"Hey, Miss Ashley."

"Hey," Ashley replied. Her heart quickened a beat. She turned to see where Gram was. Nowhere in sight. But why was Art calling her at home?

"It's cooling down and I thought maybe you'd like to go for a ride?

"Where?" Ashley asked, a cautionary note in the word.

"Was thinking the lake," Art said in his most smooth talking voice.

"Nope, I don't drive out to the lake with guys." Ashley used her business tone as if she was talking to the state DMV folks.

"How about a drive to Huntsville. We could go for a milkshake at the A&W."

Her stomach churned and her throat choked with bile as Maybelle's words spun through her mind. She didn't want to be an old maid. Everyone in her class was already married. Or they were like Carolee, divorced with a couple of kids. Ashley wanted to be married, but to a good man. Couldn't hurt to go for a drive and a milkshake, get to know him a bit better. Maybe he was husband material. Maybe he was ready to settle down. Maybe he'd sown all those wild oats.

"You can pick me up at half-past seven then. I'll go with you to Huntsville for the milkshake or maybe a root beer float."

"You can order whatever you want," Art said. "See you soon."

"Y'all better come to the door. No honking the horn from the street. Gram will have a fit!"

He chuckled, a low intimate sound that had her heart skip a beat. "For you pretty lady." Before she could correct him, he'd hung up. Now she had to tell Gram she was going in to Huntsville with him.

THE METALLIC BLUE 1961 Pontiac convertible with a white top and white leather interior was in mint condition. With Art as the owner, she didn't expect anything less. Her long hair was up in a ponytail with a tightly tied scarf to keep it from blowing around. Of course the top was down, not that it did much good in air so heavy it felt like a thick wet blanket on every inch of her skin. She almost asked him to put the top up and turn the air on; but in the end she didn't. She might not get to go for a ride like this again.

Art kept both hands on the steering wheel, glancing over at her from time to time. When she caught his eye, the wink and the grin on his face told her he was having a good time. Surprised at how relaxed she was, Ashley laid her head on the back of the seat and watched the scattering of clouds and an occasional bird in the bright blue sky rush by.

At the A&W she ordered a root beer float and a side of fries. Art had a hamburger basket and root beer. Even though the A&W had a drive-in, they went inside to eat.

Ashley relished the cooler air. She took the headscarf off and finger combed the end of her ponytail, working the tangled ends apart. Normally she loved the feel of her long hair swishing against her back but on days like this she was tempted to chop it off at her ears.

"Penny for your thoughts," Art said.

"Just thinking about cutting my hair to about here." Her fingers simulated scissors just below her ears. She laughed at the look of horror on Art's face. "What?"

"Never cut it." Adamant, he shook his finger at her. "Don't you know in the sun or in the moonlight your hair is like a silver-gold halo? You look like an angel." His mouth held in a firm, serious line. His gaze held hers. "You're mighty pretty but with your silver blond hair you're beautiful."

Her face flushed with anger and her mouth flopped open a couple of times like a fish out of water before words came. "I'm more than my looks and my hair," she said, pointing her finger at his chest. "I've a brain, you know."

"Of course I know that," he said, relaxing back against the booth's back. "You're one of the smartest girls in town."

"I'm nineteen, I'm not a girl," she said, her tone sharp, indignation fusing her spine.

"And a mighty pretty woman at that." He took a drink of his root beer and leaned forward when he set it back down. "Smart enough to want to go places?"

"I do want to do some traveling. I may have been born here but I don't much like the heat and humidity. I've been to the Gulf but would like to see the oceans." Ashley nibbled on a fry. How did he do that? — one minute her back was up like a cat hissing for a fight and the next she felt like a cat that's settled down and purring.

"The weather don't bother me much. I've got air in my ride and in my bedroom in my apartment. But I want to travel some. Been between here and Chicago but never been west."

"Gram is more like Denton. She got window units for our bedrooms but just closes the house up in the morning and opens it up at night. Guess that comes from growing up when air conditioning was only for the rich." She sighed at the thought of traveling out west. "Are you thinking about going to California?"

"A friend of mine went to Oregon and Washington," Art said, his eyes lighting up as he talked about the future and traveling. "He says you can spend one day at the beach, sleep in your own bed and the next day be in the mountains or the high desert. That sounds pretty good to me. He's sent pictures of him and his buddies. Said there's always a job for a good mechanic."

"Is this friend from around here?" He's so different when he's just being himself.

"Nope, buddy of mine from high school. Went our separate ways but we keep in touch a couple times a year. Usually just a post card. Maybe a phone call if I know where he's at."

Art's voice dropped as if he was sharing a secret as he went on talking about the Pacific Northwest. He was especially keen on traveling to Fremont, a major city in Oregon. Ashley leaned closer so she wouldn't miss a word. She'd truly like to see these places. Learning more about him, she mentally ticked off the positives: friends he keeps in touch with, good with customers, ambitious, hard worker.

Finished with their meal, they headed back to the car. When Art put his hand on her elbow, she matched her steps with his. At the car, when he suggested they put the top up and turn the air on for the return trip to Declan, she was pleased he'd asked her permission first.

"Guess this was our first date," Art said as he walked her to the door of Gram's house.

"Guess so," she replied, a bit on the wary side. She hoped he didn't try anything and spoil a wonderful evening.

"So I hear you don't kiss on the first date." In the soft porch light, he grinned as if he already knew her answer.

She still shook her head.

"How about a second date?"

"Are you asking me if I'll go out with you on a second date or if I'll kiss you on a second date?"

"Both," Art said in a serious tone at odds with the twinkle in his eyes.

"Yes, I'll go out with you on a second date if you still want to, knowing I don't kiss on a second date either."

"How come?" Art asked, his brow arched in question.

"How come what?" Ashley responded, a hint of suspicion in the wariness.

"How come you don't kiss a guy good night after going out on a date?"

Ashley bristled. "Do y'all think Carolee got pregnant without kissing?"

"Now Miss Ashley, I know you know a bit more about these things. No one gets p.g. from a kiss," Art leaned a bit closer as if imparting some special news.

"But no one gets p.g. without some kissing," Ashley replied, standing her ground, arms folded over her chest, eyes narrowed, staring at Art.

"One kiss and nothing more, I promise."

"I'll think about it but don't get your hopes up," she countered. With a last look, Ashley reached behind her for the front door knob, turned it and on a pivot stepped inside. "Night Art," she said and closed the door.

$\mathcal{T}$WO WEEKS LATER, Ashley rose from the bench where she and Maybelle always took their break. Smoothing her skirt, she checked that her blouse was tucked in. With a flip of her head, her long hair swirled. She caught it with one hand, twisted it once before letting it slide and hang down her back. Casting a surreptitious glance over her shoulder for a quick peek at the first bay in the service department, she was grateful neither Maybelle nor Art noticed. She was flattered that he still pursued her. The gossip vine that quickly shared everyone's business had been silent when it came to him for over a month. Maybe Gram was being a little too Grammy. He kept telling Ashley she's the one for him.

As she and Maybelle sauntered across the lot, her chest tightened and her heart did its little happy dance. Thinking about Art made her body hot and jittery. Gram may be right to not trust him, but she couldn't think why. The more time Ashley spent with him, the more she liked him. She looked up Oregon and Washington in the atlas and thought she'd like to visit there some day. Gram may be right but, then again, she might not. Ashley decided she would keep going out with Art and see what happens.

The weekend after the Fourth of July, they went on another date. Art picked her up in the car, said he had a picnic lunch for them. Why she didn't think to ask where he wanted to have that picnic she didn't know. At the stoplight, with his blinker on to turn right, she did know. The lake.

"Ashley! Wait! What are you doing?" Art hollered as she swiftly unbuckled her seatbelt, opened the car, and scrambled out the door. "What the hell?"

"You know what the hell," Ashley said. Her arms folded across her chest, her foot tapped a sharp staccato, she glared daggers at him. "I told you I wouldn't go out to the lake with you. Are you deaf?"

The light turned green. Art pulled his car to the curb and got out. "I just want you so bad, Ashley. Can't you understand that? I dream about you. There's no one else for me. You're the only one I want."

They faced each other on the sidewalk on Main Street. People walked by, a few slowing their steps to take in the show.

"I'm done with you, Mr. Kenner. You aren't listening to me and I'm tired of saying the same thing over and over. I'm not going out to the lake with you. I'm not putting out for you," Ashley growled the words. She stood on the sidewalk, stance wide, hands on hips and stared him down. With a final "I'm done with you," she turned on her heel and started back to Gram's house at a brisk pace.

Tires squealed as Art peeled away from the curb. Without turning around to look, she marched on. Nausea threaten to erupt right there on the sidewalk. Head high, she put one foot in front of the other. But knowing she'd done what was right for her didn't stop the niggling voice. Tears welled and a few escaped and trickled down her cheeks. *Y'all going to end up an old maid, living the rest of your life here in Declan.*

An hour later Ashley sat on the porch talking with Gram, sipping on a glass of iced sweet tea when Art pulled up to the curb. A moment or two passed before the engine went quiet. Ashley heard the car door shut. Gram watched him approach but Ashley didn't even look his way. When she heard his foot hit the first step, she stood and went into the house.

"Miss Ashley," he said as the screen door shut behind her. He sounded contrite but she was in no mood to listen to him apologize. Assuming he was going to that is.

Her Gram said in a stern voice, "My granddaughter is a lady. You'll do well to remember that young man."

She knew Gram had more to say but Art's footfalls down the porch steps told her he'd left. When she looked out the living room window, he had peeled away from the curb leaving a wide swath of rubber on the road.

"HEY, MISS ASHLEY," Art said to her a few days later as she walked past him on her break.

"Hey back." Ashley kept on walking down the hall to the break room as if he'd said nothing important.

"Miss Ashley, I'd like a minute of your time, if you please," he said in what she knew was his best gentlemanly manner.

Ashley stopped, turned towards him, arms folded over her chest. "What?"

"Can we go sit on the bench outside? Please?" He pleaded with his hang-dog look on his face and his chocolate-lava-cake eyes.

"Whatever you have to say, say it. I'm missing my break time standing here," she said, toe tapping, noting his gaze had slid south to her breasts.

He raised his gaze to her face, took a deep breath and slowly let it out before saying, "I was hoping you'd tell me what I need to do to win you back."

"Y'all can start by treating me like a lady instead of a ho."

"I don't treat you like that!" Art's face reflected the horror she heard in his voice.

"When you buy me a hamburger and shake and then expect me to go out to the lake with you to have sex, you are treating me like one," she shot back, showing no mercy. "Y'all may not be paying me in cash but you are bartering food for sex. Pretty much the same thing in my book."

Art raised his left hand and placed his right over his heart. "I promise I will never try to take you to the lake again. I won't ever push you to make love with me."

*J*UST AFTER LABOR Day weekend, Ashley sat at her dressing table, elbows on the top, chin in her hands. Staring into the gray eyes in the mirror, she reflected on the conversation she and Art almost had about eight weeks ago.

She stood and crossed the small room to her bed and grabbed her newest possession and now favorite stuffed dog. Lying on her back, Ashley held Fido in the air, his soft fur and long floppy ears caressed her arms. "Need to get you a new name, dawg. What was I thinking when I decided to call you Fido? Don't know that I was doing much thinking actually." She hugged the dog, lifted his ear and said, "Art spent twenty dollars at the carnival to win you for me. Can you believe that? Twenty dollars."

Rolling to her side, she looked Fido in the eyes. "You know he wants me to come to his apartment with him. Says he wants to show me his place and fix me dinner. If I say 'yes', he'll think I'm going to go all the way with him. Do you think that would be so bad? He sure curls my toes with his kisses and sometimes, when I let him touch my breasts and all, I get so squirmy and out of breath." She flung herself on her back and considered the cracks in the ceiling as her hand rested on her belly.

Ashley flounced back to her dresser and resumed her earlier pose. "Well, what if I did go all the way with Art? Would that be so bad? What young lady these days saves herself for marriage?"

Solemn gray eyes stared back from the mirror as she fiddled with a strand of platinum blond hair. "Yesterday I heard that Carrie

Sue is pregnant. She just graduated high school and even had a scholarship to college. Now she'll be working at the A&W and raising a kid. Carolee is on welfare. Mom didn't say 'no' and look what happened. If Gram hadn't insisted I come and stay with her when it was time for me to be in school, I don't know what would have happened to me. Memories of too many middle-of-the-night moves to new towns, sleeping in the car, hiding under blankets in the backseat while her mom worked in bars reminded her of why she still said 'no.'"

She propped Fido to sit to one side of the mirror and talked to him. There was something to be said for a stuffed animal that couldn't talk back or give opinions.

"What I need is to find a good man and wait until I'm married to have sex so my kids don't go through what I did." Her throat burned and she swallowed back tears. "I do want to marry and have kids. Just not right now." She pulled her hair up and back in a ponytail, turned her head this way and that, watching the long tail swing from side to side. With a sigh, she let it fall, the silver cascading down her back. "Just wish he'd listen to me. I like him and he's a good worker. If my dad and mom had married, if he'd been a steady worker, we'd have been a family. This morning Gram said she'd heard from Mom and she was coming home for good this time."

The Carlyle women were full of grit and determination so something must be really bad for her to move back to Declan. She's always been so feisty. Must run in the family because Gram and I have a strong streak of feisty too. Ashley tilted her head. A frown creased her forehead right between her eyes. "Gets in our way some times — but better to be too much that way than to be a doormat."

Ashley fumed; tears glistened. She barely restrained herself from stomping her foot. Of course her mom would want to meet Art! Of course she'd stop by Uncle Ed's and invite him to dinner! Of course she'd play matchmaker!

Why Gram didn't stop her, Ashley didn't know. Resentment was still simmering in her gut two weeks after Fran's arrival when Art sat down to dinner with them. Her mom had set dinnertime for seven so she could rope her into helping. Sitting at the table, Ashley now knew why.

"Ashley fixed the salad," her mom said, passing the salad bowl to Art. "And this is our family's special homemade dressing." She eased the bottle towards his plate.

Art picked up the bottle of dressing. "Didn't know your daughter was such an accomplished cook," he said, and smiled.

"Yep, chopping up lettuce and stuff for a salad takes a lot of skill." She hoped Mom heard the sarcasm but if she did, she ignored it.

"And, she helped with the casserole," Mom went on.

"Same skills, chopping." Ashley glared at her.

"Well, it's all delicious," Art said. He matched movements with words by forking more salad into his mouth.

After her initial exchange with her mom, Ashley spoke only when she needed to. Gram was unusually quiet throughout the meal. Her mom and Art didn't seem to notice they were the only people at the table talking. Ashley was surprised they were so easy with each other and had so much to talk about. Although awkward at times, dinner passed quickly. They had dessert on the front porch, deep-dish-berry cobbler Gram made with store-bought vanilla ice cream if someone wanted it.

As Art made ready to leave, her mom said, "It's been a pleasure meeting Ashley's young man. Hope y'all can join us for church and Sunday dinner afterwards. Fried chicken." She smacked her lips in appreciation of the meal to come. "My mom makes the best fried chicken in the state."

He rolled his eyes heavenward and ran his tongue around his lips. "Sure is. I remember it from the charity auction last year. Which service do you attend?"

Startled at his question, Ashley's head swiveled so hard her neck cracked. Her eyes squinted, her brow raised in suspicion as she watched the exchange between her mom and Art.

"Usually the ten o'clock service," Mom replied.

"What if I pick you ladies up at half past nine? Give us plenty of time to get there, get parked and get inside."

Ashley's mouth gaped open. Never in a million years did she think Art would say 'yes' to that invitation. She caught the surprised look on Gram's face. As Art turned and trotted down the steps and to his car, her mom turned back to them. A wide smile on her face she said, 'That went well.' Breezing past Gram and her, her mom entered the house. "Time to clean up. There's dishes to do."

After that night, Ashley's routine changed dramatically. Art spent most of the day on Sundays with them, going to church and having dinner afterward. Usually he took all of them for a drive before bringing them home by six. He never came back inside although he was always invited.

The phone rang at eight-thirty on weeknights. Their conversations were seldom long. She figured he just wanted her to know he's home and not out gallivanting around. Friday nights they went to the movies and Saturdays they went into Huntsville or maybe to Birmingham. One Saturday they went to Monroe, Mississippi for lunch and another time they spent the day in Nashville.

His invitations to his apartment had stopped and he seemed to genuinely enjoy the time with her family. Gram still had a modicum of reserve but her mom welcomed him with open arms, sometimes literally.

Art spent the day with her family on Thanksgiving. He helped peel potatoes and baste the turkey. They had football on the television and even though Ashley wasn't particularly into sports it was fun to watch her mom and Art debate plays. After dinner, Art helped clear the table and while Ashley washed the dishes, he dried. Her mom put them away. Gram had been banished from the kitchen because she'd done most all the cooking.

Ashley stepped out onto the front porch when Art left, his hands full of foil wrapped turkey, dressing, sweet potatoes and pie.

"I forgot what it's like to belong to a family," he said, leaning toward her. "Thank you for including me."

He shifted, put his packages on the porch rail and trailed his fingers down the side of her face, to her shoulders. His caress created shivers wherever he touched. "I like seeing you affected by my touch." His lips whispered over her forehead, resting for a long second on her temple. "You smell like summer." His hands slipped over her shoulders, drew her closer, as his head lowered. "I love you, Ash." His mouth brushed over hers, once, twice and on the third pass, stopped. Minimal pressure, just enough to ensure she knew she was being kissed. Her breathing hitched and she tilted toward him. She lost her balance and he caught her, pulled her close and deepened the kiss.

When he let her go, she stumbled. He steadied her.

Her heart sang with the words, "I love you, Ash". He'd said it first so it must be true. Even Maybelle told her she'd told Walt she loved him first. But when Ashley tried to say the words, nothing came out.

"Don't forget your food," she said when he let her go. "Here." She gathered up the foil packages and handed them to him. Daring a glance at his face, she saw a furrowed brow, a confused look in his eyes and his mouth half open as if he was trying to think of what to say. "See you tomorrow," she said.

"Yeah, see you in the morning," Art replied. He paused another moment before turning and making his way to his car.

She waited on the porch until he pulled away from the curb. Back inside, her mom was at the kitchen table, sipping a cup of coffee. Gram was stirring flour into the yeast mixture for a pan of her pecan sticky buns. Ashley stood in the doorway for a minute watching her mom and Gram.

They weren't talking but the air didn't feel full of contentiousness.

Her mom turned and motioned her to join her at the table. First she went over and gave Gram a hug and kiss on the cheek.

"I'm looking forward to taking one of those sweets with me in the morning."

"Do you have to work?" her mom asked as if this was news to her.

"I do have to work. Maybe not a full day. It'll depend on how busy they are. Lots of people out and about on a holiday weekend. I know Ed hopes to do a lot of business."

"That Art working?" Her mom asked, a twinkle in her eyes and a grin on her face.

"Expect so. Cars still need to be worked on even if it is a holiday." Ashley ignored her mom's mushy look.

"Well be sure to take him one of Mom's pecan buns," Mom said. "He's sweet on you, you know. And he's treating you good. Has a job and makes decent money so you'll never go hungry."

Her mom looked like she was going to cry. She rose, took her cup to the sink, emptied it and rinsed it out. "Night now," she said setting it on the counter to air dry.

Ashley sat barely breathing. Her gut clenched and bile rose in her throat. No hug good night, just two words and she was gone. Those are the two words mom always said when she left during the night.

Ashley started after her but Gram's voice stopped her.

"She's not going anywhere. She's staying put."

Tears welled in Ashley's eyes. For once her mother was going to stay awhile. "I thought she was going to cry," Ashley said and walked to the counter. She stood close to Gram who was now kneading the dough. "Let me do something to help." She picked up the measuring cups and scooped two cups of pecan pieces and a cup of brown sugar into a bowl.

"Just those memories coming up of what was. Your mom has a whole lot of sorrow buried inside her and sometimes it just comes up and wants to spill out. She'd feel a whole lot better if she let it loose instead of pushing it back down."

Ashley and Gram finished making the sticky buns, leaving a dishcloth covering them for the night. The last of the baking dishes and utensils were washed and put away when Gram gestured for her to sit at the table.

"You know you already have your mom's blessing for you to marry Art. If you love him and he loves you, you have my blessing too. I may have my doubts about that young man but I've been known to be wrong." She put her hand on Ashley's cheek, a soft smile on her lips. Love shone in her eyes. "Don't let that get around, you hear?"

"He wants to move away from Declan," Ashley whispered.

"Your mom and I'll be just fine if you do," Gram assured her. "You follow your heart. You've got a good one that's honest, loyal and true."

She took three of Gram's buns to work: one for her and two for Art. He seemed a bit distant but by the end of the day was more like himself. What did surprise her was he begged off spending Saturday with her, said he had things to do at his place. A wave of nausea swept through her. She wondered if he was seeing someone else. She shook her head. In this small town, she'd hear if he was.

𝒯HE SUNDAY AFTER Thanksgiving, Art showed up to take them to Church and had Sunday dinner with them. Instead of spending the rest of the afternoon with her, he'd asked Ashley to meet him at the bandstand in the town square at eight. Her mom had a secret smile on her face so Ashley figured Art had a surprise for her. Whatever could it be?

Garlands of evergreens wound around the railings, pots of poinsettias marched up the steps, twinkling lights outlined the intricate carvings on the octagon-shaped structure and the soft-silvery light from the moon created patterns on the bandstand's floor. Whatever he's got planned, he sure picked a beautiful spot, so romantic with the lights and all.

Ashley waited on the top step, curiosity and anticipation about what he'd planned curling in her stomach. Usually they spent

Saturday together and yet yesterday he hadn't seemed to want to spend time with her at all. She shivered as the specter of her sitting on the front porch sipping sweet tea with her mom and Gram in five years or ten danced through her mind. Dread slithered through her veins. Maybe he was going to break up with her. After all, she hadn't told him she loved him. Why hadn't she? She'd thought about it but when she opened her mouth, even in the privacy of her room, the words just wouldn't come.

His gait was determined as he neared, his arms full of items he'd taken from the trunk. She didn't know exactly why, but she knew it was important for her to wait where she was. Her gaze took in other couples strolling the grounds, hand in hand, leaning into each other saying words meant only for themselves. She recognized them and knew they recognized her and also knew Art was striding across the lawn to be with her. One of the hazards of living in a small town. Everyone knows your business. If he broke up with her, she wouldn't cry. Everyone would know.

"Hey," she said, her soft voice expelling air like a whispered kiss.

"Hey back," he answered.

"What you got there?"

"A blanket to keep us warm and some nourishment."

She moved to the center of the bandstand. He carried his load up the steps and inside. He flicked out the blanket and let it settle over the wood floor before setting the cooler to one side.

"Here," he said. He took the top off and extricated bowls of fruit, two glasses and a bottle of sparkling apple cider.

"Ohh," Ashley drew out the word, a bright smile on her face, "my favorites. Y'all brought my favorites." Another idea popped up. "Are you trying to seduce me, Art?"

"Nope, I'm setting the scene. I want you to know I've paid attention to what you like."

He handed her down to the blanket, then poured her a glass of sparkling apple cider before he joined her. "I want you to know

I plan on always treating you with the respect you deserve. Hope you've noticed my changed ways these past months."

"I have noticed you being a true gentleman," she said. "I've noticed all the little things you've been doing and appreciate your effort."

"I'll always be on my best behavior with you. Scout's honor."

"Were you even a Boy Scout?"

"Yep, almost made it to Eagle before I stopped and went to work."

Sitting on the blanket, they munched on strawberries, blueberries and drank cider. They talked about hopes and dreams. Neither had good prospects if they stayed in Declan. Their talk strayed to what might be if they moved away, moved away to Fremont, Oregon, walked along the beach, played in the snow and hiked through old growth forests. While neither said anything specific, the conversation implied they'd be together.

The night grew cooler. She commented she was getting chilled. When he didn't kiss her or put his arm around her, she was a mite disappointed.

"Time to get you home," he said.

Together they cleaned things up. He drove her the few blocks home, walked her to the door and kissed her good night. It wasn't exactly a quick kiss but it wasn't one of his long, passionate drugging ones either.

Confused by the evening's events, she went inside and got ready for bed. She had no one around to talk to who was neutral. If she talked to her mom, she'd tell Ashley he loved her and was showing it. Gram, well, she liked him better but still had her doubts. Even Maybelle wanted her to marry Art.

After that evening they were back to their routine of phone calls at half-past eight, Friday night movies, Saturday spending time together and Sunday church and dinner. Since it was Christmas time, they went shopping in Huntsville and Birmingham.

Although their non-work routine was the same, things had changed at work. Art had his breaks and lunch rescheduled so he spent them with Maybelle and Ashley.

Some days Walt made it over and the four of them had a grand time talking about what the future held in store for them. Walt and Maybelle talked about moving to a suburb of Birmingham where he was looking into setting up his own carpentry shop. Maybelle was excited to be a partner, running the business part and all. They'd even driven around and found a couple of places that had a house in back or over the shop. They'd set their wedding date: March twenty-sixth. Of course, Ashley would be a bridesmaid. "If you were married, you could be my Matron of Honor," Maybelle had announced. She'd given Art a wink.

Ashley's world was changing whether she wanted it to or not. By this time next year, Maybelle and Walt would be living in Birmingham. A shiver rustled through her as the specter of siting on Gram's porch with her mom and Gram after a long day at Ed's, sipping iced sweet tea in the spring and summer, hot tea in the fall and winter year-after-year stretched out before her.

Christmas Eve, Art escorted Ashley, her mom and Gram back to the house from the midnight church service. Her mom and Gram went inside leaving Ashley and Art on the front porch. Art shifted, wiped his hands on his pants, and cleared his throat. He cleared his throat again and lowered his voice.

"Let's sit over here," he said and gestured to the porch swing.

The chains creaked as the swing moved back and forth. Ashley's boots shuffled across the porch with each movement.

"We get along pretty good and all that. So …" Art dove in for a quick kiss.

Ashley stilled for a moment and then kissed him back, opened her mouth so he could taste her. Art slowed the kiss, pulled back, created space between them. Ashley missed the kissing and snuggled closer, tugging his arm around her shoulder.

"So I've been thinking maybe we should get married and all." He stopped and groaned. "What I meant to say is, Ashley you really are the one for me. Will you do me the honor of marrying me, of being my wife?"

While she'd known something was up because he'd gone to extra measures to please her tonight, she was surprised by the proposal. Until her mom came home in September, Art hadn't been to a church service in years. But since then, he'd escorted her mom, Gram and her to every Sunday service and the special Christmas Eve midnight service. Tonight he'd stood tall beside her and sang the hymns, his baritone blending with her soprano. Afterwards he stayed by her side and visited with other parishioners, seeming at ease with both the old and the young.

Her favorite Old Spice Aftershave, with a hint of that special scent that was Art's alone, drifted around her. Memories of his sterling efforts, the time and expense he'd spent to woo her, to let her know she was special, the one for him, floated through her mind. He'd even told her he loved her and he was proposing without her having said the words back. That took courage.

"Ashley? Did you even hear me?" Art asked, an edge of irritation in his voice.

"Of course I heard you," Ashley replied. "I was just thinking on your proposal is all."

"Need more thinking time?" He leaned down and brushed a soft kiss on her temple. His breath caressed her check. "Anything I can do to help you make up your mind?" He leaned in to nibble on her earlobe. She leaned away.

"Three little words would help?"

"Are you tired?"

"What are you talking about?"

"You said you wanted to hear three little words and 'are you tired' is three little words."

Ashley pushed out of the swing. Art caught her around the waist before she'd taken a second step. She stopped, stood rigid, stared ahead and said nothing.

"I know I wasn't funny and I know those aren't the words," he said his breath feathering across her neck. "Let me try again."

He stepped in front of her, rested his hands on her shoulders and caught her eye. "I love you, Ashley Carlyle. You're the only one for me. I'll try to always treat you like the lady you are." He leaned an inch closer. "I love you and would be honored to have you be my wife."

"Love and marriage are serious, Art. There's time for fun and stuff but if our marriage is going to last, we've got to be serious about making it work. Just because I love you—" She shook her head at the look of victory on Art's face. "Listen to me, Art. Just because I love you don't mean I'll marry you. I need to know you won't cheat on me, go running off and leave me. I need to know you'll be a good husband and a good father to our kids."

"I love you, Ashley. Our wedding vows will say 'for richer or poorer, in sickness and in health, forsaking all others until death us do part'. I'll say those words to you now."

Art took Ashley's hands in his, led her back to the swing and sat her down. His gaze steady, his voice firm and clear he said, "I, Arthur Kenner, do take you, Ashley Carlyle, to be my wedded wife, to have and to hold in sickness and in health, for richer, for poorer, forsaking all others until death us do part."

His declaration was more than she'd expected. Her heart did its happy dance, her lungs expanded with joy, her throat filled with laughter. Ashley launched herself into his arms. "Yes, yes I'll marry you."

The swing rocked, the chains creaked and the porch light came on. Art ignored the warning light and held her close. "I promise you'll never regret it," he said and sealed his promise with a kiss.

~

ABOUT THE AUTHOR

Judith's imagination has always been active and through books she's been a princess rescued from the tower by the handsome knight, a missionary in India, explorer in the Amazon jungle, a priestess of the Goddess, and a nun to name a few. She's lived with people from all walks of life including different tribes of indigenous people on five continents in tents, wood cabins, igloos, castles, mansions, high-rise apartments, penthouses, dungeons, basements, and cottages.

You can learn more about Judith and her Sacred Women's Circle *series of novels at:*

judithashleyromance.com

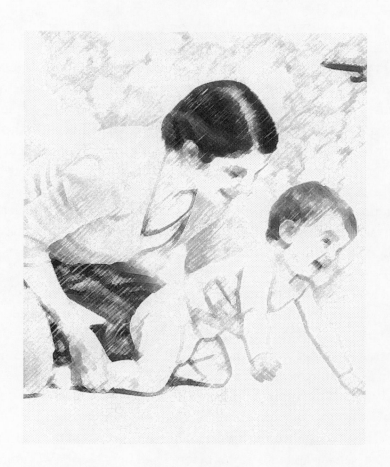

Christmas with You
Jane Killick

*T*HE UNCOMFORTABLE NOISE of someone moving in my house pulled me from sleep. I listened, tense in the dark, to the static of night until the sound of nothing was loud in my ears. Even though I heard no one, I sensed a presence. I imagined burglars tiptoeing across my carpets, surveying my belongings and silently slipping Christmas presents into their swag bags. Once I had thought it, there was no going back to sleep without checking it out. I got out of bed.

Flannelette pajamas with pictures of little bunny rabbits all over them was hardly the outfit to strike fear into the hearts of burglars but, unfortunately, that's what I was wearing. I suddenly realized why all those Americans in the films and TV shows keep a baseball bat under the bed. Being British, the best I had to offer was a half-deflated football somewhere in the back of the wardrobe.

I looked around for a weapon. In the half light, I saw yesterday's discarded jeans and jumper, the curtains billowing in the breeze from the crack of the open window, and my make-up stuff on the dresser. Beside it was my hairbrush. I grabbed it and I held it as tight as I would have held a knife, ready to defend myself.

I stepped out onto the landing.

A year ago I wouldn't have been so brave. A year ago I would have called the police and hidden under the duvet until the horrible people went away, but that was before I had Ben. No one was going to break into my home and threaten my baby. No one.

I stopped outside Ben's room and listened: all was quiet. I opened his door just a crack and peered inside to see him sleeping in his cot, the breath from his tiny nose gently ruffling the fur of Ducky, the little cuddly duck that lay beside him. I closed the door again, relieved to see he was okay.

Turning to the stairs, I realized I could see better than I should be able to in the middle of the night. The soft glow from a light downstairs filtered up to where I was standing. A light I thought I had turned off when I went to bed. I gripped my hairbrush tighter and descended, softly tiptoeing on the carpet of each stair.

The light came from the living room. I recognized it as the distinctive dim yellow glow of the energy-saving lightbulb. It filtered through the mottled glass in the door and out into the hallway. The pattern of the light fell across my bare feet as I stepped off the last stair onto the smoothness of the laminate floor. I stopped to listen: and heard nothing. Only my increased breath sounds and the thump of my heart. Maybe there was no one else in the house after all, maybe I had imagined it, maybe I'd simply forgotten to turn the lamp off.

Something moved beyond the glass door. Quick and white, almost ghostly. I stopped breathing, fearing even the faintest sound would give me away. I had to act quickly and I had to act decisively. Scare them away, don't give them time to realize they're being threatened by a woman in flannelette pajamas with a hairbrush. I took a long, silent, breath and prepared myself.

Two quick steps forward and I grabbed the door handle. I threw open the door which swung back against the radiator with a clang. I ran inside and raised the brush, ready to stab the white figure standing in front of my Christmas tree. "Get the hell out of my house!"

The white-shirted, tall man turned around. I stepped back, pressed myself against the cold radiator to clear his path to the door.

The man didn't run. He looked at me, startled. His face ashen, as white as his shirt.

And familiar.

"Alex?" I gasped, the brush wavering in my hand.

"Bloody hell, Sylvie!" he said.

"Alex!" My husband, standing there in his white work shirt and black work trousers when he was supposed to be half way across the Atlantic. "I thought you were a burglar!"

Shaking from the shock and the adrenaline, I brought my brush down on him anyway, bashing out my frustration on his arm.

I was so relieved not to be confronting a burglar, I didn't feel the hits touch him.

"You scared me half to death," said Alex.

"*I* scared *you*?" I failed to have any sympathy. "You're supposed to be at work."

"I thought I'd surprise you," he said.

"You did that all right."

Upstairs, Ben started crying. We both acknowledged it with a flick of our eyes towards the ceiling.

I wondered why Alex was skulking about downstairs in the middle of the night instead of coming up to bed. Perhaps he had secretly slipped another couple of presents under the tree, although it was difficult to tell with the higgledy-piggledy collection that was under there already. The room looked somehow different without the Christmas tree lights on, kind of hollow and lifeless. Even the tree itself looked almost dead standing in the corner under the glow from the lamp's energy-saving bulb.

"Why did you come home without telling me?" I said.

"I wanted to spend Christmas with you," said Alex.

Ben's wailing got louder and I felt it pull me away. "Tell me in a minute, I'll go see to Ben," I said. "You put the kettle on."

I picked up my red-faced little boy from his cot and held him close to my chest. So small, but with the rise and fall of his lungs and a heartbeat that was strong against my body.

"Did Mummy and Daddy wake you?" I said in that sing-songy voice that came naturally. "Silly Mummy and Daddy."

I swayed him, I bounced him, I hugged him. Friends tell me I will miss this closeness when he gets older; his softness and the feeling that hugging is enough to protect him. I suspect they're right. It's hard to imagine him, a few years down the line, grown into a sulky teenager.

Ben stopped wailing almost as soon as I picked him up, and turned to regular crying. After a few minutes it subsided to sniveling.

I got a tissue, wiped his tiny nose and brushed the tears from his cheeks. Checking his nappy was dry, I laid him back in the cot. He was drowsy and looked like he would go back to sleep easily. Poor boy. He must have been frightened to be woken up in the middle of the night like that.

Alex was in the kitchen waiting for me, sitting at our solid oak table that cost us a fortune. There were no mugs in front of him. There were no mugs out on the counter. I listened for the kettle, but it was silent. "Where's my tea?" I said.

"You want tea?" said Alex, looking around at the time display on the microwave. "At three in the morning?"

"I wouldn't usually," I said. "But *someone* woke me up."

I shook my head and took our expensive chrome-finished kettle over to our expensive filter tap to fill with water.

Everything in my kitchen cost more than we had intended to spend. Every time we sat down to decide on all those little accessories, we always went for the nicest things. It went with the bespoke oak cupboards, the mosaic of blue, green and cream tiles on the walls and the LED lighting scheme we installed. We had a lot of disposable income in the days before I got pregnant. I tried to honor the amount of money we ploughed into our new kitchen by keeping it neat and tidy, despite the baby stuff which seemed to have taken over every room of the house.

"So, what happened with work?" I asked, as I pulled a Scooby Doo mug and a British Airways mug from the cupboard and dropped in a couple of teabags.

"Mike came through in the end," said Alex.

"Mike, little Chinese guy?" That's how I distinguished him from Mike the big fat white guy who Alex also worked with (although, not to his face, obviously).

"Yeah, he said he could swap shifts after all."

The kettle reached boiling point and clicked off. I filled both mugs. "Bit last minute, wasn't it?"

"I think it was some family thing he didn't want to talk about," said Alex. "He was just suddenly at the airport, wanting to work."

To people outside the industry, it might seem strange that the airlines fly all over the Christmas holiday the same as on normal days. But they have to. Commercial airplanes spend so much of their lives in the air, that there simply isn't enough room to put all of them on the ground at the same time. Before Ben was born, we'd take advantage of this. Alex would offer to work Christmas Day, I'd fly out with him, we'd spend a couple of days in New York or Los Angeles or Alicante and come back again after an indulgent Christmas holiday.

This year, we'd hoped to spend Christmas together at home, but Alex's shift pattern put him on a flight leaving Heathrow for New York last thing on Christmas Eve and there was no getting out of it. Or so we thought.

"Wasn't your flight supposed to take off just before midnight?" I said, fishing out the teabags and adding in a swirl of milk for us both. "It doesn't take three hours to get back home from Heathrow."

"Does it matter?" said Alex.

I guess it didn't. I knew there was something he wasn't telling me, but when it's Christmas Eve and there are last minute presents to be bought, I can give him a bit of leeway.

"The important thing is," he said, "we get to spend Christmas together."

His words, as always, softened my heart. I came over to kiss him, but I had two mugs of boiling hot tea in my hand and he pulled back from my lips to avoid a painful spillage.

"What do we tell the family?" I sipped my tea. It was very hot, as I liked it.

"Nothing," he said, deadly serious.

"But my Mum is ..."

"No," he insisted. "As far as she knows — as far as any of them know — we're sticking to the original plan."

Our plan had been to delay Christmas. Alex had been due to get back from New York on the 27th, we'd have his parents over for Christmas dinner on the 28th, then go over to my family for a repeat performance on the 29th. We'd have the 30th to recover before Alex piloted a Boeing 777 back to New York again on New Year's Eve.

"We'll spend Ben's first Christmas here together," said Alex. "Just the three of us."

I smiled and nodded as I finally saw the light. As far as everyone else was concerned, Alex was in New York. Allowing us to have some quiet time together. Sounded heavenly.

"In fact," he continued, "we're spending it all ready."

I looked at the display on the microwave: 3.27am. After midnight. It was Christmas Day. "Happy Christmas, darling," I said.

I wanted to seal the moment with a hug and a kiss. But as soon as I had hopped off my stool, Alex yawned a wide lion-like yawn, stretching out his lanky guerrilla arms in the most unattractive way. He wished me happy Christmas while he did it, but the yawn turned it into, "Yappy Yismass."

"Maybe we should go to bed," I said. After all the excitement, I was feeling tired too. And I knew Ben would be up at six wanting to be fed, so we were best to get in a few hours while we could.

"Yes," said Alex, "or Father Christmas won't come."

*I*T'S MAGICAL COMING down in the morning to the peaceful, snug feeling of Christmas. It was the only day of the year that most people don't have to work. There were exceptions, like nurses and firefighters and the workaholic at the shop down the road, but there was just the feeling everywhere of it being special. Even the normally busy road outside had barely a car going by.

I turned on the fairy lights and the tree lit up with multi-colored twinkles that reflected in the glass of the baubles and strands of the tinsel, just as I remembered the trees from my childhood. We'd decided to get a real tree for Ben's first Christmas which gave the living room a faint smell of pine and musty damp soil. The tree was not entirely happy to have been moved from its natural environment and stuck inside next to a radiator, and it showed its displeasure by dropping needles. All the brightly-colored parcels under its branches had a layer of green sprinkles on top of them.

I had slept beautifully. It may have been for only two-and-a-half hours after I went back to bed, but Alex managed not to snore, steal the duvet, or overheat me with his body heat and I slept like a baby. As did my baby boy who woke up on schedule at six o'clock and took his milk without a problem.

I went into the kitchen where Alex's cold, undrunk tea and my empty mug still sat on the table. I cleared them away and was going to put them in the dishwasher when I realized it hadn't been emptied from the previous night's wash cycle. That was usually Alex's job when he was home, but for some reason he was spending ages in the bathroom doing whatever it is men spend ages in there doing, so I unloaded it myself. The kettle went on, I took out Ben's breakfast cereal — he's got to the stage where he loves solid food, or loves smearing it all over his cheeks and sticking it up his nose at least — and went upstairs to collect both my men.

"Breakfast!" I called on the landing. My big man didn't respond, so I went in to see my little man.

Ben had done a poo-poo, so I changed his nap-nap and cleaned his bot-bot. Then I promised myself to make an effort to have more conversations with adults using real words.

I dressed Ben in clean clothes and brought him downstairs to the kitchen. Ben was half way through his crunchy fruit cereal and starting to push the spoon away when the phone rang.

"Hello?" I answered.

"Happy Christmas, Sylvia." It was Mum.

"Happy Christmas to you too. And Dad!"

She asked how I was, how Ben was and how Alex was. In return, I asked how they both were and how they were enjoying Devon.

Alex walked in in the middle of it. I waved frantically and mouthed that it was Mum on the phone. He nodded an acknowledgment and crept in.

"What was that?" I said down the receiver.

"So terrible British Airways makes him work. On Christmas Day of all days, and you with a new baby and everything."

"I know," I said, injecting grave disappointment into my voice as I silently giggled at Alex. "Terrible."

"You shouldn't be alone on Christmas Day," Mum was going on. "We could still come up from Devon you know, keep you and little Benjie company."

"No, no!" I said rather too enthusiastically. "I wouldn't want to interrupt your little seaside getaway. I'll see you on the 29th."

"If you're sure..." Mum was saying, as Alex was making gestures for me to hang up.

Ben thought this was very funny and started laughing at his Dad, banging his open palms on his high chair table and shouting. "Da! Da! Da!" I was worried it sounded too much like Daddy and she might twig our little secret.

"Sorry, Mum, I gotta go — Ben's rubbing breakfast in his hair." A white lie, but I'd make it up to her on the 29th.

"Of course, Sylvia," she said. We exchanged 'love you's and I hung up.

I glared at my husband. "You are a very bad man," I said.

"We should unplug all the phones!" he said. "So we can really make sure we spend the day alone together, just the three of us."

"We can't—" I began to say, thinking of all the reasons why cutting ourselves off from the outside world was a bad idea. Then I thought of all the reasons it was a good idea. "Okay."

I ran round the house giggling like a toddler, unplugging all the landline phones from their sockets (we had three) and taking the battery out of my mobile. While I was at it, I unplugged both TVs from the wall. Not even the Queen's speech was going to interrupt our day.

I got back to the kitchen and found Ben digging his fingers into a bit of cereal which had been dropped on the tray and drawing pictures with it. He also seemed to have an itchy head and so, as I inadvertently predicted, he was rubbing breakfast into his hair at the same time as having a scratch.

"Alex, didn't you think to stop him?"

But Alex wasn't listening. "What are we having for dinner?" he said.

I had a traditional Christmas dinner all ready to go for when his parents came to visit. "There's a turkey in the …" I trailed off. "Damn."

I threw open the door to the freezer. I'd had a hell of a time the previous week, pulling out all the shelves and making sure we ate up all the frozen meals I had in there to make way for the turkey. I squatted on my haunches, face to drumstick with the leg of the dead frozen bird. With hands either side of it, I grabbed hold of the cold carcass and pulled.

It had been a job and a half to get the blinking thing in there in the first place and it didn't seem to want to come out three days early.

"Give us a hand," I called over to Alex. I turned round, but he was keeping Ben occupied playing peak-a-boo by bobbing up and down beside his highchair. Ben thought it was hilarious. It didn't, however, help me retrieve the turkey.

I took a deep breath, gathered up my strength and gave it one last yank. The turkey broke free of its icebox and I staggered backwards, just about managing not to go arse-over-tit on the floor.

I dumped the turkey on the table. It landed with a thud which only just about managed not to crack the wooden surface. I kicked the freezer door shut behind me and stood looking at the frosty vapor steaming off the bird.

Alex looked too. "So that's dinner," he said.

"Yep," I said.

"Looks a bit cold."

"Yep."

"You could blast your hairdryer at it," he suggested.

I glanced at him sideways.

"Or defrost it in the oven," he said.

"I can't cook a turkey from frozen," I said. "We'll all get salmonella."

Alex thought about it for a moment. His expression suggested a stream of ridiculous ideas going through his head. "How about we open a tin of baked beans?"

I don't think I stopped laughing from that moment on. Alex is so funny sometimes. Silly, quite often, but in a funny way. We decamped to the living room, after another quick nappy change, and sat watching the fairy lights cycle from red to orange to yellow to green to blue on the Christmas tree.

Father Christmas, it seemed, had visited while we were asleep because there seemed to be even more multi-colored parcels at the base of the tree than I remembered.

"Presents!" said Alex with an excited child-like voice. He pronounced it 'pwessents' like a little boy who hasn't yet learned to speak properly.

I gave him another one of my sideways looks. "How old are you?"

"Pwessents! Pwessents! Pwessents!" he said, bouncing up and down on the sofa.

Ben, sitting on my lap, started bouncing up and down too. "Wessy!" he managed.

I laughed. "Okay, okay" I knew when it was pointless to resist men ganging up on me. "You're so keen, Alex, do you want to pick the first present?"

"Oh no, ladies first," he said.

So, that was his strategy, eh? Get me to do all the work. I got off the sofa, bringing Ben with me. He wasn't interested in the presents, he was too young to know there were toys inside the pretty paper, he was mesmerized by the ever-shifting colors of the twinkling lights and how they made all the shiny bits sparkle. I sat him near the tree, but not close enough for him to grab hold of the tinsel and pull the whole thing crashing down on top of him.

"Ben, which present shall we open first?" I said, trying to interest him in the parcels. "This one?" I pointed to one wrapped in blue paper with images of reindeer. "This one?" A snowy white square one with glitter. I took a sneaky peek at the tag, which read 'to Sylvia, with all my love, Alex'. "Oh no, that's for Mummy." I didn't want to selfishly pick my own present to unwrap first, so I went for a red parcel, knowing for a fact exactly what it was because I was the one who wrapped it. "What about this one? This one's for Ben!"

I brought the parcel over to him. It was sort of lumpy rugby ball shaped, but only about as big as my little boy's head. He wasn't sure what to make of it, he was still mesmerized by the lights. So I put it in his lap and took both his wrists, like I did when I showed him how to clap, but placed his hands on the parcel. Which he dropped.

Alex laughed. "You'll have to show him, Sylvie."

I found the edge of the paper and tore it a little bit. The sound caught Ben's attention. "What's this?" I said. I tore a bit more. He liked the sound and was happy to let me take his hand and use it to tear more, revealing a patch of white fur. Together, we kept tearing, until all the paper was gone to reveal a cuddly snowman, complete with carrot nose, top hat and red woolly scarf. "Ooh, look Ben! A snowman. Can you say 'snowman'?"

"No-no!" said Ben.

Alex laughed. "Is he refusing or is that 'snowman' in Ben-speak?"

"No-no," Ben insisted. He had the poor snowman by his carrot nose and was swinging it about, without a care for its welfare.

"More presents!" demanded Alex.

The way we do Christmas presents — the way we always did it in my family — is we take them from under the tree one at a time. The rule is, the person who last opened a present gets to pick the next one from under the tree, as long as it isn't a present for themselves. That way, everyone can enjoy the opening of every single present, even if it is only a brand new pair of gardening gloves for granddad.

According to the rule, it was Ben's turn to pick a present. I tried to get him to point at the one we should open next, but he didn't seem to understand the game, and so I pretended he'd chosen one wrapped in gold-color foil. "This one's for Daddy," I said, reading the tag.

I held it out toward Alex, but he didn't take it. He looked to Ben. "Do you want to help Daddy open it?"

I encouraged Ben to crawl with me over to Alex's feet and we unwrapped the present together while Alex remained on the sofa like King of the Living Room. It turned out to be a spare phone charger to take on his travels.

We carried on like that for ages. Alex, lording it up on the sofa, giving instructions while me and Ben crawled backwards and forwards on the carpet which became increasingly covered in torn wrapping paper.

By the end, I was exhausted and lay down on the floor, my head near the small pile of things people had bought for me. Next to that was a much larger pile of Ben's presents. People love to give things to a new baby, although where we would put all his new toys, I really didn't know.

"Look at Ben," said Alex, chuckling.

I turned my head. Ben was sitting not two feet from his collection of new gifts, picking up discarded pieces of wrapping paper, tearing them in half and giggling.

"You spend all that money on toys," said Alex, "and all he wants to play with is the wrapping paper."

"Yeah," I said.

"I had a wonderful day," said Alex.

"But it's only lunchtime," I said, looking over at where the time is usually displayed on the television set, except it wasn't because it was dark from where I'd unplugged it. It certainly felt like lunchtime, I was getting hungry.

"I'm glad I spent Christmas Day with you," he said, sounding suddenly serious.

The doorbell rang. "Who the hell's that?" I said. That was the one thing I hadn't been able to unplug. I decided to lay there and ignore it.

"You should get that," said Alex.

"It's probably only carol singers or something."

"It's Mike," he said, sounding so certain, I sat up.

"Big fat Mike?" That made no sense, he lived the other side of London and was likely far too busy juggling his two sets of children from two marriages.

"The other Mike."

The doorbell rang again. Twice. Insistent.

I pulled myself to my feet, deciding the sooner I answered the door, the sooner I could get rid of whoever it was. Glancing behind at Alex's strangely intense expression and nearly slipping over on a bit of shiny wrapping paper, I went out into the hallway and to the front door.

Opening it, I was surprised to find it really was the other Mike. Only about as tall as me — short for a guy — in overcoat, shirt and tie, his dark black hair unkempt from the wind and a face so pale he looked ill.

"Mike!" I said. "What are you doing here? It thought you were in New York."

"I'm sorry," he said. "I tried to call, but I couldn't get through."

"Yeah, we unplugged all the phones."

He went even paler. "Then, you haven't heard?"

"Heard what?"

"The news."

"News? We unplugged the TV too."

He swallowed. This was hard for him. "Flight BA117."

I recognized it as the flight Alex was supposed to have been on. "Didn't it take off? Engine trouble?" Cabin crew can only hang around for so long waiting for a flight to take off before their shifts expire and fresh staff have to be brought in. In that scenario, without a car and with the lack of public transport on Christmas Day, it would be difficult for Mike to get all the way over to his parents' place. He probably just wanted a bit of company. "Why don't you come in?"

He accepted my invitation and followed me into the living room.

"Alex, Mike is …" But my husband wasn't there. It was just Ben, reaching over for another piece of wrapping paper to tear in half. "Oh, he was here a minute ago."

"It's what I'm trying to tell you, Sylvia," said Mike. "Flight BA117. It's been lost."

"Lost?" I turned to him. Everyone in the air industry knew what 'lost' meant. It meant air traffic control had lost contact. That could be because of system failure, a hijacking or even a crash. In any event, it was almost always bad.

"I'm sorry, Sylvia. Alex told me your parents were away and you'd be here on your own with Ben, I thought it would help if you had someone with you."

"But Alex is here," I said. I looked round. He wasn't in the living room, but I knew he was in the house.

"No, that's what I'm saying, Sylvia. Alex was on flight BA117 when it was lost."

I shook my head. "No. He swapped with you at the last minute. You went on the flight to New York instead and he was …"

"We didn't swap, Sylvia. He asked me to, but I said I couldn't." He looked down at Ben playing happily on the floor. "I'm so sorry."

Mike looked like he was about to cry. I touched his arm. For comfort, at first, but then I realized how solid his arm felt in my hand and how the sensation of the scratchy softness of the wool blend of his overcoat felt against my palm.

I stared at the place on the sofa where Alex had sat. Where he had declined to open any of the presents, insisting instead that I be the one to crawl around the floor with Ben and tear off the wrapping paper.

I began to understand what he was saying. But I didn't want to believe it. "No."

I rushed into the kitchen. No Alex.

On the worktop was last night's mug of tea that he didn't drink, the kettle he hadn't put on and, on the table gently defrosting, the turkey he didn't help get out of the freezer.

I remembered the kiss that I had wanted last night and the way he pulled back from me so our lips never touched.

He hadn't touched anything since last night, since he appeared out of nowhere in our living room.

"Alex!" I screamed. I ran from the kitchen, up the stairs, shouting — *screaming* — all the way. "Alex! Aleeeeeexx!"

Not in the bathroom, not in Ben's room.

I stopped at the entrance to our bedroom. He had to be in there. He just *had* to.

But I was afraid. In case I walked in and there was no one.

"Alex?" I called gently. I stepped inside.

There was our unmade bed, the pillow depressed on my side and the duvet ruffled where I had pulled it over me. But, on his side, all the bedclothes were smooth.

I thought I heard his voice, carried on the breeze from the crack of the open window. "I'm glad I spent Christmas Day with you."

"Alex?" I looked up. Through teary eyes, I thought I saw him at the window, standing partly hidden by the curtains.

I rushed over. "Alex!" I grabbed an armful of material, but his body melted away in my arms. I pulled the curtains, bashed them, thrashed them, searching for Alex in their folds of material. I grabbed and I yanked until I pulled the rail off the wall and it collapsed on top of me, covering me in a shroud of curtain.

"Alex! Alex! Alex!"

Mike was suddenly there. "I'm so sorry, Sylvia."

I looked up at him, his face blurry through my tears. "He got on the flight to New York?"

"Yes," said Mike. "I should have swapped with him. If he could, I think he would have done anything to spend Christmas Day with you."

I grabbed Mike's scratchy overcoat, feeling the all too solid body of the man who didn't get on the flight to New York. "I think he did," I sobbed into his chest. "I think, in some way, Alex did."

~

ABOUT THE AUTHOR

British author Jane Killick lives the single life in Buckinghamshire, England. She trained as a radio journalist and still works for the BBC. Her novels, Fairy Nuff *and* If Wishes Were Husbands, *find the fun in women's search for the right man and add a magical twist.*

Learn more about Jane and her work at:

janekillick.com

Career Conundrum
Christmas

Jamie Brazil

*T*ONIGHT WAS THE night. The defining moment of my life. Staring into the china cabinet, I selected my most precious pieces. My mother's Spode plates and Georg Jensen silverware, an antique Orafors decanter for the wine, and Aunt Helen's Baccarat water glasses. The smell of the Christmas tree and roast turkey filled the house with family magic.

One by one, I held the water glasses up to the light and examined them for water spots or stray specks of dust. I wanted everything to be perfect. After tonight, everything would change. I had a job offer across the country.

If I accepted, I'd be the senior appraiser at an internationally renowned auction house in Los Angeles. Heading up the department for 20th century fine and decorative art, it was a job I'd wanted since childhood when my father let me hold up his bidder's paddle. We vied for everything from Tiffany letter openers to Lalique vases and Roycroft trestle tables to fill his store. Dad and the store were both long gone, but the seeds had been sown. Antiques were in my blood. I'd made a career of them.

But a job wasn't everything, was it? I wanted a husband and children, too. Yet I couldn't wait forever. The clock was ticking. After five years and no marriage proposal, this was it, my boyfriend Ben or my career. I had to make a choice.

Thumps sounded at the back of the house, followed by the squeak of the hinges and a gust of Connecticut winter wind. I set the glasses down on the dining room table and hurried to the kitchen. Bursting through the backdoor with her four rowdy kids, my three nephews and, thankfully, a niece, my sister Rebecca held out my grandmother's old moo cow creamer. "I brought this for the party. For you, Sara. It wouldn't last five seconds at our house."

As her kids peeled off coats and snow boots, Rebecca placed the moo cow creamer in my hand. It felt heavier than I remembered.

And cold. I ran my hands over its smooth surface, nostalgic. I was touched by the gesture, but before I could thank Rebecca, she'd already turned her attention on her troops, calling for order as they filed into my kitchen.

Quickly moving to the refrigerator, I filled the cow with cream. Granted, the moo cow creamer wasn't of the same quality as the other table decorations, but it was very welcome. Special. As a child, every holiday meant a visit with the moo cow creamer. It was the only thing of service at my grandmother's family meals with personality. It spoke to me.

Its gentle brown eyes were calming, and Grandma used to add that extra dollop of cream to my hot cocoa as we tried to wait up for Santa. Not that I ever made it. Only a year ago my grandmother passed away. This was the first time for me to host Christmas dinner. And now the moo cow creamer was mine.

What could go wrong?

Nothing.

The rest of the guests arrived. Dinner was flawless, with me at one end of the table, Ben at the other, and sixteen friends and relatives between. Aunts, uncles, siblings, nephews, and my one cherished niece, Caroline, at my right hand. At seven, she was the youngest of Rebecca's brood. Quiet, thoughtful and inquisitive, she liked to ask me questions about every sparkling treasure in my china cabinets and jewelry boxes. I don't know why she looked up to me, but she always did.

"Did you call L.A. and tell them you're not coming?" Ben called from the far end of the table. "Because they're sure not going to give you a job cooking turkey there."

I frowned. My turkey wasn't that bad. A little dry, but I'd read that sometimes happens with a free-range twenty-eight pound bird. Why did he always point out the negative? My dressing was moist. My potatoes fluffy. No lumps in the gravy. Even my yams were yummy. "I haven't decided," I called back.

Caroline sipped her eggnog, a treat for the holiday, and made a face. "Eww."

"I can make that better." I reached for the moo cow creamer and poured a dollop of cream into her glass. She stirred it in, tasted it again, and smiled.

The moo cow creamer always saved the day.

Still holding its looped ceramic tail, I turned the cow to face me. The eyes were the same eyes I'd known all my life. Only now, they seemed even more alive and I could have sworn its lips moved as I heard a faint voice in my head that said, "Moo, moo, move."

I shook it off. It had been a long day in a hot kitchen. Light-headed hallucination happens now and then.

After pumpkin pie and ice cream, we cleared the table then settled into the living room. The children tore the wrapping off toys and electronics and Ben volunteered for the white elephant finale. He handed out one gift to each adult. Socks, gloves, heated windshield scrapers. Mine was the last box and after I opened it, I stared. It was a ring. I looked up to Ben. Was this what I thought it was?

In front of all my relatives he stood proudly and crowed, "I'm going to give you a chance to do something big with your life, Sara. If you promise not to cremate anymore turkeys, I'll marry you."

It wasn't the proposal of my dreams, but it was a proposal. My first.

"What are you going to do, Auntie?" My niece leaned into me, eyes wide as she marveled at the diamond in the box. What was I going to do? Ben had asked me to marry him. He'd also insulted my turkey. In front of everyone I cared about. I knew he loved me, but did he respect me?

"Auntie?" Caroline asked again.

"I'm going to get some hot cocoa for everyone." I stood and raced to the kitchen, my heart thumping double time. Rebecca followed on my heels.

"Are you nuts?" she whispered. "You aren't going to find another decent guy like Ben again."

"It's just that I've waited for so long for him to ask, and now…" I turned and dug through the cupboards for the hot chocolate pan Grandma always used.

"Now what?"

I stood in front of the stove, blinking back tears. "Now I don't know."

I didn't know. Confusion wasn't like me. In my job I was confident, I almost always had the answer to everything, and even when I got stumped, I knew the solution was only a matter of research and history. I had history with Ben, too. But when I thought about it, it was a rocky history. Nothing I did was ever good enough. He hated my career. And antiques. All the things I loved meant nothing to him. I was certain he'd be a good father and provide for the family, but was he good for me?

"Don't screw this up. Ben's a catch." Rebecca crossed her arms. "He's got job security and a 401K."

"What about me? I've got a 401K, too." I earned twice as much as Ben at my job in Manhattan. Sure the hours were long, and my daily commute from Fairfield almost killed me, yet I couldn't imagine doing anything other than appraising and cataloging treasured collections.

Just because you sell rich people's stuff in a hoity-toity auction house doesn't make you smart."

"Dad was proud of me." I stirred the cocoa into the milk as it steamed.

"Dad died alone and broke," she shot back.

I bit my lip, burying the hurt. As much as I loved my sister, when it came to our father we never did see eye to eye. He passed his passion for history and antiques on to me, and I hoped someday I might pass that love along to my own children. In the meantime, Caroline reminded me of myself more and more. If for some reason motherhood didn't happen for me I'd see to it my niece inherited the Georg Jensen silverware.

"He died doing what he loved," I replied quietly.

"This is a no-brainer. Marry Ben. You'd have nothing in L.A. except a barren apartment, an empty bed, and a sixty-hour-a-week job."

I opened my mouth to object, but stopped. She was right. The company condo in L.A., only a block away from their landmark headquarters, guaranteed long days. My life would be work, work, work. Work I loved. But I loved family, too. A familiar numbness washed through me as defeat slumped my shoulders. "I don't want to argue with you, Becky. It's Christmas."

"Then get your dry-turkey-cooking butt back in there and say yes."

"It's free-range! It was supposed to be a little dry." Why did everyone hate my turkey?

Rebecca stomped back to the living room where I heard her consoling Ben and making excuses for me. Taking the cocoa off the stove, I reached for the moo cow creamer. Did I want to be with Ben all my life? I stared in the cow's ceramic eyes. What did I want?

The voice in my brain was clear this time. "Moo, moo, more!"

I couldn't argue with a moo cow creamer. Marrying Ben meant a lifetime of putting his needs first while burying my own wants and desires. I deserved to be appreciated. To be cherished. "Thank you," I said softly to the moo cow creamer.

"What are you doing?" Caroline appeared beside me, tugging at my elbow. "Are you getting married?"

I knelt down. "I like Ben a lot, but I'm going to Los Angeles. Sometimes a girl has to do what a girl has to do."

"You'll be so far away." Her face crumpled. "I'll miss you."

"I'll miss you, too." I placed the moo cow creamer in her hands and held them tight. "But we'll always be connected wherever we are. Like your great grandma, and me, we will always find a way to be there for each other. Listen to the moo cow creamer. It's yours now."

Caroline stared at the moo cow creamer with curiosity, then held it to her ear. "I think I hear something."

"What's it saying?"

"She said don't worry. Someday you're going to be a great moo, moo, mom." With that, Caroline ran back to the living room.

Stunned, I sat at the kitchen table. I'd wanted a sign, a direction, and it had been delivered. I couldn't imagine a better Christmas present.

I picked up the phone. Before I talked to Ben, I had a message to leave for the auction house.

YES.

Confidence swept through me as I dialed. Even though I'd be alone in L.A. on New Year's Eve, no family or friends, just a party of one, I was certain this was the right decision. This future was my choosing. I'd continue to follow in my dad's footsteps, doing what I loved most. As the phone rang on the other end of the line, I knew one thing for certain, to the core of my being: never look a gift moo-cow-creamer in the mouth.

~

ABOUT THE AUTHOR

Jamie Brazil is a lifelong morning person who is happiest when the sun is rising. When she isn't writing romance and adventure, she works in television and sales. Musicals, character-driven fiction, and morning dew on her Bloodhound's whiskers are three of her favorite things.

You can learn more about Jamie at her website:

jamiebrazil.com

The Hogmanay Stranger
Maggie Jaimeson

ℛACHEL PACED IN the conference room beneath Michele and David's condo in the Pearl District. Sunshine played peek-a-boo with the clouds over the Willamette River as yesterday's storm blew eastward. When David first took over booking all of Sweetwater Canyon's gigs each year, he used his office at home. But soon they were doing so well that he hired a part-time assistant and took over an office downstairs.

With only two months until the holidays, she had a special funding request and David Blackstone was the man with the purse strings. Because of his management and marketing capabilities, Sweetwater Canyon was finally making a living with their music. No more breakdowns on the road. No more wondering if they would return home even more broke than when they left. No one was a millionaire, or even a hundred thousandaire — except David with his consulting business — but no one was starving either. Each woman had sufficient income to survive on her own if needed.

Rachel's da had sent her an invitation to come home to Scotland for Hogmanay. She hadn't been home in eight years and she was dying to go. Letters and Google Hangouts had kept them in touch, but nothing like seeing each other in person. Her da had invited the entire band and their families to his home and B&B in Dunoon. Hogmanay was a traditional time to welcome friends and strangers to your home, and to enter into the new year together with a clean break from the past — looking forward, not back.

Rachel wanted to share Hogmanay with both her families — her da in her family home and with the family she'd come to know in America since she'd joined Sweetwater Canyon five years ago. If she didn't extend the invitation and work out the financing now, they would all make other plans. The logistics could be difficult, but that wasn't her prime worry. It was the cost to fly all five women and their families to Scotland during one of the busiest travel times of the year that had her prepared to beg for assistance.

David sauntered into the conference room and smiled. "So, what was so important you had to call me away from Michele and little Susie? I can't believe it was only a few months ago she was barely walking on her own. Now I can hardly keep up with all the places she finds to climb and get into trouble."

He turned and reached into the small refrigerator for a pitcher of water. "Can I offer you any?" he said, holding a glass next to the raised pitcher.

"Sure." Rachel ran nervous fingers through her hair.

He looked at her with narrowed eyes. "Is there a problem? Where's Noel?"

"Noel's home with Claire. No problem ... exactly." Rachel shifted from one foot to the other. "I have more of a question. I need an advance or a loan or something."

"Have a seat." David placed the glass in front of her on the conference table and sat in a chair facing her.

She flopped into the chair and then sat erect, her fingers drumming on the table. She hated asking for favors but this meant the world to her. Somewhere deep inside she knew it was important to spend Hogmanay with her da. She didn't know why this year was more important than any other, but it was. This was the first time he'd actually extended the invitation. He hadn't made it to her wedding, hadn't even met Noel yet. Though she and her da loved each other, since her maw's death they'd been a bit closed ... not as forthcoming in their conversations. Rachel saw this opportunity as the first real chance they had to define a new life without her maw.

She had left so soon after her mother's death, and then been consumed with her new husband, moving to America, his infidelities and the divorce a few years later, that she'd never had the time — taken the time — to reconnect with her da. It had been eight years since she'd been able to hug him. Now with Noel and Claire and a real family of her own it seemed even more important.

She wanted — no, needed — this time for the two of them to discover how they could both move forward and still be a family together and part of the extended family she now shared. She very much wanted Claire to know her Scottish roots and especially her grandfather. She also wanted her da to be a regular part of their family — more than a person seen on a computer screen once a month.

David took a long, slow draught from his own glass of water. "Are you and Noel having financial problems?" He asked, his voice soft.

"Oh, no. No, no, no. It's nothing like that." Rachel clasped her hands together to stop her fingers from tapping. "Da wants us to spend Hogmanay with him."

"That's great." David tilted his head and quirked an eyebrow. "Isn't it?"

"Oh yes. Absolutely. Claire is thrilled and can't stop talking about it, and Noel has never been to Scotland and I'm excited to share it with both of them, but …"

"But?"

Rachel took a deep breath. She'd talked about this with Noel, but she still hated asking for an advance. It's just that she wanted to make it a present for everyone, and they couldn't do that easily on his teacher's salary and her usual take for the band gigs.

"Rachel?"

"The deal is I'd like to take everyone with me. Our family home is also a B&B and Da will put everyone up and have meals and all that, but I wanted to pay for the airfare so no one would feel they couldn't come because they couldn't afford it."

David nodded slowly. "I see."

Rachel rushed on. "I don't want to sound like I always hit you up because you're … well … you know … rich."

David nodded. "We are very comfortable."

"I know you and Michele can afford it for sure, but Theresa is trying to pay for Kat's college and Sarah and Tom are still deciding what to do about the ranch and have lots of bills for rebuilding and it didn't seem fair that I would pay for some and not others, so I figured I'd just pay for everybody but I can't exactly afford it and so I'm asking for an advance or a loan or whatever you think is right."

David chuckled. "You're sounding like Kat with that sentence going on and on."

Rachel let out the breath she was holding. "I just don't like asking." She purposely paused and took another breath. "But all of you are my family too. You've been my only family until I met Noel and I just can't imagine spending New Year's without all of you. And it's the first time I'll be home since Maw passed, and I'm not sure how I'm going to take it or how da will be about it. They were engaged on Hogmanay you know." She swallowed against the lump in her throat and the memories of her mother's illness and having to leave so soon after her death.

"It's not a problem." David covered her hand with his. "Let me pay for everyone as my Christmas present to the band."

Rachel stood. "No. That's not what I meant. This is why I didn't want to ask. I knew you would do the rush in and save us thing just like you did when Annabelle broke down."

"I'm not saving anyone and, if I remember correctly, it was that motor home breakdown that provided me with the best opportunity ever — marketing for the band and getting Michele back in my life. I've been thinking what to do about gifts. It's been such a wonderful year and this is the perfect way to celebrate it — all of us, together, in Scotland. I can probably even book a couple of gigs to help pay for it all."

Rachel shook her head. "Admit it, this is much more than you would normally spend. We are talking thousands of dollars to fly everyone there. No, I want an advance or a loan. My idea. My treat."

"What if I can get a couple gigs?"

"I don't want us worrying about playing during the holidays. I just want us to enjoy each other. We can sing and play if we want, but nothing formal, nothing that we absolutely have to do." She paused and stood still, looking out the window. This part of Oregon even reminded her of Scotland. She had to share it with everyone. She turned back to David. "Please, lets do this my way for once."

David shook his head in resignation. "Why are all the Sweetwater Canyon women so stubborn?"

"We have to be because we seem to fall in love with stubborn men." Rachel smiled. "Thanks for the offer though. Now, how are we going to arrange this?"

David reached for his computer bag and pulled out his laptop. "Let's see what we can do." He typed something on the keyboard and then nodded. "Here's the deal. Michele and I will pay our own way."

"No. I want to be fair. I pay for everyone."

"If you want my help, Michele and I pay our own way. I'm not charging you for a loan to pay for something I can do on my own. Also, with Susie, we will be wanting to go first class or business class to have more space and some sleeping room."

Rachel let out an audible sigh. "Okay. I can accept that."

David nodded. "I will make all the arrangements for everyone so we can leave at the same time and arrive at the same time. If we get the tickets together we can get a group rate. Also, I can use my miles to get upgrades for everyone to at least business class."

Rachel thought about arguing on the miles but she knew she would lose that one too. Besides he probably had enough miles to last him for years. She had to admit that traveling in business class would be a lot more comfortable than coach.

"Thank you," she finally said. "So, you'll let me know the damages and the terms of the loan?"

"I will. I'm estimating the charges will be somewhere between three and five thousand dollars. That's about two months pay for you on our current schedule. Shall we say three years at no interest?"

"No. That's not fair," Rachel said. "The bank would charge me a lot more than that."

"I'm not a bank," David said. "I'm family. You just said so yourself."

"But even family deserves interest on a loan. Business is business. How much would you be making on that money if you didn't give it to me?"

"That's not the point."

"How much?" she asked again.

"Two percent."

"Liar. You would have it in some great stock that is making gagillions."

He chuckled. "You must think very highly of my investments. There is no stock that makes gagillions."

"Okay, an exaggeration. But I know two percent is not realistic."

"This particular money is in a money market account. That keeps it liquid. Money market interest right now is less than one percent. So, by charging you two percent I'm gouging you. Do you feel better now?"

Rachel narrowed her eyes and studied him. She had no idea what money market rates were right now. "Deal." She finally held out her hand. "Shake on it."

David shook her hand. "You'll also sign a promissory note. You wanted this to be business."

"Thanks, David." She looked straight at him. "Really. Thanks. This means a lot to me."

ℛACHEL STARED OUT the window of the limousine hired to bring them all from Glasgow airport. She didn't know how he managed it, but as usual he had everything arranged to make the trip as easy as possible. She watched for her home as the hired car lumbered up the steep winding drive to the top of the hill. Positioned high amid a woodland garden, the home — now inn — enjoyed sensational views over the Firth of Clyde.

Claire dozed curled on Noel's lap. Both Kat and Theresa had drifted between reading a book and napping during the hour ride. Michele held a sleeping Susie while snuggled into David's arm. The two-year-old had been so good on the long flight that Rachel had almost forgotten they had such a young child with them. Sarah and Tom snuggled together in the last seat at the back. Still newlyweds, it seemed they couldn't stand to not be touching for even a second.

Noel squeezed Rachel's hand. "You okay?" He whispered.

She nodded. "A little anxious."

"It will be great." He drew her closer into his side. "With all your friends here, there is nothing that can happen that we can't handle together."

She gasped as the view of the house appeared in the window. The main house still fronted the firth. Its three-story Victorian structure loomed tall on the steep hill. The bright white stucco, trimmed in black, presented a happy welcome. It was much better than the slate blue and gray she recalled when she'd left Dunoon with her ex-husband and worried that her father had to face his grief alone.

The limousine came to a stop and Rachel scooted toward the door to be the first out. Her father appeared at the top of the drive and her breath caught. He looked good. Healthy. Smiling. Not much different except more gray in his hair. She ran to him, tears streaming down her face.

He wrapped her in his big strong arms. "I missed you Rachel. I'm so happy you could come and bring your friends."

She buried her head in his chest, inhaling deeply the smell of pine boughs and firewood that she always remembered for this time of year. Why had she taken so long to return home?

After a minute, her father released her. "Let's meet your husband and daughter. Shall we?"

She turned and Noel and Claire were right in front of her, waiting quietly. Noel held out his hand. "Good to meet you sir."

Her father shook Noel's hand heartily. "Gavin. Please call me

Gavin. Sir makes me feel old."

"Gavin then." Noel smiled and knelt on the ground to be at the same height as a sleepy Claire. "Claire, this is your granda. "

Claire looked up shyly. "You talk funny, like mommy."

Gavin laughed. "Aye. I do, lass. And you talk like an American."

"I am American," Claire said.

"That you are. Let's get everyone settled shall we?"

Rachel introduced all of her friends and their family.

"Leave the luggage for now," Gavin spoke to the group. "We'll get it sorted shortly after all the rooms are assigned. We have the entire inn to ourselves for Hogmanay."

Rachel helped direct each family to their room. Claire went with Noel to unpack in a room with a queen bed and a small side room with a twin for Claire. Michele and David were in a room next door with a child's bed for Susie. Sarah and Tom were one level up, and across the hall were Theresa and Kat, each with a double bed.

All the rooms were taken except the one small one in the back corner, facing the hill. It was originally designed as a housekeeper's quarters. To her knowledge, Rachel's father had rarely rented it except in emergencies when a traveler was stuck late at night with nowhere to go. Rachel thought it could serve as a quiet place to get away from everyone else if needed.

When all were settled in rooms they reconvened in the living room.

Claire ran to the Christmas tree festooned with packages. "Mommy, does Santa come after Christmas to Scotland? Nobody opened their presents here."

"For many years celebrating Christmas was banned here," Gavin said. "That means we were not allowed to celebrate it publicly."

Claire wrinkled her nose. "You mean Santa wasn't allowed to come?"

"Santa still came, but in secret," Rachel answered. "When I was a little girl, Santa came on New Year's Eve. We call that Hogmanay."

Claire laughed. "That's funny. Hug muh nay? What does that mean?"

"It means many things," Gavin said. "In olden times, the solstice was celebrated by the Celts and the Vikings and many other cultures. They called it *oge maiden*, meaning new morning. It is when the shortest day of the year is past and from that point forward the days get longer. The solstice usually happens just before Christmas, around December 21st. However, because of disagreements between the Church of Scotland and the Catholic Church long ago, the public celebration of Christmas was banned. So, instead we celebrated on New Year's Eve — when we say goodbye to the old year and welcome the new year. *Oge maiden* over hundreds of years became Hogmanay."

"It is also called hoog min dag or the great love day." Rachel added and winked at Noel. "You will see," Rachel looked around the circle of friends and family. "We'll be participating in many of the traditions over the next few days."

Gavin looked at the clock above the fireplace. "It is time for dinner and then I bet you are all tired from travel and want to get to bed early. Best to get your sleep now. Tomorrow is the last day of the year and all the celebrations will keep us awake through the night and into New Years'.

*A*FTER ALL WERE sated with food and off to their rooms to sleep, Rachel curled up in one corner of the settee in front of the fire, her hand draped along the armrest. Her father occupied his usual large leather chair to her right, a glass of Talisker in his hand. The day had gone well. Claire and her granda had hit it off, and Noel was quietly comfortable with him. Her da seemed relaxed, happy.

He took a swig of his whisky. "Your family seems to fit you well," he said.

Rachel smiled. "Yes. Noel and Claire are more than I could have ever wished for. I didn't know how much I needed them until they came into my life."

They both looked to the fire in companionable silence.

"I'm sorry I ..." they both said at once.

"You go," they both said at once again.

Her father reached over and placed a hand on her arm. "Please, you first."

Rachel inhaled a deep breath and let it out slowly, concentrating on not letting go the tears filling her eyes. "I'm sorry I didn't write more, left so early, couldn't talk about Mum. I feel like I let you down."

Her da immediately moved to the settee and drew her into his chest. "It is I who let you down, Rachel. I knew Kavan was not the man for you, but I was so lost in my grief I had no energy to fight about it. Then you were gone to America and it was as if I lost my daughter too."

No longer able to hold back, Rachel wept into her father's shirt. She cried for all they had missed together. "You could never lose me, Da. Never."

When she'd stopped crying, he gently pushed her away from him and ran a thumb beneath her eyes to dry the last vestiges of tears. "Tomorrow is Hogmanay. We will purify the house together and put our grief in the past. I've been waiting to do this and now that you and your family are here, it is right to move forward."

Rachel nodded. "Are you done grievin', Da?"

"One is never done," he said. "But it does not hurt as much as it once did. And it is no longer every day that I long for her. I will always have the memories of your mother as a vibrant, loving woman. Eight years is a long time to grieve. It is time to move forward." He paused and let out a sigh. "How 'bout you lass, are you done grievin'?"

"The same as you ... I think. Though with leaving home and all that has happened, I fear I have perhaps moved on faster. I fear ... perhaps ... I forgot things too soon."

He patted her hand. "No, not too soon. You are young. It is right that life is alive for you. There is no need to dwell on the past."

"Do you think …" Rachel paused. She couldn't ask that question. It wasn't her place.

"I know what you ask, lass. I have thought of it often myself. I believe Evelyn would want me to love again. But I admit I haven't been looking. There are a couple women in the village who have set their caps for me, but I canna think of them that way. It will happen when it's right. How would you feel about it, Rachel? Would it hurt you if I met someone?"

Rachel looked into the fire. Her father deserved to find love again. She'd had her second chance already and he deserved the same. "I want you to be happy," she finally said. "It will be strange, I suspect. But I know you would only choose the finest woman and how could I not love her too?"

"Aye," he said and clasped her hand with a smile. "I will let ye know when I find her."

$\mathcal{K}$AT TIPTOED DOWN the stairs in the early morning. Her sleep cycle was completely bonkers now. The eight-hour difference was driving her batty. They were eating dinner last night at lunchtime and going to bed at dinnertime. Now it was five in the morning, but back home it was prime time for date night. Ugh. There was no way she could sleep.

She quickly wrote a note to her mom, so she wouldn't think she'd been kidnapped in the middle of the night or something. She placed it on the fireplace mantle where it would be easy to see. She shrugged on her raincoat and galoshes near the front door, tucked a paperback novel under the coat, and carefully let herself out. A strong wind added more chill to the already moist air. She'd been hoping for snow, like they had on Mt. Hood back home. Evidently the weather in Dunoon was very similar to the weather in Portland. Rainy. Who would've known?

Pulling the hood tighter around her face, Kat thumbed the flashlight app on her phone to help see the gravel path in the dark. If there was a moon tonight, the clouds obscured it. She could see a few lights on the firth below, but not many with the misty fog hanging over the harbor. She turned toward the back and slowly made her way down to the greenhouse where Rachel's father kept all the plant starters. It would at least be dry and warmer in there, and she loved sitting alone, surrounded by plants and reading a good romance novel.

Hmmm. The light was already on inside. Someone must have forgotten it when they took the tour of the property yesterday afternoon.

The door creaked like the opening of a horror movie. She couldn't stop her heart from automatically beating faster. "Silly," Kat said aloud. "We are in a tiny village in the early morning. There aren't going to be bad guys in here." She laughed a little anxiously at her wandering imagination.

"Maybe there are," a male voice responded and she jumped back and screamed.

A hand snaked over her mouth from behind. "Don't do that," he said. "I'm just teasing, I'm not a bad guy."

Kat stomped on his instep, just as she'd been taught in self-defense class.

He yelped.

She grabbed a trowel from the table next to her and brandished the pointy end at his throat. "Who are you? What are you doing here? This is Cullen property and I'm sure you don't belong here."

The man didn't look much older than Kat — maybe eighteen instead of seventeen. Hard to know. His longer, shoulder-length hair curled naturally around his face. His clothes looked a bit ragged. Jeans with holes in the legs, a flannel shirt that looked like it came from the Goodwill bin. Did they have Goodwill in Scotland?

"I would appreciate you not stabbing me with that," the young man said.

Kat did not change the position of the trowel. "I said who are you?"

"Nobody. Just looking for a warm place to spend the night."

"Nobody is not your name. Who are you?"

He lifted his hand slowly, palm facing the pointy end of the trowel. "I can talk better if I don't think you are going to cut my throat with that thing and infect me with whatever dirt or other chemicals it has on it."

Kat waved it side to side. "Talk."

His hand grabbed her wrist and twisted until she dropped the trowel. He kicked it under the potting bench.

"Why you ..." Kat couldn't think what to say. "I'm leaving now. I'm going up to the house and reporting you."

The young man grabbed her wrist again. "Please don't do that. I'll just leave."

He looked so tired and downtrodden that Kat couldn't help but think he was either running away from home or homeless.

"I suggest you let go of me or I will scream my head off and then you'll never leave."

He let go and headed for the door. "I'm outta here."

She ran ahead and stood in front of it. "Wait! Maybe I'm being a little harsh." What was she doing? He might be a murderer and she was asking him to stay? This never turned out well in the movies. "It's cold and rainy out there. Where would you go?"

"Just a minute ago you were threatening to cut my throat and now you're acting all Mother Theresa?"

Kat waved a hand in front of his face. "Look, I was just taken aback ... you know I didn't want any Jason, *Friday the Thirteenth* stuff happening. It was just a reaction. But I'm not like the innkeeper who puts out baby Jesus when there's no room, either. You know?"

The guy laughed. "You are somethin' else. Americans are always so ... weird."

Kat pulled herself up straight. "Look I'm trying to help you here and you're gonna trash talk my country?"

He shook his head and held out his right hand. "Let's start over. I'm Ian. You are?"

Kat worried her lower lip. Finally she shook his hand. "I'm Kat. We're visiting Rachel's dad. Mr. Cullen. We're staying at his place. Well the B&B place I guess. We're all in a band together and Rachel recently got married and so did Sarah, and before that so did Michele, and well we are all like family, but we're not, but we are. Do you understand?"

"I'm not sure I do, you talked so fast I might need a translator."

Kat laughed. "You're funny. I'm the one who needs a translator with that accent."

"You're in Scotland, lassie. This is how we talk. You're the one who has an accent."

The door rattled behind her and they both jumped. Ian's eyes grew wide.

Kat slowly turned to see Gavin's large frame fill the door.

"Your maw's worried about you," he said, not looking at her but at Ian. "Who's this then? How did you get to meetin' a lad already? You've barely been out of my site except after we all went to bed."

"It's not what ye think, sir," Ian said.

"Then what is it?"

Kat stepped in front of Ian and shook her head to warn him not to get in trouble.

Ian pushed her behind him again. "I was crashin' here to keep warm," Ian said. "I'm sorry. I'll go now. Happy Hogmanay to you."

Gavin stopped him with a strong hand to his shoulder. "Have you nowhere to go lad?"

"I do." Ian responded. "I do."

"And where would that be?"

"Um … east of Dunoon. I'm going to meet my sister but got a late start and got a bit tired and saw the greenhouse and thought to get out of the wind and rain."

"Did ye now?"

"Yes, that's it," Kat offered, now standing side by side with Ian. "And I got up early 'cause I couldn't sleep and came down here to read and here he was."

"And what's your family's name, lad? I know most everyone in these parts."

Ian swallowed, his eyes darting to one side and then another as if looking for escape.

"I see," Gavin said. "You're on your own then. How long? You best tell me right."

Ian let out a big breath. "My da kicked me out when his lady friend came home last week. He said there wasn't enough room for her and me and I were old enough to be on my own."

"And your da is?"

"It doesn't matter now, does it? He doesn't want me back." Ian kicked at the gravel.

"You're welcome to stay with us if I have his permission, lad. But I'm not harborin' a runaway. So, tell me who he is and I'll go round and talk to him."

Ian said nothing his eyes cast down.

Kat pushed at him. "Tell him, Ian. If you're telling the truth, Gavin will take care of it. I know it."

Ian looked away. "It's McKay. It won't do you any good to talk to him."

"Your father is Calum, then?" Gavin's voice lowered.

"Yes, the same. The one that is in the papers every week." He looked up and locked his jaw. "I'm not like him, Mr. Cullen. And I'm not goin' back no matter what you say and no matter what my da says. So you might as well just let me go now and be done with me."

"Don't be so anxious to get out in the cold, lad. I understand it all now. How old are you? Sixteen? Seventeen?"

Kat stared straight at him. She wanted to know too.

"Seventeen and ready to work."

Gavin clapped him on the shoulder. "We'll see about work after the holidays. You come with us for now. It happens I have a small room left in the inn. You bring us good luck this day. A stranger at our door. So you come on up and get some breakfast and I'll get you settled. Then you can help us get ready for Hogmanay."

Ian didn't move. Kat saw him swallow several times. She didn't know who his father was, but Gavin evidently knew him and he must be bad enough that he wasn't even going to go talk to him.

"I've got to get breakfast started," Gavin said. "Kat, you see that Ian here gets back to the house." He looked at Ian. "I'll find you a clean T-shirt and you get washed up for breakfast. We'll talk later about what you can do to work for your room and board." Then he turned and walked out the greenhouse door.

Kat couldn't stop smiling. "See. I told you Gavin would take care of everything. I knew Rachel's dad would be cool, but he's even better than I thought. You know his wife died eight years ago, right? I mean he's been running this place pretty much on his own. I'll bet he's really looking forward to the help and all."

Ian didn't respond, but he followed her without hesitation as she led the way back up the hill to the main house. Who would've known that an early morning visit to the greenhouse would end with a handsome boy staying at the Inn? She smiled, barely stopping herself from skipping her way up the hill. This might be an even more amazing new year's then she thought.

THERESA PACED THE floor in the room she shared with Kat. After hearing Kat's story over breakfast she was still seething. How could Gavin take in a perfect stranger, especially with Kat here? Kat had always been a bit too accepting of people but Theresa had never considered she would have to be protecting her against some hoodlum in Scotland.

A solid knock on the door stopped her pacing. "Come in."

The door opened and Gavin stood in the frame. "From your terse instructions, I gather you are upset."

"Close the door," Theresa mumbled. "I don't want everyone here to be listening to us."

Gavin closed the door behind him but didn't move further into the room.

"Look at it from my perspective," Theresa started and began to pace again. "If Kat were your daughter and you were visiting America and a strange boy with a criminal family history accosted her, would you be happy if I then invited that same boy to stay in my home where he could convince her to do who knows what?"

"Because the father is rotten it doesn't mean the boy is too," Gavin said. "He's a lost lad with nowhere to go and little skills to survive. Would you have me put him out in the cold?"

Theresa sat on the edge of the bed. "No, but isn't that what social services are for? You do have social workers here don't you? Don't they have special arrangements to come help those children?"

"May I?" Gavin pointed to the other bed in the room.

Theresa blew out a big breath and nodded.

"He's seventeen," Gavin said as he lowered himself to the other bed and faced her.

"Exactly, and that's a big problem. Kat's been hurt before and I don't want it to happen again. This young man is obviously a man of the world already. Kat is innocent, trusting. She sees life like one big romantic movie."

"I think you are selling her short," Gavin said. "She was ready to protect him from being sent to the police. I think she understands on some level that he comes from a bad family."

"She would. She sees herself as the savior of animals and anyone who is orphaned. That's how she sees this boy, as an orphan who needs saving — not the predator he could be."

"Predator? That's being a bit harsh."

"Is it?"

"Yes, you know nothing about him."

"I know men," Theresa said. "They all want one thing from girls."

"Really?"

She stood and looked down at him. "Yes. And it is my job to protect my daughter from them."

"I see."

"No, you don't see. I have been a single parent since Kat was two-years-old. I've been the father and the mother, and sometimes the big sister when needed."

"I'm sorry," Gavin said. "It sounds like it's been a rough time."

Theresa looked away and, after a few moments, sat down on the edge of the bed again. "I'm sorry. I must sound like an ogre."

"No. You sound like a mother who loves her daughter very much. Evelyn was the same with Rachel."

"I know I can't protect her from everything," Theresa continued. "I already failed her once by not being understanding of a … a particular situation. What can I do to make this Ian go away?"

"I could try to find you a place elsewhere, if you prefer," Gavin said. "There are probably no inns with rooms but I could talk to a neighbor if you like."

"No. She would blame me for being too paranoid and it would certainly drive her back here. She would sneak out just to learn why I didn't like the boy."

"Then we are at a stalemate," he said. "It is Hogmanay. A day when the entire country celebrates. Even if social services would take him — which they wouldn't because he's seventeen — they aren't open and no offices will be open until the day after New Year's. I've known this family for a long time and I've never once seen a police report where Ian has gotten into trouble."

"That doesn't mean—"

"I promise," he interrupted her. "I promise to share the burden of watching out for Kat. I promise I won't let anything untoward go on between them."

Theresa sighed and shook her head. "I guess I don't have much choice."

"Come on, Theresa. If you give the lad a chance, you may even find out you like him." Gavin stood and opened the door. "We're going to be cleaning most of the afternoon, so now is the time to get some rest. Once the festivities start you'll be going until the wee hours of the morn."

$\mathcal{E}$VERYONE JOINED GAVIN in the living room. Ian had cleaned up as best he could. The clean shirt that Mr. Cullen had supplied hung loosely on his thin frame. Truth be told he'd never really celebrated Hogmanay. His da had always left him at home to tend the animals while he went out and caroused. Then he'd come home sometime the next day, delivered by a friend or a woman he'd met in town, and Ian would help carry him to the bedroom. It was then he swore he'd never drink whisky because of what it did to a man.

The fire flamed high and the lights of the Christmas tree glowed brightly. While they had all napped, Ian and Gavin and two young girls had worked at cleaning the inn from top to bottom — changing all the sheets, airing out the rooms, adding new towels, and readying the sideboard with the traditional Hogmanay meal. Ian couldn't help but count his blessings that he was here instead of home.

"Ian, will you pass out the gifts and then we will all open them together?" Gavin said. "There is one for each of you."

"Da, it wasn't necessary," Rachel said.

"Of course it was. You are my guests and you must be prepared for all the celebrations to come."

Ian crawled beneath the tree and located all the packages, calling out the names and greeting each person with "Happy Hogmanay."

"Da?" Rachel shouted when Gavin had disappeared.

He hurried down the hall from the back room with a package he handed to Ian. "It is not brand new, but it is well earned."

Ian's eyes widened. He couldn't remember ever receiving a Hogmanay gift. "Thank you, sir," he said. "It is beyond the call."

Rachel also held out a package to Gavin. "Da, for you. I made it myself — well, with help from Theresa who actually knows how to knit."

Gavin hugged Rachel tight and Ian swallowed hard. What a family this was, filled with love — as it should be.

"Well, what are you waiting for?" Gavin asked. "Let's see what Santa brought us, shall we?"

Claire was the first to tear open the wrapping paper but was not able to cut the ribbon that secured the square box. Rachel reached over with scissors. As Claire opened the box, others began to exclaim their own surprise. Each person had been given a warm wool sweater. The women and girls received a tartan cape with the Cullen colors and the men received a tartan cap.

"The colors are beautiful," Theresa exclaimed, holding the poncho in front of her, dark and light blues with small strips of green, yellow and black.

"Blue is for the Cullen family tradition as police officers," Gavin said. "The light blue is for the family's Scottish heritage."

"The gold is for the family's military service," Rachel added. "And the green is for their Irish heritage."

"Your family is both Irish and Scottish?" Sarah asked.

"Yes, the Gaels, what you call the Irish," Gavin said, "conquered most of Scotland around the fifth century. The language and mixing of the cultures are particularly evident today on the western coast and the highlands in smaller villages like Dunoon and in the Hebrides. It's near impossible to find a Scottish family without Irish in their blood too.

"And the black?" asked Michele.

Rachel looked at her father and answered in a soft voice. "Black is for mourning those who were lost."

"What about yours?" Claire asked, pointing at the still unopened box in Gavin's hands.

"Oh, I almost forgot." He bent low in front of Claire. "Would you help your granda open it?"

"Yes!" She tore into the wrapping with the same abandon she had used on her own present. Then she opened the box and pulled out two mittens in a navy blue color with gray cuffs. "Mommy and Theresa made them," Claire declared.

Gavin immediately put them on. "They are perfect." He wiggled his fingers and Claire laughed. "Now that everyone has warm things it is time to join the processing of fire."

Outside, behind the inn and part way down the hill a large stone circle enclosed a six-foot basket-weave woodpile. Three-foot wax tapers were neatly stacked nearby.

"Everyone get a candle," Gavin instructed. "And the honor of the first lighted torch goes to the newlyweds."

Gavin lit the large candles that Tom and Sarah had selected. They smiled and kissed in the light of the candles, and then each helped to light others.

"Now we carry our fire and join the door to door procession of torches," Rachel instructed. "This is one of my favorite parts of the evening. We all gather together in the village and go house to house."

"Not the entire village," Gavin corrected. "We've grown a bit and have divided up into neighborhoods. But certainly we will process with our nearest neighbors."

$\mathcal{S}$OON THEY JOINED several other families carrying torches as well. Kat compared it to a caroling party in that they went house to house and sometimes sang. But it was also quite different in that everyone had these big candles and with each house, more joined the procession. Kat walked with Ian, while her mother and Gavin walked just ahead.

"This is amazing," Kat said. "You are so lucky to get to do this every year."

Ian smiled but kept his head down.

"Is something wrong?" Kat asked. "Aren't you having fun?"

He turned around and stared down the long line of the procession. He smiled and turned back. "I've never done this before."

Kat's eyes widened. "Never?"

"Me da always went out to celebrate but that meant I was to mind the house. And … well … the procession doesn't stop at my house. People kind of avoid us."

Kat didn't know what to say. One part of her wanted to thrash Ian's dad. Another part of her wanted to hug him tight and kiss him like crazy. Instead she kept moving forward in silence.

"Sorry," Ian said. "I didn't mean to bring ya down."

"No. You didn't do that. I'm just sorry your family is kind of screwed up."

Ian let out a guffaw. "Screwed up is putting it mildly"

Kat took his hand in hers as they walked side-by-side. "As far as I'm concerned, you are part of the Sweetwater Canyon family now."

Ian swallowed hard and looked away.

Kat squeezed his hand. "I hope that's okay with you."

"It's …" Ian withdrew his hand and took a handkerchief from a pocket to wipe his face. "Good."

Though Kat was surprised at his tears, she looked away to give him some privacy. She knew he wouldn't want her to say anything. Guys were like that. Not so good with emotional stuff.

"It's not all that great, really," she said, picking up the pace as they climbed a hill to the next house. "I mean we are a bit crazy, what with the band and all, but we put up with each other most of the time."

Ian bumped her shoulder with his. "So, I have to put up with you then?"

Kat laughed. "Oh yes, more than put up with me. You have to do everything I say, and right now I say last person to the next house doesn't get any treats."

They both took off, running to the front of the line with their long candles bouncing above the others.

Each house provided a part of the Hogmanay feast and a good Ceilidh — a social gathering. At one house they offered shortbread to the walkers. The entertainment consisted of storytellers both young and old. At the next, the main meal of venison pie and a side dish of rumbledethumps — a type of potato casserole with turnips and kale and topped with cheese — fed each of those traveling with the fire procession. Then they moved to another home where music played and everyone danced and dessert was served. As they passed each house, the members of that family joined them in the procession as well.

All of the neighbors ended at the Cullen's inn with Kat and Ian being the first ones there, holding open the gate to the backyard. The long line of families rippled down the steep stone steps like water cascading over river rocks. Each person grounded their fire just outside a circle of stones surrounding a giant pile of wood. When all the other tapers were out, Gavin touched his to the kindling and paper at the bottom. It took off immediately, crackling and singing as the flames climbed to the top of the pile.

"Happy Hogmanay!" Gavin declared as he walked from one person to the next offering a dram of whisky and sharing old stories of Hogmanays past.

RACHEL SAW KAT taking a drink of whisky and then coughing. She ran to her side. "Your mother is going to kill me for this."

"Then we won't tell her," Kat responded still barely able to talk. "Besides it's legal for me here."

Ian looked sheepish. "Sorry, I figured one dram wouldn't hurt. And she is seventeen."

"She may be seventeen, but I doubt she's ever had alcohol and whisky is not the way to start. And, in America the age is twenty-one so you can imagine how her mother would feel about this."

"Twenty one? I can't imagine they all wait 'til then."

Rachel sighed. She wasn't going to get into American teen ways with Ian.

"It tastes awful," Kat said, swallowing multiple times. "I don't know why anyone would like this."

"I'm glad *you* don't like it," Rachel said. "So, don't try anymore. Come on, we need to get set up. We will be expected to start playing soon." She half dragged Kat in her wake to the other side of the bonfire.

"Good neighbors," Gavin began. "I am blessed to have my daughter, Rachel, here again after eight years. She comes back with her family and her friends." He pointed to the women arrayed to one side of the bonfire. "This is the Sweetwater Canyon band all the way from America — Portland, Oregon."

The band played the traditional tunes Rachel had taught them before the trip, and they also did a few of their own original tunes. Claire joined in on fiddle as she could, and Rachel asked her father to join them with his fiddle as well. She couldn't help but tear up remembering the times she and her father would play together for her mother while she was ill.

Eventually, Rachel invited all musicians to get out their instruments and join them. She knew that Kat, Theresa, and Sarah would struggle to pick up some of the tunes they'd never heard before, but that was the nature of many Ceilidhs — musicians played as best they could, sometimes sitting out and at other times taking the lead. She'd forgotten how wonderful and warm it was to play with so many people who cherished the old tunes.

During a pause, Gavin asked, "Rachel, do you remember any of the dances?"

"Oh, I don't know."

"Please, mommy, please. I know you do. You've taught me a couple."

"Only if you dance with me," Rachel answered and took Claire onto the lawn.

Gavin started a jig with his fiddle and the other musicians joined in. Claire and Rachel stepped together. When the musicians changed to a reel, Ian sidled up to Kat and took her hand to teach her. Other dancers joined in. Soon, it was one big happy party with musicians trading off, dancers coming in and out, and people milling about having a grand time. The whisky was plentiful, but no one seemed to be over the top as they counted the minutes until midnight.

The women of Sweetwater Canyon gathered near one end of the yard for a moment of quiet with just the five of them.

"Thank you," Rachel said. "Thank you for being my family for all these years and for giving up your own New Year's celebrations to come here with me."

"To us!" Michele raised her class.

"Wait, let me refill." Rachel poured a little more whisky in her glass and offered it around the group.

"Not me," Sarah demurred.

"Come on, Sarah," Rachel teased. "One dram is not gonna hurt you. It may even loosen you up a bit."

"I don't need any loosening," Sarah retorted. "Besides it's not good for the—" She cut off her response with a hand to her mouth and all her band mates quickly closed in.

"You're pregnant?" Michele asked.

Sarah blushed and nodded. "Two months. But we weren't going to say anything until after the first trimester."

Screams of happiness welled from the group.

Gavin poured another dram for each of the men. "Sounds like we are in need of a toast," he said. He called the attention of all those gathered. "A toast to the new bairn. May he—"

"Or she," the women said together.

"Or she," he repeated, "be the light in your eyes, the lilt in your step…"

"And the longin' for the day she leaves home," Rachel finished with a laugh. "And may she not give you as many headaches as me."

The evening continued with singing and storytelling. As the church tower rang out twelve times, all the neighbors gathered round the bonfire. Crossing their arms they held each other's hands in a full circle as they sang *Auld Lang Syne*.

Ian made sure he was at Kat's side. For the first time in his life, he actually believed he was an accepted part of this community. For the first time in his life, he felt like he had a family.

He stared at Kat as she sang all the verses. Her voice pure, her eyes glistened in the light of the bonfire, and Ian marveled at how his decision to sleep in that greenhouse had changed his life. At least for tonight, he wouldn't think about the future. He would only think about now. And about Kat.

The song ended and Ian turned to Kat, softly brushing a kiss across her cheek. "Happy New Year," he said. "Thanks for trusting me. This is the best Hogmanay I've ever had."

"This is the only one I've ever had," Kat said, her wide eyes and broad smile alight with the reflection of the bonfire. "I want to come back every year!" Then she grabbed Ian and planted a strong kiss on his mouth. "Now that's a proper kiss."

Theresa scurried over. "Time to turn in," she said to Kat.

"I'd like to stay out for awhile. Please?" Kat drew out the please.

"I don't know. It's very late. It's …"

"Mom, it's not like I don't stay up late for New Year's at home. And it's not like I get to be in Scotland every day or anything."

Theresa looked from Kat to Ian and then back to Kat again.

After a long pause she sighed long and loud. "All right, but don't go wandering off. Stay here by the bonfire or in the house. And no whisky! Understand?"

"Yes ma'am." Kat executed a perfect military salute then hugged her mom. "Thanks."

"I'll be out here until the fire is out," Gavin said, appearing behind Ian with a hand resting on his shoulder. "Nothing to worry about."

Theresa laughed. "You really don't remember much about teen-agers do you, Gavin? They have a way of getting into trouble without even moving a step."

Kat rolled her eyes. "Mom."

"I'm going. I'm going." She hugged Kat again and then walked toward the Inn without looking back.

Gavin watched Theresa as she slowly took the steps back up the hill. Her face was strong. Her high-boned cheeks and animated fine lines in her face told of a life that was hard but had also had its share of laughter. He couldn't help but wonder in that second what his wife would have looked like at this age. She would be softer, he decided, because she'd known love. Theresa knew the love of a daughter and of friends, but not the good love of a man.

For the first time since his wife's death, Gavin felt a stirring of interest. He shook his head. An old man's folly. It would be impossi-ble to try a long distance relationship with an American, her teenage daughter and an ocean and thousands of miles between them. He turned back and looked into the dying embers of the bonfire. It was a good thought for a few moments though. It felt good to even consider it.

$\mathcal{S}$MOKE FILLED THE room and Kat choked on the smell. She was between her bed and the wall. How did she get here? Last she remembered was saying good night to Ian and then climbing the stairs to the room she shared with her mother.

"Out! Everyone out!" Ian shouted as he ran up and down stairs and halls. "Out now!"

Her mother called out, "Kat, where are you?"

She heard hands patting the bed. Kat tried to answer but her voice didn't work. Too much smoke.

Bells rang and sirens blared.

A door opened.

"Theresa, You have to come now," Gavin said.

"I can't find her. I can't find her!" Her mother's panicked voice screamed.

"She must already be out of the house. Come. I don't know how long the structure will hold."

The door closed with a slam.

Kat fell back to sleep.

She woke again but the nightmare was worse. She could feel the heat now. Flames licked the outside of the bedroom window. She crawled on the floor to the door, but she couldn't get it open. The handle was stuck. She heard shouting as if it was far off. Maybe it was just a bad dream. Realistic, but just a dream. She decided to go back to sleep and hope that next time she woke it would be breakfast time.

*T*HERESA SHOOK IAN hard. "Where is she? Where is she?"

"I don't know," he said. When we turned in she said she was going to bed. Wasn't she in the room with you?"

"No! I felt the bed, she wasn't there!" She ran off to check with others.

Ian stared hard at the inn. It had been here all of his life. It was more than one hundred years old. The left side, where the fireplace had been was completely engulfed. If Kat was in there, he hoped she was on the right side, where her room had been.

He looked down the hill where the local fire truck was still lumbering slowly around the turns. There wasn't enough time. He knew she was in there. She wouldn't let her maw worry like this. If Kat were okay, she would be checking on everyone else.

Ian took off his T-shirt and wrapped it like a bandana around his nose and mouth and then sprinted toward the front door.

"Ian!" Mr. Cullen shouted behind him. "No! Wait for the truck."

Ian ducked inside the door, keeping low to the ground.

The fog of smoke immediately assailed him and he coughed. He couldn't see anything. He moved forward until he bumped into something. A railing. It came off in his hand. He crawled on hands and knees to the kitchen. He soaked his T-shirt with water and put it back around his nose and mouth and then made his way back to the stairs. He'd have to find his way to the second floor. She had to be there, trapped somewhere.

One. Step. At. A. Time. His knee stuck in a hole and he pulled out. His hand slipped off one side where the rail gave way. He counted each step to keep his bearings. One step. Two. Three. Four.

Finally he was on the landing.

He crawled to the right and listened at the door. Nothing. He pounded.

"Kat! Are you in there? Kat?"

Was that a scratching? Or his imagination.

He felt his way up to the doorknob. It was stuck. It wouldn't turn. The solid wooden door was too heavy for him to break down.

"Kat! If you can hear me, push on the door. It's stuck."

Again he only heard a small scratching sound, like a kitten was asking to come out.

He wrapped his hands around the knob and pulled with all he had. Nothing.

Ian took a part of the broken railing and pounded on the door near the frame, hoping to dislodge it even a little.

Again, he grabbed the knob and with all his strength yelled at the top of his lungs as he pulled. It opened and he fell backward coughing.

Crawling again he found Kat had fallen in the doorway. Her finger tapped almost silently on the floor.

Ian unwrapped the T-shirt from around his own mouth and tied it around hers. "Breathe," he told her. "I've got you."

He put his arms under her armpits and pulled her along with him as he crawled and scooted back to the stairs. Again, he counted the stairs as he moved back down them, one at a time. First he moved down a stair and then he scooted her down the stair. Him. Then her. Him. Then her.

Sometimes she would moan as her body hit one stair and then the next. He couldn't help it. He couldn't carry her without falling.

When he finally got to the last stair, two firemen were there to help. One took Kat in his arms. Ian collapsed. His energy spent.

$\mathcal{I}$AN WOKE IN the hospital. Mr. Cullen sat next to him, legs stretched out as he leaned back in a chair.

"You're awake." He leaned forward to pat Ian's arm, and smiled.

Ian tried to sit up but started coughing. "Kat?" He eeked out her name.

"She's fine. You saved her, you know. I don't think the firemen would have found her in time. She's recovering in another room."

"Where?" he coughed again. "Want to … see her."

Mr. Cullen pushed him back against the pillow. "Take it easy. Don't do too much. She's fine, thanks to you. Her mother's with her, has been the last two days. If you hadn't given her your soaked T-shirt it might have been too much. We might have lost her."

Ian relaxed against the pillow.

"Is it my fault? Did I forget something? The bonfire? The fireplace?"

"No. Nothing like that. It was no one's fault." Mr. Cullen paused. "It was an electrical fire. Old wiring."

"The house?" Ian whispered.

"Gone. All of it." Mr. Cullen looked to the ceiling. "Nothing salvageable."

"Nothing?"

Mr. Cullen didn't speak.

Ian didn't know what to say. It was one thing to be kicked out of a house he never liked. But Mr. Cullen had raised his family there. Had nursed his wife and buried her there. He couldn't imagine what that must feel like.

Ian looked at the ceiling too. They were both screwed.

"Ian, I want you to know that no matter what happens you have a home with me. I don't want you to worry about where to live."

"Thanks Mr. Cullen but it looks like neither of us have a home now."

"Something will work out," Mr. Cullen said. "You just rest. You concentrate on getting better. Let me worry about where we will live."

GAVIN LOOKED OUT to the Firth of Clyde one last time. Then he turned back to look up the hill where his home and inn had been. It hadn't taken long to level the burned hulk and cart it away. The village had helped. Instead of spending their holiday relaxing as planned, they'd all shown up with shovels and dump trucks. They laid out food for everyone who worked that day. They brought extra clothing too.

When Theresa had offered for him and Ian to come to Oregon and stay with her on Mt. Hood, he was surprised. She didn't seem to be the same frightened and cautious woman he'd met that first day when Ian showed up. Then she was a woman who believed the world was a dark place and no one was to be trusted — particularly men.

Of course, Ian saving her daughter's life might have put a little kink in her outlook. But certainly not enough to wholeheartedly invite two strangers to America to share her home. Not that there was a romance or anything. She was just being kind. She said the climate in Oregon was very similar to Dunoon. He wondered.

Ian yelled from the car. "Everyone is ready, Mr. Cullen. Are you ready?"

Gavin waved and held up a finger to show he needed another minute.

The car door closed and he turned back to the hill once more. He remembered when he and Evelyn had first bought the old house in that summer more than twenty years ago. Rachel had been six and just starting school in the village. The sky had been clear blue, the air offering them new life and so many plans. They had blindly taken on the task of making it into a B&B, welcoming visitors from around the world. They had raised Rachel together. And they had said their goodbyes in that house.

He looked at the empty space again where the house once stood. He realized he had been standing still the last eight years since Evelyn's death. Rooted to their room together. Rooted to their life together. Not looking forward or backward, simply standing still, moving through each day in a fog. It wasn't until Rachel returned with her family and her friends that he realized he hadn't been living, he'd merely existed.

"Evelyn," he said as he looked toward the hill where she was buried. "I'm awake again. I don't know exactly where I'm going or what is to come. But I am free now. Thank you for loving me. I hope that one day I can pass it on."

He turned away and walked to the waiting car not looking back again. From now on he would only move forward.

It was a new day. A new year. A new life.

~

ABOUT THE AUTHOR

Maggie loves to learn. With careers ranging from counseling families with special needs children, to leadership in academic computing, she has had plenty of opportunities to learn, meet new people, and travel widely. Throughout it all, writing has been her first love. Her publications include four non-fiction books, over thirty-five short stories, and nine novels. She now writes full time as Maggie Jaimeson for adult fiction and Maggie Faire for young adult fiction. Her fiction is often cross-genre including SF, Fantasy, Suspense, Women's Fiction and Romance. She continues to write non-fiction under Maggie Lynch.

You can learn more about Maggie at:

maggielynch.com

A Marine's Christmas Proposal
Susan Lute

$\mathcal{D}$AVID RANDALL, ONCE upon a time the top of his class at Stanford Business School, and more recently, Captain in the US Marine Corps, took a break from unpacking to watch his nephew run his toy truck around the boxes scattered through the living room.

"Brrrmm. Brrmm."

Elijah turned his toy toward the open front door and ran as fast as his short little legs would go.

"Not so fast, buddy." David scooped him up just before the kid drove over the highly polished black pumps stepping purposefully through the entry.

"More trouble than a platoon of Marines, isn't he?" Lilly Hunter's amused laughter followed right behind David's snort.

"It's a tossup."

His aunt closed the door on the setting December sun before planting a kiss on Elijah's temple. "But he's such an angel — aren't you young man?"

Setting her oversized black purse on the wood stove he hadn't had a chance to heat up to ward off the winter's chill, she took in the chaos erupting from the boxes the movers originally left neatly stacked against one wall.

Chaos reigned. For a Marine, even one who'd made the hard choice to become a civilian, it wasn't a good thing.

"Looks like you can use some help."

He frowned. *In more ways than one.*

He knew how to be a Marine, even one who was no longer on active duty. What he didn't know was how to be mom and dad to a three year old.

His aunt was dressed in her usual business attire, dark gray jacket over pale pink blouse and gray wool skirt. As administrative assistant to the owner and CEO of Banks Sportswear, she was from the old school and refused to relax her wardrobe to business casual.

Graying hair hung in long curls to her shoulders making her look more vibrant than your typical great-aunt.

"Michelle's coming over later."

A worry line etched between her perfectly formed brows. "She's working too hard. I was hoping to see her here this morning. I have something for her in the car."

Working too hard was his little sister — he would always think of her that way — doing her third year of general surgery residency at Oregon Health and Sciences University.

"She's breaking away this afternoon to watch Elijah while I go to the interview."

Lilly ran a hand over the box on the coffee table marked *Christmas decorations,* in his sister Sarah's neat handwriting. Dark brown eyes welling with sorrow asked a silent question.

David shook his head, heart crunching in pain. "Not this year. It was her favorite holiday. I can't."

Losing one of his soldiers had never been easy. Losing Sarah and Tom in a senseless traffic accident ripped his heart right out of his chest.

"Down!" Elijah demanded, kicking his feet, surprising David out of his misery by coming dangerously close to an important part of his anatomy.

On a choked laugh he released the boy, almost dropping his nephew before the kid's lethal weapons got planted firmly on the floor.

Lilly chuckled.

He shrugged, fighting his own smile. "He gets a little excited."

"So I see." His aunt knelt to Elijah's level. "Do I get a hug?"

Elijah threw himself into her arms as David's cell erupted with a country song. He plucked it off the box where he'd put it safely out of his rambunctious nephew's reach, and watched from the kitchen while his aunt reigned kisses all over the little boy's laughing face.

"Randall here."

"Captain. Wilson. I ... um ... how did the move go?" First Sergeant Brian Wilson, six months after retiring from managing troops, was now in charge of Human Resources for the Pacific Northwest Bank. The First Sergeant's promise of a sure job was one of the reasons David had left the Corps, packed everything he owned, and moved with Elijah to Portland. The other was to be close to the only family both of them had left.

The uneasy sound in Wilson's voice kick-started David's alarm. In all the time he'd known the retired Marine, the man had never been caught off guard. "Still unpacking. I'm all set for the interview this afternoon. My sister is going to watch Elijah."

"How's the kid handling ... everything?"

A delaying tactic. This couldn't be good.

"He's doing okay." Except that an inexperienced uncle could never replace his parents.

"There's no easy way to say this, Captain. I just got word the bank is downsizing. They've put a freeze on hiring and canceled all interviews."

"Choo-choo!"

Wincing when Elijah plowed into his legs while pretending to be a runaway locomotive, all David could envision was his draining bank balance.

He ruffled the boy's blond hair. "Any chance they'd make an exception?"

"I'm sorry, Captain. I tried. I know how hard it was to get here this fast."

A Marine never panicked. "Any scuttlebutt about openings at other companies?"

"None. The job market is tight."

Not a surprise. The feelers he'd put out hadn't brought any results until Wilson had called about the business analyst position.

"I can ask around. See what I dig up."

"Appreciate it." David disconnected and tossed the phone on

the counter. His first assignment as Elijah's parent — to support the kid — and he was failing.

He straightened his spine. He could do this. Get a job. Keep it. Be a dad. Take care of Elijah like Sarah would want. She'd been the glue that had held the three siblings together when their family had broken apart. Now it was his turn.

He turned to Lilly as they had all those years ago. "Banks Sportswear doesn't happen to need a business analyst, do they?"

IN THE EARLY hours before the hallways of Banks Sportswear began to bustle with employees going about their business, Charlee Banks stood at the window in her father's office staring at Keller Fountain. She uncurled her fists, reminding herself she'd get more with honey than by backing her sole parent into a corner.

Sneaking a calming breath, she faced him while schooling her voice into a reasonable tone. "At least let me explore the *possibility* of maximizing our share of the domestic market."

"No. If I'm successful in Tokyo, we won't need to worry about the domestic side of the business. Bill will take care of it."

Bill Danvers was the Operations Manager of the domestic division, a position Charlee had coveted from the moment she'd insisted her father give her an office and work to do.

She watched him pack his briefcase, his automatic refusal to consider her ideas chafing like bad fitting panties. He'd been working on the Japan angle for a year. Her job — reluctantly bestowed by the elder Banks — was to get the company in position, staff wise, to handle the added business. It wasn't the work she wanted to do.

She loved her father. For as long as she could remember, it'd been the two of them. But Charles Banks, CEO of the family business had always been a hard act to follow. Especially when he denied her the opportunity to make a difference in business.

She was in danger. Danger of never breaking free of the image of a brainless daughter who had no ambition, a role he continuously thrust her into. And to be honest, it wasn't all his fault. For a long time she played the spoiled rich girl to the hilt.

Charlee flushed with an embarrassment that still stung.

She'd just turned thirty. It was high time she did something more with her life; proved to her father she could fill a better role in the company than Barbie-doll.

One week was barely enough time to consult with the business analyst she'd chosen, much less develop a plan Charles Banks couldn't refuse, but she would make it work. After all, she *was* his daughter. She'd learned a thing or two from the old man about how to get what she wanted.

Lilly Hunter, her father's administrative assistant joined them. "Our plane leaves in two hours."

Her father closed his briefcase. "I'll be back in time for the Christmas party. I need everyone ready on this end when I get here. No more talk about hiring business analysts, or wasting time and energy to fix what isn't broken."

Knowing she was planning to ignore those orders, Charlee gave a stiff nod. Her father might think his was the last word on the subject, but the domestic market was nowhere near a closed agenda item.

"We'll be ready," she said in a deceptively calm voice.

He sighed heavily. For a moment the CEO took a bench on the sidelines. "Look honey, I've worked hard to build this company so you wouldn't have to scramble through life. You should be traveling, exploring the world, or whatever it is young people do for fun these days. I gave you an office and work to do because you said that's what you wanted. It's not what *I* want for you."

"I know, Dad, but it's what I need."

Lips firming into a disapproving line, he turned to Lilly. "Have you got our tickets?"

"In my bag."

Lilly had been Charles' right hand for as long as Charlee could remember. The older woman exuded a pragmatism and calm professionalism she tried very hard to emulate.

Lily's look of sympathy spurred her on. She didn't want pity, just the chance to show the MBA she'd worked hard to get wasn't just a pretty piece of paper, or a waste of time, as her father had told her often enough.

"Aren't you dating that fella ... what's his name?"

"We broke up."

"Oh. Well. I'll call—"

"You're going to miss your flight."

He gave her a brief hug before heading for the elevator. "Let's go, Lilly."

"I'll be right there." Elbow resting on the hand at her waist, her chin settled on the other, a manicured finger tapping to a silent rhythm.

The speculative look in Lilly's eyes made Charlee more nervous than her father ever could. "What?"

"I haven't had a chance to tell you. Alice broke her leg yesterday while you were in Pendleton."

"How?"

"She slipped going down the stairwell." Lilly held up a hand to ward off Charlee's immediate concern. "She's okay. Recuperating at home. But she'll be on medical leave until the doctor releases her."

Dismayed she followed Lilly to the bank of elevators lining the opposite wall in the outer office, where her father waited. "I'll send flowers and a basket right away."

"Taken care of." The elevator doors pinged open. Lilly paused, her expression lit with surprising humor. "I've arranged for a temporary replacement. He'll be a little late. I told him to stop by Human Resources first."

"He?"

The lights on the Christmas boughs decorating the outer office couldn't begin to compete with the sparkle in Lilly's laughing eyes as the elevator doors slid closed.

*O*N THE ONLY room he'd completely organized, David pulled the blanket up to Elijah's chin, gently brushing a lock of hair off the boy's forehead.

Raised by his aunt from the age of ten, when his parent's divorce had torn David and his sister's safe world apart, Portland was the first place he'd thought to come when he'd become responsible for his nephew.

Both with serial marriages under their belts, the last time he'd seen his parents in the same proximity was at Sarah and Doug's funeral. Neither had offered to stay and help with Elijah, and David hadn't invited them to take on the little tyke.

Though he had zilch in the way of parenting skills, watching them climb into separate vehicles after brief good-byes to their remaining children and grandson, he'd vowed not to let a little thing like lack of experience stand in the way of giving Elijah a loving home.

"David? It's nearly seven," Michelle whispered from behind.

Burying the sour memory, he tugged on the blanket one more time, straightened his tie and followed his sister downstairs to the kitchen. The boxes he'd emptied after putting Elijah to bed last night were re-stacked against the wall.

All except the Christmas box. That one he'd put in the spare bedroom closet. It would be their first Christmas without Sarah and Tom. Elijah didn't need the reminder. Just this year he didn't either. Instead he planned to spend the holiday quietly putting the house in order and getting the little guy settled in their new life.

He checked his watch. The first step in that mission was not being late for his first day at Banks Sportswear.

His aunt, the miracle worker. He didn't know how she'd done it, but somehow she'd scrounged up a job. It was a temporary solution, of course, but would get them through the next month, at which time he would regroup. Somewhere in Portland there was bound to be a position that fit his qualifications.

"Coffee." Michelle handed him a travel mug. "I wish I could help more with Elijah, but as soon as you get home from work I have to head back to the hospital."

Dressed in green scrubs, her straight, blond hair pulled into a ponytail, Michelle had come straight from the night shift, having traded with a fellow resident so she could watch Elijah while he went to work.

David one armed her into a bear hug. For as long as he could remember, Michelle had wanted to be a surgeon. She'd worked too long and hard to get where she was to be sidelined now. And he and the squirt weren't going to be the ones who knocked her off course.

"We'll work it out. Don't worry. Whatever time you can spend with him will be enough."

David cleared his throat, untangled himself, and grabbed his suit jacket. "Wish me luck."

"Always."

Barely making it to HR on time, an hour and a half later, he stepped off the elevator onto the fifth floor.

At odds with the theme of cheery Christmas decorations littering the elegant outer office, an understated, cute blond muttered angrily at the computer screen she thumped with her palm.

David's brows shot up. The black power suit over crisp white shirt wouldn't encourage most red-blooded men to take notice of the curves hidden underneath. His long neglected libido noticed anyway. Short corn-silk hair slicked back from a delicately shaped face should have discouraged the drop kick of his pulse. It didn't.

"Stupid, flipping machine." She gave the monitor another thump. "What have you done with my letters?"

Spirit was something he'd always liked in a woman. He just didn't have time for boy-girl games at the moment..

Still he couldn't help teasing. "That's one way to get the ruddy machine to talk."

Irritated blue eyes, the color of the Mediterranean Sea, snapped to his — and grew round with surprised appreciation.

David's temperature rose about twenty degrees.

"Can I help you?" Her voice held a breathless quality that had him thinking of candlelight dinners and slow dancing in the moonlight.

Resisting the sudden urge to tug his tie loose so he could breathe, he pushed back the unwanted desire building in his gut. "Human Resources sent me. I'm looking for Charlee Banks."

As quick as a minnow darting through water, all that feminine interest died a swift death. Gorgeous blues narrowed. The husky, come-hither timbre left her voice. "You've found her."

Lilly hadn't given him much information about his new boss, but it was easy enough to search the internet where he'd discovered the owner of the sportswear company had a hellion of a daughter who'd given Paris Hilton a run for her money. Then suddenly, six years ago she'd disappeared, finally resurfacing at her father's company. There hadn't been much written about her since.

"I'm David Randall, your temporary administrative assistant."

She didn't blink. "Can you get my letters off this infernal machine?"

Meaning if he couldn't, he wouldn't be staying.

A Marine wasn't so easy to intimidate. His mission was to keep this gig long enough to find another with a longer life cycle. A knock-your-socks-off sassy woman would have to take the back seat.

He waved her out of the chair. "I'll bring the letters to your office as soon as I've retrieved them."

If his situation weren't so desperate, he'd find the lack of trust laughable.

Holy—! THAT MAN'S shoes can go under my bed any day or night.

When her stomach did a slow, appreciative somersault, Charlee cut the thought off at its proverbial knees, and turned Alice's chair over to the hunk shooing her out of the way.

Tall and built for ironman triathlons, his dark hair was cut military short. Eyes the color of chocolate lingered on her face before settling on the monitor. A jaw carved from stubborn rock dared her to let her hair down and have fun as her father had instructed. The kind of fun that came to mind was not what the elder Banks meant and certainly wasn't an item on her current agenda.

Charlee caught herself sighing like a high school girl on her first crush. Taking a mental step back, she managed to sound just the right shade of uninterested. "You type, file, and answer phones?"

He frowned, punched a key. The copier began to hum as he pinned her with an assessing stare. "Yes."

Charlee didn't mistake the flutter in her belly for anything other than what it was — a challenge to step out of the strictly business life she made for herself and kick up her heels.

It was way too tempting. But she'd spent her teens and early twenties being everyone's fun-time girl. That girl who lived only for kicks and thrills was behind her. It was hard enough to live down her past without putting her toe back in *that* water.

"Where did you find them?"

"In the word processing program, under today's date. Your assistant is very organized."

When he flashed her a dangerous smile, she rounded the desk out of reach. There was no doubt about it. Her temporary assistant had been around the block a time or two — intriguing to say the least, but too hot to place on the menu.

Charlee pulled free from her growing preoccupation and made a beeline for her office. She didn't need a playmate. What she needed was someone who could keep the office running while she devoted every available minute to devising The Plan.

"Coffee. I need coffee. It's in the break room. Just down the hall." She waved a hand in the general direction.

"You want me to bring you coffee?" The disbelief deepening the edges of her new assistant's baritone brought her to a halt at the door to the inner sanctum.

Putting on a brave face, she spun to face the scowling man. "Um. Yes. If you don't mind."

He wasn't happy. Well good. Neither was she. The replacement Lilly had found for her was a distraction she didn't need.

"Lots of cream. No sugar." Though it was a cowardly thing to do, she ducked into her office and closed the door softly behind her.

Going straight to her desk, she dropped into the chair, covering her face with her hands. What was she thinking, playing the pampered boss? If she couldn't be professional with the employees, how would she convince her father she had what it took to take the company to the next level? She hadn't stepped out of line like that since leaving that other life behind.

She planted her palms flat on the desk. That had to stop. Now.

Grabbing the notes she'd already made for her next meeting — the most important one of the day — she mentally put David Randall where he belonged. At the desk Alice usually occupied. Except at that moment, he stepped into her office to deliver the coffee she'd stupidly demanded.

"Your coffee." He slipped a sheet of paper on the desk next to the steaming cup. Her calendar for the day.

His frown said she should put a bandage on her earlier gaff. Instead her tongue ran in another direction. "My ten o'clock is Richard Kemper. When he gets here, buzz me."

The disapproval that distorted his face, pulling his brows together, only served to make him yummier. Was that possible?

He nodded briskly.

Pretending an interest in the notes she knew by heart, she refused to stare as he retreated to the outer office.

*D*AVID PACED IN front of the copier waiting for the letters to print. He'd recognized the name of Charlee's ten o'clock. A man could change a lot in ten years, but the Richard Kemper, heir to RK Management Consulting he remembered from college had been known for his ambition, ruthlessness, and the short cuts he took to get what he wanted — a shark in business and with the ladies.

That he was in Portland was a surprise since his big brag was to go to New York City and rule the business world from there. If it was the same guy, he was the last person Charlee Banks should do business with.

Stop right there, Marine.

The decisions Ms. Banks made in regard to the business had nothing to do with him. Still, unable to put his unease aside he called his sister's cell.

Mind your own business and just do the job. You don't want to get fired on your first day.

In spite of the admonishment, instincts honed over the ten years spent in the Corp prowled in his gut questioning the façade of brisk business woman Charlee Banks wore, wondering if it was a mask to keep the larger world at bay.

"Hello?"

Elfin features and kissable lips made the boss a stunning girl, regardless of the old-fashioned librarian look she espoused. What guy in his right mind could resist that combination? Good thing he didn't have time for such nonsense.

"Hey, Sis. How's the runt doing?"

"I wondered how long it would take you to check in." Michelle laughed. "I swear you'll be better at this parenting thing than I ever will. He's fine. Playing with his trains."

Parenting. He was more afraid of failing his nephew than he'd ever been of anything the Marine Corps threw at him.

"You're off the hook tomorrow. I signed Elijah up for the in-house daycare." The elevator pinged softly. "Gotta go."

An older version of the man David remembered stepped into the lobby. Kemper had packed on some pounds, and apparently spent more money on suits than he used to, but it was the same guy.

"Richard Kemper to see Miss Banks." Kemper's brows arched in recognition behind wire-rimmed glasses. "David, isn't it? I heard you went into the Army."

"Marines."

Kemper straightened his tie, taking in the desk and David's position on the working side. "Haven't gone far since college, have you?"

"Ms. Banks is on a call. I'll buzz you in as soon as she's done."

Leaning over the desk, Kemper lowered his voice intimating they were best buds who met for a beer every Friday night. "Hey, can you give me a few hints on how to make points with the boss?"

Self-absorbed. Obtuse. Jackass!

His jaw locked, David rose to his full height forcing the shorter man to take a step back. It was all he could do not to grab the jerk by the neck and toss him back onto the elevator. "Have a seat. I'll let you know when she's ready to see you."

He kept Kemper waiting a full ten minutes before punching the button on the intercom, while shooting the sleaze ball a warning look. *No messing with the boss lady.*

"Kemper's here."

Charlee shot out of her office. "Richard. How nice to see you again."

Again?

She'd maneuvered around David, reaching to shake Kemper's hand before she clued into the tension boiling between them. "You've met my assistant, David?"

"Er, yes. Shall we get down to business?"

"Certainly. Let's go into my office."

The possessive manner in which Kemper hovered over Charlee neatly undid David's temper.

Kemper was going to eat her alive.

Ushering the dirt-bag ahead of her, she mouthed, "Coffee!" nodding toward the break room. With a snick of the door closing behind her, Charlee was cloistered in her office with the world's worst kind of businessman.

Hands shoved in his pockets, David circumvented the room. He'd bet lots of money he didn't have to squander, Charlee wouldn't appreciate any interference on his part.

Maybe he should see if there was a permanent position that suited his qualifications right here at Banks.

Bring coffee? When hell froze over!

WHEN SHE'D PUT her father on the elevator, all Charlee had wanted was to win his respect. Instead the melting brown eyes of her temporary assistant and a boatload of sexy confidence had thrown off her stride.

Across from her Kemper sprawled in the chair she'd picked out because it was functional rather than having anything to say about her as a businesswoman. Then again, maybe it did. No frills here. Only plain, modern glass and wood, all that was needed to transact daily business.

Kemper, looking like he was settling in for a cozy chat instead of discussing serious business, hadn't gotten the memo. "I've done a little research and believe we can improve productivity while lowering Banks' overall expenses."

The right words came out of his mouth, but his eyes shifted

hungrily around her office before coming to rest on the Tiffany lamp she turned on when the natural light from the floor-to-ceiling windows faded. She tried to focus on what he was saying, something about streamlining production … solutions … trimming the workforce, but it was impossible not to compare Kemper with David.

Her temporary assistant exuded a calm competence missing in the men she'd dated over the years and certainly in the one man who'd stolen her nineteen-year-old heart, then tossed it at her feet.

Now that she thought about it, David had a soldier's bearing — tall and straight with measured, calculated movements that won her attention hands down. Her intuition said he was a man she could depend on, though how the muses knew was another topic all together.

Kemper on the other hand was droning on, talking to her like she was a wet-behind-the-ears kid. One who didn't know her android tablet from a con job. Trim the workforce? Was he kidding? She needed every single employee she had.

Charlee tapped a manicured fingernail on her notes. "Can you develop a business plan to expand our domestic market, or not?"

"Well sure. But if it's increased revenue you want, your best bet is to get into the foreign market — Japan or China."

Her distraction with David took a back seat. "My father is working on that angle. I think there's more we can do here at home, maybe even open stores under our own brand in the new shopping villages cropping up across the Pacific Northwest."

"The domestic market. Okay. But all the money is in China right now." His condescending smile made Charlee's teeth ache.

Pushing her notes to the side, she leaned forward. "That might be true, but I'm not as interested in how much money we'll make as I am with making Banks Sportswear a go-to product. When men and women want new sportswear, I want them to immediately think Banks. And I think there are opportunities to take advantage of in our own back yard. Start in Oregon, then expand across the country."

"If that's what you want, I can come up with something, I'm sure."
Kemper hitched his pant leg, crossed one leg over the other.

The I-can-change-your-mind smirk he sent her did nothing
of the kind. She was used to men like Richard Kemper. Men who
thought they could get to daddy's money though the spoiled daughter. At one point she'd been just like him, believing she could get
what she wanted because she *was* the boss's daughter.

At nineteen she'd fallen hard for her father's right-hand man.
She'd gone after Brian like a shark after her last meal, believing he'd
loved her too, that he would welcome a merger.

Her total self-absorption scared him off, and the bad cliché she'd
least expected, her fiancé in bed with another woman, was the
result. Because of her misguided belief that everyone in her world
was intrinsically good, she'd given him more than the innocence
of her body. In the end it wasn't her naïveté he wanted, just her
father's business.

She would never love like that again — full steam ahead. It was
a lesson learned the hard way, leaving a slice of rejection and the
knowledge she would never be good enough.

Charlee lifted her chin. Clearly David Randall was hands down
the better man. She just couldn't afford the price of admission.

"Are you busy tonight? I can go back to my office, come up with
some ideas we could discuss over dinner."

She recognized the corporate climber unsuccessfully hidden by
an expensive suit, and knew exactly how to handle him.

She let a brow slide up. "Seven?"

His satisfied grin had a condescending quality that almost
changed her mind. "Maybe afterwards we can go to this great place
I know for drinks."

Predictable. "I don't—"

He waved her brush-off aside. "You'll love the place. I'll pick
you up at six-thirty."

"I'll meet you at Stanfords. On the waterfront. At seven."

His surprise that she didn't fall immediately in with his plan almost had Charlee's eyes rolling. But she had to hand it to him. He recovered quickly. "Sure."

As she walked him out, Charlee felt David's gaze on her back all the way to the elevator. She couldn't help wondering where *he* would take her for an impromptu business meeting.

*D*AVID HUNG UP the phone, switched off the computer, and rolled his shoulders to work out the stiffness that was lodged between them.

He stared at the closed door of Charlee's office. Kemper had left after a fairly short meeting, giving a subtle thumbs-up on the way out.

Not liking the man's smug attitude, he'd wanted to follow Charlee back into her office, demanding to know what deal she'd made with the devil, but she was the boss, he — in the least politically correct vernacular of the day — was just her secretary. She could make whatever deals she wanted.

Charlee Banks was the boss lady. His job besides sending out her memos? Get the lay of the land, and *stay far, far away from the disturbing woman.*

So he'd shoved his distracting attraction for Charlee into a corner of his mind where it couldn't cause any harm, then spent the whole day discovering the keen mind beneath the stoic business exterior she presented.

His work assignments came via the intercom. If she were a Marine, she'd be the one planning battle strategy. A not all together unattractive quality, damn it.

Another thing he'd learned, she was a certifiable workaholic. Hadn't bothered to take more than a five minute break all day. He rapped softly on her door before stepping in.

Charlee Banks, extreme businesswoman, was sitting in a high

backed, uncomfortable-looking chair by the window. Her shoes were lined precisely underneath, feet tucked under as she made notes on an electronic tablet. A tall, Tiffany lamp at her back — the only color in an otherwise orderly room that could be found in any perfectly organized library — cast a glow highlighting sun-kissed hair slicked smoothly behind her ears. Unaccountably his fingers itched to test their softness; find out if the spikes were as stubborn as the woman sporting them, *and* if she was as repressed as the room she did business in.

The scene left him speechless. And more bothered than he had a right to be. David cleared his throat, more to move the gravel settling there than to get the boss' attention.

She glanced up at him, her eyes crowded with secret dreams that made her look more like a young Marine just starting out than the astute businesswoman he was coming to know.

"I'm finished for the day. I sent you an email about the batch of correspondence that went out electronically. Here are the ones you wanted to go by mail. They need your signature."

He placed the letters in her inbox and got caught up in an impossible fantasy as long legs uncurled and delicate feet slipped into the waiting shoes.

David turned to leave. He couldn't give in to whatever was building between them. He had Elijah to think about. Already knew he wouldn't do anything to jeopardize his job.

Priorities. He *would* keep them straight.

"What time is it?

Snagged before he could make his escape, he glanced at his watch. "Six o'clock."

Charlee grabbed her purse from a desk drawer. "Crap! I lost track of the time."

"Where are you parked?" The question was out before he could stop. Then he dug the hole deeper. "I'll walk you to your car."

If this was staying as far away from the boss as possible, he was going to have to come up with a new strategy.

"You don't have to. I'm in the parking garage on the ground floor."

He followed her to the elevators, ordering himself to keep his eyes off the sway of her hips as she walked. "What's the matter? Late for a hot date?"

He was only half joking, and if the spike of jealousy was any clue, more intrigued than he aught to be.

She gave him a careful look. "I have a business dinner with Richard Kemper at seven."

The elevator door slid open. Waiting for her to step in, unreasonable worry built in his gut. He'd done enough letters that day to know she was working on a plan to solidify, maybe even expand Banks' domestic footprint. Kemper had most likely been tagged to help with the details, but David was certain the other man was not as interested in doing the hard work as he was in boardroom meetings between the sheets.

He clamped his jaw. It wasn't his place to tell the woman how to run her business.

But no matter how hard he tried, he just couldn't stay on the sidelines. "You're not serious about working with Kemper, are you?"

"I'm as serious as a hundred dollar bill." Her clipped tone didn't encourage further input on his part.

Back off, Randall.

Despite his best effort, he couldn't follow his own advice. The elevator opened into the parking garage. "You know what he's about, right?"

"I've got his number."

She's a big girl... and a beautiful woman.

"He doesn't have business on his mind."

"And you don't think I can handle him?" If she was on the firing range and he the target, the sparks flying from her eyes would light a cannon.

Frustrated, he pushed his hand through his short hair. "I didn't mean— Guys like Kemper take advantage of—"

Charlee pressed the remote lock on her key chain. Headlights flashed on a modern version of the classic Thunderbird. Metallic silver. Classy. Understated. Just like its owner.

"Poor defenseless women?"

His misguided advice apparently had the same effect as swatting at a swarm of yellow jackets.

Charlee yanked open the car door, tossed her purse in. "I can handle myself. And Kemper."

Insight was too slow in coming. How many times had this beautiful woman been told she couldn't take on a challenge, couldn't accomplish what she wanted?

Her delicate brows slammed together. "I don't need instruction on how to run my business from a temporary employee. If you can't do the job I'm paying you for, I'll get someone who can."

$\mathcal{A}$FTER A ROUGH night's sleep, David switched off his laptop and set it aside. A quick job search had turned up zilch. And nothing of interest at Banks either.

He owed Charlee an apology. Instead of holding the line, he'd stepped over it. If one of his Marines had pulled a stunt like that, the kid would be doing pushups until he got the message. Do the job. Nothing less. She was right. She should fire his ass.

It was just . . . for some reason . . . and nothing he could make sense of, his new boss brought out previously unknown protective instincts. He couldn't figure out why, but there it was.

And since he was being honest, he may as well admit . . . he had major hots for the woman.

On a resigned sigh, he went to refill his coffee. Elijah careened into his legs.

David lifted the three-year-old and sat him on the counter.

"Hey buddy. You're up."

A tired Michelle leaned into the wall. "He's all ready to go."

The scamp pointed at a cupboard. "Cereal!"

"Coming right up." He got Elijah, with his cereal, settled at the table.

Hugging his sister, he gently pushed her toward the door. "Go home to bed. You don't have to come over every morning. I'm pretty sure I can get Elijah dressed and fed."

"It's my way of helping." Michelle covered a yawn with the back of her hand. "When are you putting up the tree?"

David's insides went cold. "I'm not going to do one this year."

His sister's attempt to smile was heartbreaking. "Sarah would want us to decorate a tree with him."

He shook his head. He couldn't. Not with Sarah's special ornaments. One for every year since she turned thirteen.

"I hope you change your mind." Michelle planted a kiss on Elijah's forehead. "Be a good boy for Uncle David."

"Good boy!" his nephew pantomimed.

The silence filling the house after her departure mocked David. In the last two days he had not batted a thousand.

"Okay buster, eat up so we can blow this pop stand." Ruffling his nephew's hair, David knew Michelle was right. Didn't change how his heart hurt at the thought of celebrating Sarah's favorite holiday without her. The child slurping down his cereal wouldn't even remember. "You get to play with other kids today. Won't that be fun?"

Elijah scowled. He banged his spoon on the table. "I play with you."

"For a little while," he agreed.

Three months ago he'd gotten a call that irrevocably changed his life. The miracle was Elijah hadn't been with Sarah and Tom when they'd been hit by another driver.

From the moment he'd picked up the frightened boy at the

neighbor's who'd been watching him, David had known he would honor the request in Sarah's will and become Elijah's guardian.

Even so, when Elijah asked for his mom and dad, he'd settled for the easy way out and told him they were away for a while. When he'd seemed to accept that explanation, David had finally told the truth — that they weren't coming back.

Elijah had stuck to him like glue ever since, which was another reason why it was making more and more sense to find a permanent position at Banks. With the on-premises daycare, he could check on the child anytime during the day.

According to his aunt he had four to six weeks before Charlee's regular assistant returned from medical leave. So without further interference in the boss's agenda, he'd go to work, make like the best assistant she'd ever employed — which meant becoming indispensable and keeping his thoughts to himself. Instead of giving him the boot, she'd give a glowing reference to his future boss.

Elijah called from the table, "Done."

One look at the boy and David shook his head. Looked like the kid was wearing more of his breakfast than he'd gotten in his mouth.

Sarah's favorite lullaby drifted softly through his mind. *First comes love. Then comes marriage. Then comes Elijah in a baby carriage.* Well, he'd skipped the first two steps, going straight to the baby who'd turned into one heck of an active little boy.

When a picture of Charlee all curled up in her office chair intruded on his daddy moment with Elijah, he quashed the idea that a woman's hand was needed — and not just any woman.

They were two bachelors. David intended to keep it that way.

CHARLEE WAS AT her desk working, or at least attempting to work, by seven-thirty. She hadn't slept much. And she had a headache.

A dinner spent fending off Richard's unwanted advances hadn't been fun. On top of that she had a nauseating feeling he'd put more effort into trying to get her to have that drink afterward than he had coming up with a workable proposal.

Making matters even more peachy, her night had been plagued by restless dreams of a chocolate-eyed, sexy man whose concern had been well founded. It rankled that David hadn't been as blinded by ambition as she and Richard, in their different ways, had been.

Most frustrating of all, she didn't want to play Richard's games. And she really *liked* David. If he wasn't her employee *she'd* ask *him* out on a date.

On an exasperated sigh she carried her empty cup to the break room, hunting aspirin and wake-up juice. Thinking she deserved a reward for not pushing Richard into the Willamette River, she downed two of the pills kept stocked in the cupboard and grabbed one of the pudding filled pastries delivered on a daily basis.

Treat in one hand, coffee in the other, she'd almost made it back to her office when David came out of the elevator, his long, harried stride eating up the ground to his desk. He carried a little boy. Tears streamed down cherub cheeks. Miserable hiccups interspersing with silent sobs shook his small frame.

"Sorry I'm late." David sounded like he'd run up the stairs instead of coming up the elevator. He sat the boy on the corner of his desk, a comforting hand brushing tussled blond hair off the little guy's forehead.

The child clung to David. Sobs broke out in earnest.

Charlee's heart stumbled. "You've brought a ... helper."

David shifted uneasily. She would never have guessed the man could be uncertain about anything. Her pulse hitched in alarm.

"This is my nephew, Elijah."

She approached cautiously so as not to upset the boy further. At least that's what she told herself. "Hi, Elijah."

He peeked at her, his sobs slowly reducing to hiccups once more.

"I was going to take him to the daycare center, but he wouldn't stay. He's not comfortable with strangers, so it might take some time to get him settled." Blond and dark brows pulled together in equal degrees of uncertainty as the man and boy regarded each other.

David switched his gaze to hers. "I'm really sorry about this. I couldn't leave him crying like that."

Keeping her distance from this man got a hundred times harder. Sympathy cuddled up with her alarm at the charming picture the two made. She hadn't liked strangers much as a kid either, nor did she trust them. "I would have done the same."

Her father had put in long hours to get Banks off the ground, often leaving her in the care of others as a result. Elijah, sucking his thumb, his other hand nestled against David's chest as the shudders quieted, dredged up all the old loneliness.

"Where are his parents?"

The guarded anguish in David's dark eyes said it all. He wasn't going to tell her they'd gone off on an extended vacation.

Her heart went out to the child who's gaze had zeroed wistfully on her doughnut. Finally she just gave in. "Can I hold him?"

"I don't know if he'll—"

Charlee held out her hands. Elijah let go of his death grip on his uncle and leaned toward her. It was probably the power of the doughnut, but she didn't care. She'd take all the help she could get, if it would stop the tears streaking down the boy's face.

She scooped him up, warmed by David's surprise and grateful smile as Elijah's hiccups ended when he took a bite of the pastry. The scent of clean baby mixed with cream and sugar was ... wasn't something she'd experienced before. It made her breath catch, her gaze fly to the man who was tumbling her world one hundred and eighty degrees.

The ringing phone broke the moment. Eyes locked on her as if he were trying to divine her greatest secret — that she didn't know how to do a real give-and-take, boy-girl thing — David answered the summons. "Charlee Banks' office, how—"

What did he see? The all-business boss reaching out of her self-imposed bubble to hold a heartbroken toddler? Laughable, right?

"Just a moment." He pushed the hold button. "It's your father."

Clearing her throat, she gave Elijah back. "I'll take it in my office."

Making Elijah comfortable against his chest, David nodded. The tangle of awareness coursing alongside her pumping pulse was not the response she expected to have toward an *employee!*

Bad boss! Step away from the yummy man.

"Pretty." Elijah pointed.

Not ready to give up this rare moment and return to the *bubble* that now suddenly seemed to lack something important, Charlee glanced over her shoulder to see what had caught the boy's attention. "Christmas lights. Yes, they're very pretty."

"Christmas?" He grabbed the piece of gooey pastry she offered and shoved the bite in his mouth.

"We'll talk about that later, Bud." David carried now calm child to the elevators, leaving her with a brief, "I'll be right back."

Left adrift by his abrupt departure, she retreated from the bewildering attraction to take the waiting call. "Hi, Dad."

"What took so long?" her father barked from across the Pacific.

Typical. For the first time his curt manner didn't bother her. "Having a bad day?"

"Sorry. Back to back meetings. How are things on your end? Are you ready?"

"We were ready before you left."

Swiveling her chair to look out the wall of windows so she wouldn't keep 'seeing' David with his nephew, she kicked off her shoes.

"I want you to double check. I'm sending a lot of work your way."

Propping her heels on the low sill, she retrieved the half eaten doughnut, licked the pudding oozing from the bite she'd given Elijah, pretending for very solid ethical reasons she wasn't interested in the boy's uncle. Not in *that* way.

"Dad, your department heads know their jobs. Relax. You're in Tokyo. Enjoy yourself," she returned his advice. *If you can,* she muttered under her breath, then snorted. Kettle. Black pot.

"I didn't get where I am today, baby girl, by slacking off."

"This much I know." For the first time Charlee questioned how closely she wanted to follow in her father's footsteps. "Look, give us all a break and take a few days off while you're there. Before you have a heart attack. Or better yet, before you give me one."

"Can't."

"Why am I not surprised?"

"You can't take time off either. As soon as the holidays are over, I want you to come run the office. Here. In Tokyo."

Charlee dropped her feet to the floor. Her pulse sprinted into a marathon. "What do you mean?"

"Just what I said. You've been pushing for your own division ever since I gave you that office. It's time."

Caution took over. "What made you change your mind? Just days ago you were—"

"I know. Lilly said I need to have more faith in you."

"Lilly said."

There was a moment of silence, then her father's voice, quieter. "Yes. I love you, baby. And I'm proud of you. You know that, right?"

His words should have sent her to cloud nine. Instead they left her a little hollow inside. She'd waited a long time to hear them. But now she wondered if there wasn't more to life than getting her parent's approval. She sighed in disgust at her own contrariness. "I know, Dad."

"You don't have to decide right this minute."

"That's good because I'm kind of tied up with this domestic project."

"I thought I told you to let that go?" The was a moment of silence during which she didn't know how to respond, then ... "You're stubborn for a kid, aren't you?"

"I come by it honestly."

"All right. We'll talk when I get home."

Since it wouldn't do any good, Charlee didn't argue. "What time is it there?"

"Going on midnight."

"What time do your meetings start?"

"Too early."

David poked his head in, holding out a steaming cup she hoped was coffee, since she'd let hers go cold while talking to her father. She motioned him in.

"Get some rest." She hung up before he could come up with any more surprises. "If that's coffee, I'll kiss your feet."

His brows shot up, lips angling into a sexy grin. The room suddenly got too warm. "Greeks bearing gifts."

"Should I beware?"

Oh, heck yeah.

*D*AVID ORDERED HIS stoked body to behave. Talk about begging.

"How's your nephew?"

"Settled. I'll check on him at break."

The boss closed her eyes, savoring that first sip as though life couldn't get any better. He swallowed hard. He could think of a number of ways it could. And they all included the remarkable woman in front of him.

Who would have guessed Charlee had a way with unhappy children, that she could soothe a boy whose backup was an uncle who only knew how to tell the troops to take the hard hit, get up and keep moving forward?

When she trained those gorgeous blues on him, he almost threw the fight. But a Marine didn't give up. Ever.

"How ... when did his parents die?"

A bucket of cold water in the face wouldn't have been more effective in slapping him with reality. David took a step back. Physically and figuratively. "A car crash. Drunk driver. Three months ago."

"So Christmas isn't going to be easy."

He was slipping. And she saw too much. "How did dinner go last night?"

The sympathy he didn't know how to handle retreated behind her business-as-usual mask. For a brief second, he regretted resurrecting her defenses.

Leaving her coffee to cool on the precisely organized desk, she leaned back in her chair. "As expected."

"He put the move on you," David couldn't stop the words. A muscle ticked along his jaw.

She shrugged, the narrowing of her eyes warning she knew exactly what he was doing — deflecting the spotlight away from himself and the 'feelings' he didn't want to discuss. "I can handle guys like Kemper."

David suspected she'd been doing just that for a long time.

He shoved his hands in his pockets, locked his elbows. She was absolutely right. He had enough on his plate with Elijah. He didn't want to get involved with his boss' problems, even though he could do a better job for her than Kemper. And do it without angling for a little sack time.

Despite his good intentions, his mind raced with the possibilities — of helping her out with an analysis of Banks' domestic business that would do her some real good.

The Corps had taught him to surmount any obstacle or challenge that got in his way. Charlee was definitely a challenge. And unexpectedly, she'd somehow become one of his own. "I shouldn't have—"

"This is your first—" They spoke at the same time. Charlee continued without him. "Assistant job."

It was his turn to shrug. "The day after we moved to Portland, the job I came for was cut from the budget. You needed a temporary secretary. I had no other prospects."

Her lips did that funny little amused twitch he was coming to look for.

"What did you do before moving to Oregon?"

His spine snapped to attention. "I was an active Marine."

Her brows rose. David didn't generally care what people thought about the military. He loved the life and was good at it. But in this instance, seeing her renewed respect, if he was a peacock, he'd strut his tail feathers.

"Sergeant, huh?"

"Captain."

"Like Captain Kirk?" She laughed. Tried not to, but in the end let it loose.

He thought about it for a moment. "Yes."

In the outer office the elevator pinged. David went still. Charlee didn't have any appointments scheduled for this morning. "Kemper?"

Pressing her lips together, she nodded.

He headed for his desk to ward off the intruder.

"Play nice, Captain," Charlee called after him.

David slanted a look over his shoulder. He hadn't wanted to get involved, but somehow he was. "Sure."

He closed Charlee's door behind him; just reached his desk before Kemper.

"I'm here to see Miss Banks." Kemper flashed his predator smile. David wanted to haul the man downstairs and release him in traffic. But he'd given his word. Sort of.

With one hand he went through the motions of pulling up the boss' schedule. "I don't have you down for an appointment."

"I don't need one. She'll see me without it."

Charlee's door opened. She shot him a look that said she didn't trust him to stand down. Maybe she was correct in that assessment.

"Richard. Did we arrange to meet this morning?"

"I finished my analysis and wanted to go over my recommendations with you as soon as possible. I took the liberty of bringing a contract so we can get started."

"I only have a few minutes." Her tone wasn't particularly welcoming, but resigned to the inevitable.

David didn't want her to settle for a proposal from a man finagling more than a business relationship. She needed another option ... and he was just the guy to give her a legitimate one.

"David, would you make sure I have a good hour to talk to Bill Danvers tomorrow? I think we're scheduled to meet at eleven. And bring me the Macy's file. It should be in that cabinet against the wall. Also, I want to talk about the plans for the Christmas party sometime today."

She was staking her territory. Letting Kemper know *she* was the boss in this corner of the world.

Pride ballooned in his chest.

Don't be ridiculous.

Still he couldn't shove the satisfaction aside.

When they disappeared behind the closed door of her office, he rearranged one appointment, then confirmed with Danver's executive assistant.

The Macy's file was easy to find. Her regular girl was good.

Just like that his patience wore thin. The quiet was deafening. That was something he could fix.

When he entered without knocking, on the pretext of taking Charlee the Macy's file and a cup of coffee just the way she liked it, he found Kemper leaning back in the chair opposite her desk, a self-satisfied smirk aimed in the wrong direction as far as David was concerned.

"We should go to dinner. Celebrate our new association."

Charlee glanced up from the file she was studying long enough to send David a grateful smile as she took the coffee. "I don't think so, Richard."

Surprised out of his delusional good humor, Kemper straightened. "But I thought—"

David turned a spurt of laughter into a cough. Charlee clearly didn't need help protecting herself. And for having a reputation as a business barracuda, Kemper didn't have a clue he'd missed the mark.

The surprising amusement left him. A man would be stupid not to pursue Charlee Banks with integrity — if that's what was on his mind.

"The Macy's file." He laid it carefully on her desk.

She winked at him, a blink of her eye so quick and brief he wasn't sure he'd actually seen it. "Thanks. Captain. Grab your steno pad. I need you to take notes."

Steno? Notes? He'd run across the Alpha Smart his predecessor obviously used for that purpose the first day on the job while cataloging where the tools of his new trade where kept.

"I'm sorry, Richard. I appreciate the work you've put into this, but your plan isn't what I have in mind."

"I can give you—"

"I don't think you can. I need recommendations that reach as far out of the box as can be imagined. And it needs to include ideas I haven't thought of myself." She returned the file to Kemper. "This isn't it."

Beneath her stern business façade, this woman was not what David expected. She was more like an armored car on steroids the way she broke through his defenses.

"I can try again."

"Thanks for coming by, Richard. David will show you out."

The man's face turned ruddy with disbelief that morphed quickly into anger. David kept his standing ovation to himself and left a clear exit to the door.

"You're making a mistake. I hope you'll give me another opportunity to do business with you."

Dude. Give up. You've lost the battle.

Expression locked tight, Charlee didn't give an inch, instead told — as far as David could tell — the biggest lie of her life. "It was nice to meet with you."

Finally convinced he wasn't going to make the deal, Kemper nodded stiffly.

Making sure the other man got on the elevator, David was surprised by a rush of pure pride. The boss understood Marine tactics. If you want something bad enough, go over, under, or around anything in your way.

If you want something…

Kiss the girl already!

But Kemper had made the mistake of thinking Charlee was an ordinary woman. After watching her in action for the last two days, David wouldn't make the same mistake.

He liked her. She was smart, a hard worker, knew how to go after what she wanted. And she didn't give up. Maybe he more than liked her. Which wasn't possible. No one fell in l— David shook his head. Even coming up with an attack plan took longer than two days.

"Thank God he's gone." If she was a roadside bomb going off under his feet, he wouldn't have been more surprised. He hadn't heard her coming.

Taking his time, he grabbed the Alpha Smart from the bottom drawer. "Does that happen often?"

"What?" She studied him, clearly trying to decide if she should trust him.

He thought about how she'd held her own. "Guys coming on to you to get a foothold in the business."

She shrugged one slender shoulder, the wall going up not inviting sympathy. "Comes with the territory."

"It shouldn't." And that left him with a very big problem.

At the back of his mind an idea was forming. But he didn't want Charlee to think she'd traded one skunk for another. Which meant he couldn't approach her until he had a completed proposal to present. One ethical business professional to another. No business over dinner. No popping in without an appointment to use seduction as a selling tool.

She didn't give him time to brood on it long. "The file for the Christmas party is in Alice's desk file drawer."

"When's the party?"

"Friday night." She paused, her shields coming down a little. "I hope you'll come."

The familiar hard knot formed in David's gut. "I'm not sure I can. There's Elijah. No babysitter."

Slender fingers closed around his. Sharp awareness raced up his arm, a lightning strike that struck ground somewhere in his chest.

"Please. You'd be doing me a huge favor."

David couldn't help it. He turned his hand so their palms met, watched her eyes go round and liquid with the same desire rushing to take over his good sense. He swallowed hard. "How's that?"

"I trust you."

Damn it! He untangled their fingers.

She took a deep breath. "Look I know it's none of my business and that it will be difficult, but I've been thinking about it all day, and I know Elijah will always remember if you make this Christmas as normal as possible."

David clamped his jaw more bothered by their brief touch than by her advice. Doing right by his nephew was the easier road to take. "I'll think about it."

$\mathscr{L}$ATER AFTER HE'D put Elijah to bed, David followed Michelle out the front door.

Shivering in the cold, she pulled her hat low over her ears. White flakes danced in the air. "Looks like we'll have a white Christmas."

After tugging up the collar of her wool coat as added protection, he pushed his hands into his jeans pockets. "I'm thinking of taking your advice and putting up a tree."

She leaned into his shoulder like she had that first horrible year after they'd been left behind by their parents. "I'm glad. He's lost so much. We could at least give him that."

"When did you get so smart?"

She laughed and smacked his arm. "I've always been smart."

"How about tomorrow night?"

"Can't. Have to be at the hospital the next two nights."

"Friday might not work either. The boss wants me to go the company Christmas Party."

"She does?" Blond brows danced teasingly up and down. "That sounds like fun."

"I'm not sure I'm going."

"Of course you are."

"Elijah—"

Comforting arms wrapped around his middle. "Is going with me. I have two tickets for The Nutcracker."

"I'd rather go to The Nutcracker than a dull Christmas Party."

"Not true if *the boss* is going to be there." Grinning, she patted his chest.

That was the problem with sisters. Sometimes they knew you better than you knew yourself.

"You guys do the tree tomorrow night. I'll inspect it when I pick Elijah up on Friday."

THE NEXT NIGHT David wasn't sure how Charlee ended up joining them for the small tree decorating party he'd put together at the last minute. One minute they were finishing off the details for Friday's party, the next he'd mentioned they were putting up the tree, complete with pizza and hot chocolate topped with whipped cream.

The wistful look she'd cast his way had him issuing an invitation neither of them expected.

Way to keep your business life separate from your personal one, Randall.

He and Elijah had gotten to the house just before Charlee drove up. The excitement lighting up the kid's face while he 'helped' carry in the tree made all of it worthwhile. Even the butterflies taking flight in David's belly at sharing this first holiday without his sister, with a woman who was coming to mean more than she should.

The pizza was delivered just as big, fat snowflakes began to fall.

Elijah was too excited to eat, so while Charlee strung the lights she'd volunteered to pick up, David helped his nephew pull Sarah's box from the closet where he'd pushed it far into the back corner.

His breath got stuck when he opened the flaps. But Charlee's laugh at Elijah's excited, "I want to help" — as he grabbed the end of the light strand — broke the lock.

David grabbed the kid just before he toppled the tree. "Hold on there, Buddy."

Charlee laughed so hard she had to wiped tears from her cheeks.

His heart took a hard tumble. "Do you and your dad put up a tree?"

The laughter faded. "No. Well. Kind of. Dad has the same company who decorates the office put a tree up at the mansion. And there's a Christmas tree in the foyer of my condo building, so I don't really need one."

"You don't put up a tree?" David put Elijah on his feet, pointed him in the direction of Sarah's box, and stared at Charlee until she started to squirm.

She made a face. "I know. It sounds silly after pushing you to do one for Elijah."

Keeping her gaze locked on the lights she was stringing, making sure they were placed just so, her jaw firmed in self-defense. "We exchange gifts Christmas morning."

Something fragile found purchase in David's chest. He could give this extraordinary woman something she couldn't give herself. And Elijah. And Michelle. He could give them a Christmas to remember.

"Well then. Tonight's your lucky night."

Her sudden grin told him he'd hit his target. Amidst off-tuned carols and a tinsel fight at the end, they decorated the tree to perfection.

If it wasn't for Elijah, he would have given himself an early Christmas present. Charlee Banks and the chance to taste her, see how her soft curves felt in the palms of his hands.

"Mommy." Elijah stood by the box holding an ornament that had somehow been missed.

How the boy knew it was his mother's, given to her when she wasn't much older than he was ... her favorite ... David couldn't fathom. All he knew was, in that moment, he joined Elijah in missing his sister more than anything, and if he could have gotten his hands on the drunk driver who'd survived the accident he'd caused, taking this precious little boy's mother and father away—

"Mommy!" Elijah threw the ornament down.

David didn't anticipate his nephew's anguish in time. Tried to save the precious ornament, but couldn't move fast enough. His heart shattered with the delicate glass.

Crying great gulping sobs, Elijah threw himself on the couch.

David gathered him up. Tiny arms locked around his neck, but no matter how much he rubbed the kid's back, they were both inconsolable.

He held on the best he could; couldn't bear to watch Charlee, her face pale, clean up the glass shards. He'd wanted to avoid this. Instead he'd gone against his better judgment and let her and Michelle talk him into pretending they would get past Sarah and Tom's deaths.

Elijah's sobs were more hiccups when she slid her arms into her coat and stood on tiptoe to leave a gentle kiss on David's cheek. "See you tomorrow morning?"

When he didn't answer, she let herself out with one last sad glance.

*C*HARLEE PACED THE length of her office waiting to hear David at his desk. Sleep had been an elusive thing, her heart and mind completely taken with her temporary assistant and his sweet nephew.

She sucked in a breath, swung her arms out to the sides, stretching. How could she have fallen so desperately in love in just three days?

Nobody did that, right?

Except she had. David had taken her whole heart captive.

Once she'd asked her dad what he regretted most. He'd said not spending every minute he could with her mother while he had the chance.

Watching David console Elijah had made her realize she wanted to spend every minute she could with the man and boy. During her restless night, it'd all come home. The Captain and Elijah were her family. She just had to convince him.

In the outer office, drawers slid open and closed. The computer came on. When David didn't immediately come to her, she went to him.

"How's Elijah?"

David didn't look at her. "He's fine."

She inched a step closer. "How about you. How are you doing?"

"I have a lot of work to do."

She nodded. "I'll be in my office if you need me."

But the Captain didn't need her. With an efficiency that was breathtaking, and sad, breaking her heart completely, he worked as if there were no tomorrow. For the rest of the day and into Friday.

He answered questions, but didn't initiate conversation. She didn't get to see Elijah again. David dropped him off at the daycare center before starting work.

No matter how hard she tried, she couldn't break through the mile-high barrier he'd erected. Charlee was staring into the fountain below when she decided she'd had enough. Brian might not have been a man worth the fighting for, but David was.

She spent a good share of the morning in HR, looking at David's employment record, trying to add up the disparate pieces that made up Captain David Randall, a man who'd left a job he'd held for ten years for a boy who needed him. What would he do for a woman who needed him as much?

She was about to find out. When she stopped at his desk on her way out, he didn't look up.

"Pick me up at six."

That got his attention.

"I'm not going to the party."

"That's an order, Captain. Father's called an emergency meeting. You'll be on the clock." She stuck a bright yellow sticky-note on the desk in front of him. "It's black tie. Here's my address. Don't be late."

Brows slammed together. Charlee smirked. She would teach him what happened when he didn't share important information. Operation Capture The Captain had begun.

She made several stops on the way home — one to her favorite dress shop in the Nob Hill district of Portland. She indulged in long soak in the tub, and a little decorating, so that when the doorbell rang she was ready.

David didn't disappoint. Not in how his strong shoulders filled out the black suit, or in the way dreamy chocolate eyes drank her in from the tips of her newly spiked hair to the three inch heels on her feet.

"You're right on time."

"I had orders from the boss."

"A drink before we go?"

He shook his head, taking in the room and the Christmas touches she'd added, including the pencil thin tree in the corner. It'd turned out perfect, decorated in white except for the one red, glass ball she'd put front and center in the place of honor where he couldn't miss it.

A smile finally touched his lips. "You have a tree."

"I decorated it myself."

He held the door open.

Okay. So he wasn't going to be a pushover. She'd just have to work harder and put Plan B into play.

The short ride to the Benson Hotel was completed in comparative silence. Her nerves took a turn for the worst, but she didn't let it show.

When they reached the room set aside for the party, she slipped her hand into the crook of David's arm. "I had a lovely visit with your file in Human Resources this morning, and with Peter Wilson, who recommended you highly for the newly opened position of business analyst in our domestic division."

Beside her he stiffened, then propelled her toward the bar. She accepted the glass of wine he handed over, looking forward to the skirmish building on his handsome face.

"What game are you playing?"

"No game. Just wondering why you didn't tell me you were a business analyst, when you know I'm in desperate need of one."

"I'm not like Kemper," he growled.

Her father caught up with them. "Charlee. I want to talk to you about Tokyo."

Puzzled by David's remark, she didn't move her eyes from the Captain. "Of course you're not."

In HR she'd worked out a few truths. David needed a permanent job to take care of Elijah. She needed David. "Not now, Dad. I'm working here."

Stormy brown eyes narrowed on her.

Her father sputtered. Charlee ignored him, not surprised to see Lilly at his side. With clear vision for the first time in her life, she wondered why they hadn't gotten married. Now that she was getting out of her own way, she recognized the signals. They'd been involved for a long time.

She should be shocked. But frankly, she was just happy for them. And wanted to get on with her own merger.

Lilly tugged David down for a kiss on the cheek. "Hello David. I see you and Charlee are making the rounds."

Her father shook David's hand. "So this is young David."

"Oh no you don't," Charlee warned the senior Banks, pulling David away from her father and the rest of the party. This meeting was personal, not business. "We need someplace private to talk."

Cautious speculation was accompanied by reluctant feet. "Where are we going?"

She pulled harder. "You'll see."

When the key card she'd picked up earlier let them into a set of rooms decorated lavishly for the holiday, he stopped at the threshold. "This isn't a good idea."

She folded their fingers together, angled back until he stepped into the room. "It's the best idea I've had. Ever."

She dropped her wrap on a red and gold tapestry chair. Christmas surrounded them — on the gas fireplace mantle, at tables decorated with candles nestled in pine boughs, sparkling balls and red velvet bows. It even smelled like Christmas.

She'd been wrong about the man she'd thought she loved once. She hoped she wasn't wrong this time.

"Why didn't you tell me you have experience as a business analyst, that you came to Portland for that very job?"

"I didn't want you to think—"

"That you were cut from the same cloth as Kemper. I get that." Despite her *plan* to see if there was more between them than boss and secretary, her heart pinched. And she stepped away from the man who'd come to take up her whole world. "So you didn't trust me to be able to figure that out for myself?"

He suddenly closed the widening distance between them and took her firmly by the shoulders. "That's not true."

Hauling her close, he hovered a brief moment before capturing her lips, invading, encouraging a response she'd never given anyone else.

Breathless she drew back. "Still you withheld the truth."

Holding her gaze, questing fingers brushed beneath the thin strap of her black dress. "I guess I — Yes."

Heat pooled with newborn love low in her belly. "When were you planning to tell me?"

He pulled the strap off her shoulder, placed a kiss where it had been. "When I had a plan fully developed, ready to present. And when I could be absolutely sure it was love I felt, and not just lust for the most incredible woman I've ever met."

Charlee's breath caught. The flat of her palm settled inside his jacket, over his racing heartbeat, and found the truth of those words. Moisture gathered behind her eyes, but quickly disappeared as her manicured fingers caught on buttons pulling them free. "How long is that going to take?"

"No time at all. I stayed up all last night getting the proposal done." Exploring fingers edged just beneath the lace and silk covering her breasts. "Are you seducing me?"

"Yes, Captain." Her dress slipped lower, giving him more eye candy. "I think I'm half in love with you."

"I'm completely in love with *you*," The scrape of raw emotion left her in no doubt. Slowly he turned her, breath brushing the short hair at her temple, hand hovering at the nape of her neck. "May I?"

Unable to get words out, she nodded emphatically. Her dress slid to the floor. Strong arms closed her in. The flats of wide palms covered her tightening breasts, pulling her flush with his body, massaging, tweaking the begging crests.

Lips roamed down her arched neck, to her shoulder, lingered where her pulse had picked up speed. She felt the gentle nip. Shivered as lava melted between her legs.

When he took his time skimming down her stomach, slipping inside lace, a finger, then two finding a moist welcome, she gasped.

"You're fired."

He pumped once, twice, pressed his hard erection into the curve of her bottom, asked with a breathless wonder that nearly tipped her over the edge. "That's your solution?

"Yes. It. Is."

He hastily removed their remaining clothes before leaning her over the polished desk.

She informed her Captain, "I want to propose a different merger."

An arm around her waist, lips teasing her neck where it joined her shoulder, he found her sweet spot, making magic with his thumb. He edged her feet apart, nudging her opening from behind before entering with one strong thrust.

Trembling with the strain, he waited for her to catch up. His restraint brought her heart the rest of the way home.

"Is this the kind of merger you had in mind?"

She grabbed his thigh, leaned into his lap, seating him as deep as she could. Panting she gave him everything. "I was thinking. Of something. A little. More. Permanent."

He plunged, one hand holding her breast, the other taking her for a high dive. The sun exploded. David joined her with a shout at his own release.

When the shudders subsided, his forehead rested against her back. He glanced at the bed visible through the open French doors.

"Hold onto that thought. I have a present for you."

He groaned. "I didn't get you a present."

Charlee wiggled free and watched him grow hard again. With a satisfied smirk, she handed over the prettily wrapped box she retrieved from her bag. "I think you did."

His deep laugh blended in perfect harmony with hers. Pulling her close, he tore at the wrapping, quickly revealing the sister to the red, glass ball hanging on her tree. A sheen of moisture filled his dark eyes. "How did you find this?"

"I have my ways."

Carefully leaving the ornament on the table, he drew Charlee to the bed. With gentle caresses he had her ready to fly higher than before.

"You name the time and place for this merger and I'll be there. For the rest of our lives."

On that promise, Charlee fell completely for her Captain.

~

ABOUT THE AUTHOR

Susan Lute is a multi-published author of traditional and Indie books. She swears the best things in life come in unexpected packages. An ardent student of human nature, who loves ancient history, myth, and dragons, she doesn't remember thinking ... someday I'll grow up to be a writer. She writes whenever she can. In between she works as a Registered Nurse, reads, gardens, loves to travel, and works on remodeling her house. She lives in the Pacific Northwest with her husband of many years. Currently she's writing the second novel in her Dragonkind Chronicles, *and working on a new contemporary romance.*

You can learn more about Susan at:

susanlute.com

For more books of the heart from these authors,
please visit us at:

windtreepress.com

Windtree
Press